I0676618

The Skater and the Saint

Book 2

The Borschland Hockey Chronicles

D. W. FRAUENFELDER

BREAKFAST WITH PANDORA BOOKS

In association with

True North Writers & Publishers Co-operative

Durham, North Carolina

Copyright © 2013 David Frauenfelder

All rights reserved.

ISBN: 0-9885656-5-x

ISBN-13: 978-0-9885656-5-4

TO WILL AND KATE
Alleskeet ergut

CONTENTS

CHAPTER 1 - CATHY

The morning of Lily's birthday, we had a phase shift.

Not everyone can feel phase shifts when they come, but I can.

It isn't because I come from outside Borschland-- my brother Sherm never feels them.

And it isn't because I'm a candidate to be a deacon in the Church of Borschland. You'd think that spiritual people used to silence and listening would be super-sensitive to them, but they're not.

No, I think I just notice them because I was always the kid that got carsick. So it figures switching universes would get me queasy.

This time, I was with Lily, Sherm and Rachael's beautiful daughter.

I was reading her a book, about Saint Joost the Apple Sower-- the Borschic Johnny Appleseed. It was morning, and a gentle autumn sun was streaming through the narrow, high windows of the bedroom she shared with her brother Connie. We'd just had a nice run of Indian summer, but the cold weather-- and Sherm's hockey season-- would start soon.

I finished a sentence and turned the page, and the words of the book faded out, like they were dissolving in water. Instead

I seemed to see a train crossing, a memory of my childhood. The warning lights were going, and the gates were down, and the train was going by, and all of a sudden it was as if I, and the gate, and the light standard, and the road, were all moving, and the train was standing still.

There was that moment of freefall, of carsickness. Then it was over. The shift was finished, and we were somewhere else.

"*Waass ten lejts?*" asked Lily in her throaty bird voice. She was a preemie and is small for her age. "What comes next?"

At first, I thought she was asking what comes next, as in, now that we are phase shifted, what is going to happen? But she was pointing at the book that I had stopped reading. She hadn't felt the shift at all.

What comes next in my life? I wondered as I gathered myself and began to read again, disappointed that now, in this universe, it was overcast. For me the world had already shifted. After four years in Borschland, I'd finally decided that maybe, maybe, I was going to get married.

For my wacky and beloved brother Sherm it was easy. He became a star ice hockey player (I always knew he had it in him), found Rachael, his gorgeous poetess, fell in love at first sight, and had an adventure with her. Nine months after their honeymoon, their first child, Conraad, or Connie, as we call him, was born.

Lilianne, Lily, was the miracle baby: she had almost died on the day she was born, along with Rachael, who was not made for bearing a lot of children.

Four years ago, when Connie was one and Lily still to come, I came to Borschland to join Sherm, and dealt with a bunch of suitors who were mainly hockey fans wanting to meet my famous brother.

I fell in love, but not with any of those guys. No, funny as it sounds, I got a crush on the Borschic church and went back to school to be a deaconess. I figured I'd let marriage take care of itself, if it ever came.

And then, three years later, came Roald.

Roald is a hockey journalist, the son of Kadmus Greningen,

the most famous hockey journalist in Borschland. Roald works for his dad's newspaper, the *Sporttelegraaf*, as the beat writer for the minor league team, Oststaff, which is made up mostly of cadets from the Naval Academy.

As a rule, Borschic men are not talkers. But Roald is quietly charming and can tell a joke.

We are both famous in a way, because we are related to famous people, and the press in Borschland is very big on reporting on the doings of Borschic celebrities. Not a whole lot happens in Borschland, and there are many newspapers, so the paparazzi and the tabloids are quite the newshounds.

I try to stay under the radar as much as possible. But for a long time one newspaper ran something they called *Te Kathujwack*, or the Cathy Vigil. It was the number of days I had been in Borschland and single. Everybody wanted me to get married, and as long as I wasn't, it was some kind of big to-do.

They stopped on Day 1,000, which also happened to be a day that I had a date with Roald. Everyone must have figured, well, that's it. She can't pass up this opportunity. But he hadn't asked yet, and I hadn't said yes.

I didn't fall in love with Roald. He just started courting me. This is one of the good things about Borschland. You don't date per se. Any kind of contact between social equals of the opposite sex is a potential mating ritual. If a man is interested in a woman, he states his intention, and the ball starts rolling.

Which means that Roald had to ask me if I would consider marrying him based on not knowing him nearly at all when he asked. I was surprised that I said yes. That means the door is open.

Oh, you should have heard the bells ringing. Not in my heart-- in newsrooms all over Borschland. Roald was considered a bit young to get married, in his mid-twenties, and I will soon be thirty-three. But he was definitely a major catch for any young lady in Borschland, being journalistic royalty and an up-and-coming scribbler himself.

And he is good-looking. He's tall and broad-shouldered for a Borschic man, taller than me, and I'm five-nine. He's got lovely soft blue eyes and fair skin that blushes easily. His light-blonde hair is already starting to recede. But he's going to be a very distinguished bald man some day, like his dad.

And that's good, because someday I'm going to be a bald old lady, probably with a beard. It's good that Roald seems happy with my Minnesota farm-girl looks-- the blonde hair, big teeth, chipmunk cheeks, skin that burns on contact with the sun. The whole nine.

Roald seemed very sincere when he asked if I would consider marrying him, and I knew it was sincere because he cracked a joke about it, saying that my response would be "off the record," which of course it wasn't, once it got around. So I said, "You don't want to marry a deaconess from America," and he said, "It's better than marrying an American from Deaconess," and I said, "You are a bit crazy," and he said, "I know."

"Did your editor ask you to do this to sell more papers?" I asked. I had to ask at least that. But I asked with a smile on my face.

And what a gallant answer he made: "I only want the opportunity to sell myself to you, *mijne hart*."

Mijne hart is a pretty heavy-duty thing to say. It means "my heart," but it is a lot more than that. It really means my heart's desire, my longing. I've had it said to me before, but always by guys who thought they were, oh, what's the word, players, maybe? In Borschland they're called *te hoopfvolle*, the hopeful types.

Roald didn't say it like they did.

"*Ten sill wuj zujet*," I said, "we'll see," which to a Borschic man is the equivalent of a resounding yes. If I had wanted to be coy, I really should've said no, and then see if he'd come around and ask again. But I don't manipulate like that. I used to play ice hockey myself. I like the honesty of the game.

So we had that Day 1,000 date, and he met Sherm's father-in-law, the Archdeacon Conraad Martujns, who would be kind of a stand-in for my father, since Dad is resting peacefully next to Mom on a hillside in Minnesota, without a care in the world.

I thought to myself, *Dad would laugh his tail off.* I could hear him: "Young love. And in the papers, don't you know!"

For sure, I had a lot to think about on that morning with Lily, in phase-shifted Borschland. But it was going to be a much bigger day than I could anticipate. Because I was going to meet Willem on that day. And after Willem, nothing would be the same for any of us: not for me, not for Roald, nor Sherm and Rachael-- nor Borschland, either.

CHAPTER 2 - SHERM

It figured I met Willem on the day of the shift.

Once you're in the other universe, the *ujterstweerld*, the Borschic folk call it, you settle in and it's kind of like winter. You just accept it.

But the day of, everybody's borderline traumatized for a second, and it's headline news.

Most of the time nothing different or exciting happens when you're shifted out. You go about your business and the papers ask the government if they're going to send out an airship to explore the parallel universe you're in (risky for the explorers, if you shift back before the airship comes home).

But this one wasn't most of the time.

I was up early that morning for breakfast with the guys-- my closest friends on the team. We were a couple of days from training camp, which meant about ten days before the regular season started. It was going to be an international season: we had a new North American, a nineteen year-old from Canada named Urdan Kasmahlov; a bear; and a Zimrothian goalie.

The shift happened around ten-- we could tell because all of a sudden it went from sun to overcast. I checked in with my head coach, Chrojstenkaamps the immortal, did a newspaper interview, and checked in at Reinhardt Central at noon. Cathy was there, spending a little birthday quality time with the Lilymonster, and Rachael was sorting laundry for the laundry lady who came that day.

I asked Rachael what was for lunch, and she told me to warm some beef stew from the other night.

"You want some?" I yelled down to her. She was in the basement at the laundry chute.

"Not now," she said.

I retrieved the stew, lit the burner on the stove and got some stew into a pot. Then I got out the bread and hunted around for the butter dish. Empty. I fished around in the icebox. Nothing where it usually sat.

"I can't find the butter," I said as Rachael came up from the basement, red-faced and with a wisp of hair trailing into her mouth.

Rachael said, "That's because there isn't any. The Bongarteax didn't include any in the order this morning."

"Why not?"

"I don't know. Madaam van Brach told me they had to hire her brother-in-law as a stock man because he was let go from his other job, and he does not pay enough attention."

"Well, we need butter for Lily's cake," I said. I'd convinced Rachael that the birthday girl should have a part in making her own birthday cake. In Borschland they don't have birthday cakes with the name and the candles and everything. With our first, Conraad, I let that go. But I miss birthday cakes. And I wanted to see Lily crack an egg into a bowl, like kids do.

But it couldn't be that simple. When I mentioned to someone in the front office we were going to do a cake, the publicity department got wind of it and asked if they could send a professional photographer to document the historic event of a little girl in an apron.

"North American traditions come to Borschland," said the PR dude. "Very good for us to start the season."

Rachael, being a good sport, said yes, but the stress level of the day ratcheted up. Respectable Borschic people mostly like their children to be seen and not heard, and especially not seen making a mess with a mixing bowl.

Plus, we were having Rachael's parents over for dinner, as well as Cathy and her boyfriend, Roald.

Butter was for sure crucial to the day. And so were patience, and a sense of humor.

"Butter. Needed. *So vijl ken Ij.* So much I know," said Rachael. That's the Borschic way of saying *no shredded wheat, Sherlock.*

"I guess you don't have time to go get any," I said.

She just stared at me. *Who is the stupid husband in this scene,* she seemed to be saying.

"*Ergut,*" I said, the Borschic way of saying, *all right, already.* "Can I at least finish my lunch?"

"You don't have any butter for your bread," said Rachael.

I stepped out onto our street and was about to make a right turn to go to the Bongarteax, our regular grocery store. But seeing no paparazzi at the doorstep, I made a left, to go across the St. Noos Oval and stop in at Schmeecks.

After five years of being the franchise player for Te Staff, the New York Yankees of the Borschland Hockey League, I can sometimes go around in public without being followed by about two dozen photographers.

That's when I decide to change it up, take a little walk, do the unusual thing. After all, that's why I came to Borschland in the first place.

The leaves on the elm trees in St. Noos Plaza were orange and yellow, and I kicked them out of my way as I walked across the cobblestone paths between the lawns and the ponds and across the bridge over the canal that fed the big skating oval where Rachael and I had our first kiss—anyway, where I kissed her.

Schmeecks is one of the best dairy stores in the city. It's always crowded, and the clerks are constantly shouting out what people need on the cheese counter. I never saw anything like it, how fast they shout the orders and cut the slabs from the wheels and wrap them. It's the opposite of having twelve people staring at you with pen and notebooks in their hands, waiting for you to say something deep about ice hockey.

Hardly anyone noticed me as I flagged down one of the attendants, a young woman in a big apron and bonnet. I was wearing a greatcoat and a newsboy cap pulled over my eyes, so she didn't recognize me at first, but as soon as the first word was out of my mouth she placed me-- the only guy in Borschland who speaks the language with a Minnesota accent.

"Mr. Reinhardt," she said. "So good to see you."

She told me to wait. In about three seconds, the owner, Mr. Schmeeck, came out to meet me. He has a waxed moustache, a nose like a cranberry, and he's about five foot three.

"Mr. Reinhardt! What a surprise. So good to see you. What can I get for you today?" He bowed about six times while he said this, waiting for me to put out my hand to shake. Borschic people never initiate physical contact.

"All I need is a half-kilo of butter," I said, as he shook vigorously.

"Bah. Don't even think about coming in again." He worked his mustache side to side. "We will send a boy. Do you want to start an account with us? Let me give you some cheese. What about a lovely little wheel of *Schijnenfvaas*?"

We already had an account with the Bongarteax grocery store on the corner, the one with the brother-in-law who needed a job. We threw our business to them because they're cheaper on average, and Rachael is always trying to save a centime here and there, even though I get paid well to play hockey. But she always reminds me I'm a knee injury away from having my salary go from here to nothing.

"Just the kilo of butter? You need extra for some reason? Bongarteax mistook your order? I am so sorry. Of course, Lujluu is turning two and you are making a cake. I read that in *Te Taglik Staff*. She is a perfect princess, Mr. Reinhardt. Perfectly, perfectly as beautiful as her mother, thank God."

Mr. Schmeeck slathered it on heavy, like you should do with *Schijnenfvaas*. But I didn't mind. It was one of those things that you get used to.

I left the store with the butter and a wheel of cheese that

Mr. Schmeeck snuck in as a gift ("I can't let you leave without this. This batch was especially good"). Rachael would be furious. "If we don't start an account there after they give you a kilo of cheese, the whole world will know and we'll be shamed and I'll have to give my *He's an American, what can I do* excuse. Once and again." So I was thinking, *I should give this cheese away to somebody.*

Then it hit me that there is always a homeless dude who's between drinks and has gotten hungry. *Brilliant idea, Mr. Reinhardt.*

By this time a companionable group of paparazzi and tabloid types had congregated outside Schmeecks. Five or six is all, which is almost no one. A couple had gone in to the store and I recognized one of them, a regular named Gluuestische that I called Gluey for his ability to stick to me. But it was crowded, and the photogs were too busy smoking their pipes and jawing about the phase shift to figure out how to frame a shot. So they waited till I came outside with my net bag, and a couple of flash bulbs went.

Gluey called out, "Sherm, doing a bit of shopping for Lujluu's birthday?"

"Just some butter," I said, and waded out into the horse traffic on St. Noos Boulevard.

"What about the cheese?" someone else pointed out.

"A gift from Meester Schmeeck." I sidestepped the guy who sweeps up the horse apples, who was leaning on his broom, watching.

I could usually lose these dudes by saying I needed to do a little exercise, and then take a quarter mile sprint, but this time they seemed satisfied with my answers. In fact, they all turned away from me. I looked back. Schmeeck was at the door ready to be interviewed.

A little free publicity for Schmeeck, a little tongue-lashing from Rachael for me.

I walked back across the Oval, and soon found a candidate for the cheese. Or he found me. He came right up to me, as if he knew me.

"Good afternoon," he said.

"Good afternoon," I said. "Are you h--"

He stuck out his hand. "My name is Willem van Noos. Saint Noos, I'd be called around here."

"You bet you are," I said, and clutched the Schmeecks bag in front of me like a football as I shook his hand. It was creased and rough, but the grip was firm.

There were plenty of colorful bums around Staff Borsch. Some of them were from rich families. A lot of them just couldn't deal with phase shifts. Instead of claustrophobia, they had phase-o-phobia.

"May I have a moment of your time, Meester Reinhardt?"

I looked him up and down. He was pretty focused for being a homeless dude, and though he was dressed in a long overcoat, scarf, and big, floppy-brimmed felt hat, I could tell he wasn't an old man, or a young man that drinking and sleeping outside had made old. His face was strong-- not tan, exactly, but healthy, ruddy, and weathered. His eyes were blue-green, and the whites pretty clear. The guy was not an alcoholic. He just hadn't shaved his muttonchops in a while.

"If we walk and talk," I said. "I've got to get home. Family. Kids. You know."

"Briefly about myself," said St. Noos, falling into step with me. He had a good strong stride. "You know I am famous for discovering the Flowering Tree of Borschland and the Flowering Branch of Borschland that conveys eternal youth?"

"Yeah. You and St. Borsch, right?" I had been reading up on my saints at bedtime with Connie. So had this guy, apparently.

"St. Borsch? Yes, well. He was my... erm... collaborator."

"Okay." I cradled the bag against one shoulder as we walked and tried to keep a straight face.

"Anyway. You may know that the Saints of Borschland never die. Because they drank the *Bloomentisande*, the drink made from the flowers of the Flowering Tree."

That also I had read, though I figured that had to be a tall tale.

"And you may know that the Saints of Borschland return when the country is in danger. Now is such a time."

I turned and faced him. This was getting long. I needed to shake him. We were right at the skating oval. Kids were chasing pigeons. Ducks were dipping for whatever ducks like on the bottom of ponds. In the distance, the sound of a streetcar clanging its bell.

"Yes, yes. Unbelievable, isn't it?" He took a quick look from side to side, then focused on me again. Strong, blue-green eyes. "So I have come back. And I am a messenger. I want you to know that you and your sister are going to be very important people in the next several months."

"My sister and me?"

"Yes. We want you to be guardians of the Flowering Staff of Borschland. Because it has flowered after three hundred years of not flowering. And since it has flowered, the blossoms are going to be the most valuable thing in the world. Because the blossoms, once they have been brewed with boiling water, confer eternal youth on their consumer. Including me. I was the first one to drink the *Bloomentisande*."

"Wait a minute. We?"

"Yes, we. Don't worry about that now. You know the Branch, of course."

I had seen the Flowering Branch of Borschland once, in the Rijksmuseen, the National Museum, in Staff Borsch. It looks like a branch from a tree that you could use as a hockey stick, if you didn't mind it a little long and rough to the touch.

"Everyone will want this *tisande*, this elixir, and they will do whatever it takes to get it. So, Sherm Reinhardt of North America, if you don't protect the Branch, someone will strip the flowers, brew the potion of eternal youth, and become the ruler of all the continent, if not the world."

Well, I thought. *Just think of what would've happened if I had only gone to the Bongarteax. I never would've met this nut and I'd be happy, and Rachael would be happy, and we'd have butter and no extra cheese.* Although the people at the bakery would be fanning themselves with dishtowels as they discussed the weird foreigner who insisted on having his two-year old make the birthday cake instead of buying it from them.

"So," I said, "I can give you this cheese if you're hungry. But it's my daughter's birthday. I'm late already as it is, and my wife is not going to be happy."

"Oh, I know all that. I understand that distinctly."

"Why, because as a saint you know everything?"

"No, because I read the paper as soon as the phase shift came this morning."

Ha. The Paper Internet, I liked to call it. With the full story of what is happening in every Borschic celebrity's life.

"You will see me again," said St. Noos. "Soon." And he shook my hand, bowed, and bustled off, on his way to save Borschland. He hadn't even glanced at the cheese.

Eternally youthful saints who are old clearly don't need to eat.

CHAPTER 3 - SHERM

I would've told Rachael the whole story when I got home, but I didn't get a chance. In fact, when I opened the front door, I almost got a puck in the mouth.

Connie was playing hockey in the front hallway. It was long, with very smooth, shiny hardwood floors and only one rug right at the threshold, where there was a pad of stone and where the coat rack was, and where people stamped off the snow from their boots in winter. Connie thought that area was pretty terrific for a goalmouth. He'd whack a little wooden practice puck all the way down the hallway, and if it stuck on the rug, goal.

More than once, he'd actually broken the glass in the front door. And it was good, colored glass done by these expensive glass people who did seminaries and churches. Pale blue. He'd whack so hard even the practice puck could split a pane.

The puck glanced off my cheek and bounced away, and as soon as Connie saw it, he took off running. Meantime, this little Tasmanian devil thing wrapped itself around my legs. Lily was the fastest two-year old I'd ever seen. If you went to the park, you had to station police all around the perimeter of it, because she would be gone, zoom, as if into a parallel universe.

Daduj! Daduj!" she screamed. I gave her a noogie. She

screamed some more. I carried her into the kitchen on my leg.

"Oh, for Noos' sake," Rachael sighed as I came in. That was as close as she got to cursing. She was very well brought up. "Finally. You are a glacier, Sherm. Even slower. Where is it? All right. What does that bag say? I KNEW you would go to Schmeecks. Now it's going to be all OVER the papers."

Betrayed by the Schmeecks bag. And Cathy had clearly gone off duty.

The shredded wheat was about to hit the fan.

"It's *Schijnenfvaas*," I said, motioning to the cheese. Rachael liked *Schijnenfvaas*.

Rachael treated the cheese the same way St. Noos had. She pointed upstairs without looking at me. "Take care of your daughter. She's overtired. And she simply won't go down for a nap."

"What about the photographer?"

"I told him to come back at three of the clock. This child will absolutely lie down for an hour even though she is acting like she has had a dose of the *Bloomentisande*."

That meant both that she was hanging from the chandelier but also being naughty and disobedient. The *Bloomentisande* was not a drink of sweetness and light only, so they say in the Borschic storybooks. Which is why St. Noos knew if the wrong person got a hold of it, it'd be curtains for Borschland.

"And find that rapscallion of a son and fix him properly for playing hockey in the hallway again. We have TOLD him and TOLD him."

I swept Lily up in my arms. She was blonde, tow-headed in fact. She looked Swedish to me. Everyone said she would turn dark later; all the Borschic blondes did, unless there were blondes in your family, Meester Reinhardt, all the women would say.

Cathy's a blonde, I'd say. Sort of. With enhancements.

You couldn't keep Lily's hair combed, and she would scream bloody murder if you tried to braid it, which is what all little girls in Borschland did. Braid their hair, I mean.

So when we had to take Lily out in public, and she had to

have her hair braided, she'd always come out in the paparazzi pictures like she'd been tortured. In fact, she almost never looked at cameras.

Rachael called her *Te Klijnehujlenmejsjekint*, Our Little Lady of the Everstreaming Tears. She was a handful. But the name meant more than that. Rachael had had a tough time with both her pregnancies, and with Lily, we almost lost both the baby and Rachael. It's still painful to recall the whole thing. They don't have the kind of medicine here that they have in the States or in Australia. If you need a blood transfusion, for example, it's hit or miss. It was a miracle that both of them are alive.

That's why I love my kids more than life itself, and that little girl. You can't imagine.

As I took Lily, Rachael screamed upstairs, "Connuj! Connuj! You come down before your father comes up! If he has to come up, you will get a rare switching! Come down, then! Are you going to come down?"

"Shhh..." I said. "Lily. Nap. Okay?"

She gave me a look that could've killed a giant squid. I took her up to the children's room. Connie was hiding under his covers. "You lost your hockey stick," I told the mound of blankets. "Gone. I'm taking it away."

He let out a huge, dramatic sob, and the covers seemed to bunch up all by themselves.

Lily took a while to settle down, but Rachael was right, she was so tired she had black circles under her eyes. She was out for the count after half a story.

"Read the rest of the story?" Connie whispered from his bed.

"Stay up here. Mommy's pretty mad. Wait. I'll call you."

"*Ergut, Daduj*," said Connie. "Okay, Dad."

Rachael was in the kitchen, steaming. She hadn't gotten out the cake stuff. The butter was on the kitchen counter. The Schmeecks bag was on the floor. There was a new telegram, a yellow piece of folded paper, on the table.

"I can't BELIEVE you," she said, and jumped up. "I can't

BELIEVE you, you wretched excuse for a husband." She picked up a wooden spoon from the counter and was about to hit me with it. I caught her wrist. "And where is that boy? I will beat him to the edge of tomorrow."

I took Rachael by the shoulders. "Hey," I said. She wouldn't look me in the eye. "I'm sorry I took so long. What's going on? What's going on? Hey, it's okay. What is it?"

She kept shaking her head, and then her whole body began to shake. Finally she looked up, beautiful coffee-black eyes under those big, fat lashes. "I'm pregnant," she whispered, and began to cry. "I went to the doctor yesterday. The results came today." And she motioned to the telegram.

I hugged her to me. She put her head under my chin and I cupped my hand behind it. She sobbed into me, hard, racking sobs.

Oh God. Oh God. Oh God.

She was scared, but she was angry, too. We had tried to be careful after Lily. But there's no foolproof birth control in Borschland, and every little girl is taught that kids are a blessing.

"*Alleskeet ergut.* It's going to be all right," I whispered, though I didn't know. Of course. It was going to be our little adventure, along with the two blessed hellions we already had. *Alleskeet ergut, alleskeet ergut,* I kept saying, like a little poem.

Rachael's little adventure with death.

"We're going to get help," she said to my chest. "A governess. Who will live with us. I can't do this without help."

"Yes," I said. "*Ergut.* That's fine. That's fine."

She relaxed a little, then sighed.

Then I added, "And we're going to Australia for the birth."

She tensed up again. It was probably the wrong time to suggest that. She'd said no for Lily. She was stubborn. Probably the wrong time. You don't leave Borschland. You don't leave Borschland pregnant. You don't get on a plane. You don't risk never seeing your place again. And for reasons related to our last adventure, she would rather keep her feet completely on the ground.

"Maybe," she whispered. "If we are back."

Back from where? I thought. Then I remembered: the phase shift.

And the doorbell rang.

CHAPTER 4 - SHERM

It is amazing how fast Rachael Martujns Reinhardt can be totally okay again after losing it. It took her about three seconds.

After the doorbell rang, the sound of little feet on stairs told us Connie was hurrying to get the door.

Rachael yelled out in her best disciplinary mommy voice, "Connie! You have been very naughty, young man. Come back to the kitchen. Daddy will get the door."

He peered at us from the bottom of the stairs, sticking his head out from the end of the banister. Getting the door had been his plan. If it were, say, his grandfather, he'd be off the hook for a while. No one would discipline him in front of guests.

The doorbell rang again.

"I'll take him," I said.

Rachael sighed, and we turned from each other, like guards that meet in the middle of a castle wall and go the opposite way.

Connie joined me at the door, taking my hand and swinging it back and forth. He wanted me to pick him up on my forearm so he could dangle there, kicking and screaming. But he was almost too big for that. Or else I had to pump a little more iron off-season.

I undid the bolt on the door and swung it open. I was hoping for Cathy.

It was Saint Noos.

He bowed. "It's cold out," he said, "and even saints get cold."

Snowflakes had collected on the brim of his hat. I looked outside. When had it started snowing?

I frowned. "Don't you have, like, a shelter or something? Can't you sleep in a chapel?"

"I could sleep in a chapel, and have done so many a night," said the saint. "But truth to tell, I have to keep an eye on you, Sherm Reinhardt. All I said to you this morning remains true."

And I still didn't believe him, but I let him in anyway. The wind was coming up, and now the snow was blowing into the hallway.

"Who is it, Sherm?" Rachael called from the kitchen.

St. Noos held his hat in front of his belly. His cheeks and nose and bald pate were red, but otherwise he looked pretty put together. I couldn't figure out what his deal was. Unless he really was a saint.

"It's... ah..." I began.

Rachael appeared, tying an apron in front of her. She walked towards us with her head down, then looked up and stopped.

"Pardon me?" she said, her eyes wide and unblinking.

"This is... ah..."

"Dear lady," said Saint Noos. "My name is Willem. I am... I made the acquaintance of your husband this afternoon. And, well..."

"It's cold outside," I said.

"Yes," he said. "And, I've, I mean, in a bit of a predicament."

"Willem. Please, please, come in," she said, spreading her hands out in the Borschic way of hospitality. "Of course. You are welcome in our house. Are you hungry?"

Willem bowed and nodded, hat in hand, and shuffled

forward. We all piled into the kitchen, where we sat him at the table next to Connie, whose eyes got so big they might as well have crossed.

"A cup of hot coffee, perhaps?" Rachael asked.

"*Tangs Uj*," said Willem. "*Tangs Uj, mijne gastvrijische Daame.*"

"You are a gentleman," she said, and began to get out the service for coffee. "You speak like an old Borschic gentleman."

"This fine young man," said Willem. "What a handsome face."

"Thank you, sir," said Rachael. "You did not happen to bring a birthday cake along with your manners?"

"Oh, my lady," he said. "I would be happy to fetch you one. There is a bakery in the local Bongarteax just down the street."

"*So vijl ken Ij*," said Rachael, and turned an eye to me. "How well I know that. But my husband." And she made a tsk-ing sound that Willem immediately picked up on.

"Does he insist that you make it yourself?" he said.

She shook her head and busied herself with the dials and the spouts on the coffee machine.

"And is this fine young man to be given the crown of the year?"

Rachael opened a valve, and steam whooshed out of a spout.

"No," I said. "Our daughter."

As soon as I said it, there was a wailing from upstairs. Lily had woken from her nap. She was a very light sleeper, and the doorbell had probably roused her. Visitors-- Cathy, or whoever, were big news for the Lilster.

"A little one," said St. Noos.

"Yes, Saints bless us," said Rachael.

"I do, I do," he muttered to himself. I almost didn't hear him. I'm sure Rachael didn't. He stood up. "You have your hands full. I will take a cup of coffee, and then I will fetch your cake from the Bongarteax. They can make them in two squirts of a squid's ink, and they will frost them while you wait."

"*So vijl ken Ij*," said Rachael. "They are very skilled at the Bongarteax."

"It's very generous of you," I said. "I can do it."

"No," said Rachael. "I don't have my purse with me now. Sherm, darling, could you give him five schillings to take to Bongarteax?"

"Five schillings!" said Willem. "That's frightful. Have prices gone up that much?"

Rachael leveled her gaze at the saint, then at me. It was her "aren't you going to say something" look.

I didn't say anything. Five schillings was a lot for a cake. When it came to buying groceries, a schilling was like a twenty-dollar bill. You could get a lot of apples, potatoes and tinned fish broth for five schillings.

Rachael put her hands on her hips. "But we will want to make sure the cake is fine and that there is something extra for the icing piper," said Rachael. "I don't know if you know us, em, Willem, was it? But we are people who, ahem, are noticed."

"I distinctly understand," said Willem.

Rachael stared at me again. I got it. Five schillings to pay for the shame of having gotten butter at Schmeecks. I got out my wallet.

Rachael presented him with a cup and saucer. He took a sip from it, and nodded. "Perfect," he said.

"Cream?" I asked. I could have used a cup myself, but when in the doghouse I don't like to push my luck.

"I believe she has already put that in," said Willem, and smiled while taking another sip.

Rachael smiled back. "I will trust you to obtain their best cake," she said. "You are a very fine gentleman."

"And I will bring back the change," said Willem, taking a large, slurping sip. He then gave me the cup and disappeared down the hallway with the money.

Rachael waited till she heard the door close. "There is five schillings well spent," she said. "May the saints and the money find that man a warm bed and a bottle tonight."

"I think he's coming back," I said, though I wasn't completely sure.

"You think," she said. "You think. So much the worse. Please go get your daughter, put her on the potty, and then both of you come downstairs. We do have a cake to make, as well as an entire dinner, and pictures to take, before my parents arrive at the stroke of seven."

At least she said please.

CHAPTER 5 - CATHY

HAVE TO COVER EVENT said a telegram from Roald that afternoon. SORRY MAYBE COME LATER.

Journalists keep bad hours. And they are seldom off on weekends or nights. But this dinner had been on the calendar for a long time.

I sent a reply back. UNGLAABERLICKT! Unbelievable. It meant, at the same time, *I'm disappointed* and *This is your fault.* Maybe it wasn't fair, but that was how I felt. What was so important that he couldn't get a buddy to do the story for him?

It was Lily's birthday, after all. The little girl Sherm and Rachael had almost lost, and Rachael with her.

I went through all the possibilities as I got ready to go, and went to get flowers and a gift for Rachael. Was he getting cold feet? Had he met someone else? Was he intimidated by Mr. and Mrs. Martujns? Maybe he was planning a surprise. Showing up at dessert with a ring in a box.

I spend a lot of time thinking. Probably more than I should.

By the time I had picked out a little crystal *hijfenfette* bird for Rachael at my favorite crystal store, I decided I was being silly. But I was definitely going to give Roald the big interview about the crucial story he had to cover about minor league hockey players, no doubt. And I would think about getting a gauge on where we were in the relationship.

God, how I hated those words: *Where are we going?* But we'd been steady state for months now, and he'd been happy just being in my company. And I would say, *I am ready to rock and roll, Roald.*

It was already chilly and it had been snowing for two or three hours when I arrived at the door around 5 PM. I knew Rachael had her hands full with the kids and I wanted to help with dinner and the kids or wherever I was needed.

But I was not prepared for what I found when I arrived.

I knocked. A man I didn't know opened the door. He was older, but well-preserved. He was about as tall as me, and bald, with muttonchops, and a ruddy, weather-beaten complexion. The way you'd imagine a guy who spent a lot of time sailing boats for fun.

"You are Cathy, I presume," he said, in a very rich and deep Borschic voice. Borschic is a mixture of Dutch and German and West Frisian and it sounds like a fake language sometimes, or like the way you talk when the dentist has an instrument in your mouth. But this man's voice was like someone doing a voiceover for a radio commercial. Of a product that I was definitely going to buy.

"How did...?" I began, but he motioned for me to come in.

"I am Willem," he said. "Liluj is having her picture made and it is pandemonium. But we do have a cake in reserve."

Sherm had told me he wanted to make the birthday cake and have Lily help. Of course, with him, nothing is simple. From the kitchen, down the hall, I could hear the pandemonium my new friend Willem had mentioned.

"They decided to let the photographer take pictures of the cake making," Willem said.

"A cake in reserve?"

"In case this one does not come out. Which it might not, I think."

We inched our way into the kitchen. Sherm and Rachael's kitchen is not big. They live in a townhouse in the St. Noos Plaza area for a reason, but it's not because of the spaciousness of the townhouses. They could get a place farther out, with more room, but they are very thrifty and frugal.

A photographer had set up large, humming electric lights on stands and had a stand-up camera with a hood, and these took up a large amount of floor space. In the middle of the room Rachael sat at the wooden table, also in an apron, while Lily stood on a stool with an adult-sized apron tied around her, so big that the straps flowed to evening-gown length. Sherm stood behind her, as if to catch her if she fell off the stool. Connie stood next to Sherm, watching the goings-on. His eyes and little brown bangs showed above the table top.

Connie saw me first. "*Tantuj Kathuj!*" he cried, and ran to hug me. Lily, who wants to do everything her brother is doing, screamed also, and, with no easy way of getting down from her stool, held out her arms to me and in so doing smacked Rachael in the face with the spoon she'd been using to stir the cake batter. At the very same time, the photographer took a picture, and the room was filled with the charred-crumbs smell of Borschic camera flash.

Connie wrapped his arms around my waist. I knelt down so we could have a proper hug. He smelled of cake batter and had a dusting of flour on his collared shirt, which was too fancy for making a cake, but there was the photographer to consider.

"Daduj and Mamuj took my hockey stick away from me," he whispered hotly next to my ear. "I was bad."

"You'll get it back. *Alleskeet ergut.*" I can't yet conduct an official confessional in the Borschic church, but I do tend to hear a lot of unofficial ones, and I give a lot of unofficial absolutions. It just goes with the territory.

Meanwhile Lily had been caught in Sherm's arms and was bawling to be let free. Somehow Willem had gotten hold of a damp cloth and was giving it to Rachael to clean her face of the batter. The photographer was asking *medems n meesters* to please take their places again.

"Enough!" cried Rachael, and the whole room went quiet. "Enough of photographs today." She turned to the photographer, who was standing frozen with his little shutter plunger in his hand. "Excuse me, kind sir. That is all we can do. Darling?"

Sherm spoke with Lily still craning to get out of his arms. "My wife is right. That is all for today."

The photographer said, "But we have made only six plates, and none of them may come out."

Willem said, "Do you have a personal camera, Meester Reinhardt?"

"Yes, we do," said Sherm. Personal cameras in Borschland were bulky, but they were still hand-held.

"Then," Willem said, "you might make family pictures, have the films developed, and then have an engraver create a likeness from them."

Sherm brightened, and put Lily down. "Great idea," he said.

"I will send a boy to get the films," said the relieved photographer.

Lily ran to me and got her share of hugs, and I was ready to hug Willem.

After the photographer had taken down his equipment and packed it in his horse van, preparations for dinner began humming. I was put on the mission to entertain Connie, Sherm got his camera, Lily was set up again briefly at her mixing bowl, and Willem apparently began making dinner.

Dinner parties in Borschland are elaborate, with many courses. Borschic people are great admirers of French cuisine, and model their courses after the French, with local ingredients. Therefore it would have been up to Rachael to make something complicated for the first course, like a terrine, which is a many-layered casserole with each layer having something wonderful like wild mushrooms or watercress creamed with walnut oil.

Rachael was not a natural cook, however. She grew up with a cook in her house, who did not teach her much because Rachael liked to read. And now with two kids she was frequently exhausted, and with Sherm keeping strange hours and traveling for work, she often relied on restaurants to deliver dinner.

But tonight she had figured she would do a terrine, and she had all the ingredients, but was terrified to start. Willem started for her, and in half an hour the terrine was well on its way to completion, while the roast beef was in the oven, the *terveelluj* fish were dressed and ready for the skillet, and Rachael, having finished with Lily and sent her upstairs to me, was on her way with the more mundane task of julienning turnips for the turnip salad.

Sherm, who came upstairs to say hello and check on the kids, reported all this to me. "I'm not really needed down there," he said.

"A man in the kitchen is like a squid in the desert," I said, quoting a Borschic proverb.

"Willem isn't a squid," Sherm said. "The dude is a chef."

"What's going on with him?" I asked, and Sherm gave me what he knew. Apparently, after he gave Willem the five-schilling note, he was gone for about forty-five minutes and came back with a fantastic cake with gold-colored icing and artisan Bearland honey drizzles. "And he's homeless?" I said.

Sherm shook his head. "Rachael worships him already. It's weird."

That's all he said to me about Willem. He went downstairs again, came up, and around six thirty the parents, Conraad and Lynneet, arrived.

The kids officially went into a tizzy over their Grootmuttuj and Papuj. There was to be a present opening and a slice of cake for each of the children, and then they were to skip upstairs and be tucked in.

It was too much for Lily. After she opened her present from the grandparents, a she-cub of Bearland doll in an elegant evening dress, she immediately hugged the doll to her and burst into tears.

Everyone kept saying, "*Te Puupje! Te Puupje!* The dolly! The dolly!" which didn't help at all.

Rachael took her and the doll upstairs and Sherm led Connie, who protested he was not sleepy and not little like his sister. We sat in the parlor sipping cider, and gradually,

gradually, the sobbing died down to pleading, and the pleading, finally, to silence.

"Blessed be the children," Conraad Martujns pronounced, and lifted his glass.

"Blessed be," echoed his wife.

So it was not till going on eight that we actually sat down to the dinner, six places counting Willem, although he did not sit down until he had skilleted the last *terveelluj* and all the wine and cider was opened and decanted.

"Who is this you have hired for the dinner?" Conraad asked Rachael. "We have two capable women who would help you, I think."

"I haven't hired him, Papuj," Rachael said. "He has just made himself useful."

"Like a saint during a phase shift," said Conraad. "He has appeared out of nowhere?"

"Yes," said Rachael, and her eyes lit up.

Sherm said, "I met him in the park on the way home from the cheese store this afternoon. He's down on his luck and just could use a place to stay for the night."

Conraad said, "We have a place for him in the Chapel of St. Noos. He need not be cold tonight."

Right then somebody put up a wicked banging on the front door. The kind that sets little dogs into a tizzy.

Lynneet put her hand to her throat. "Whoever can that be at this hour?" she said.

"And who does not know about doorbells?" Rachael said.

"It wouldn't be Roald," I said. He knows about doorbells, but I said it more as a way of maybe magically making it Roald.

It wasn't Roald. It was one of Sherm's new teammates, Urdan Kasmahlov, the teenager from Canada. He appeared in front of Sherm, who'd gotten the door, looking like a cross between a prince of Russia and a sheik of Arabia, with a bit of skater punk mixed in.

"Hi?" he said in English.

"Why didn't you tell me you had invited him, you perfect dolt," Rachael said out of the side of her mouth to Sherm.

Conraad went *tut-tut*, and gave Sherm a look that was half sympathetic and half I told you so.

Sherm said, "I didn't invite him."

"I got a telegram," said Urdan to Sherm, and handed him a folded piece of paper.

Everyone looked around the table as Sherm translated. No one owned up to sending the telegram inviting Urdan to dinner. Urdan himself had had a tough time getting to the house when the taxi he'd hired seemed not to know Sherm's address. He'd used all his meal money for the next day paying for it.

Despite his cluelessness, Urdan Kasmahlov was a pretty dashing kid, I have to say. It was a shame that face was going to be messed up by a hockey puck some day.

A place was made for Urdan, and a welcome blessing said by Conraad, followed by a blessing of the food and the company, and finally we all sat down to the terrine, which smelled incredible.

"Oh, *drejanthus*!" said Rachael.

"*Drejanthus*? What is it?" I asked.

"A traditional herb," said Conraad. "It is very expensive, and if it is boiled in the wrong way, it smells like carrion. Rightly, it smells like this—heaven."

It did smell like heaven—like cloves, but sweeter and wilder.

"We never use *drejanthus*," said Rachael. "First of all, because I cannot cook. But second, because my darling husband cannot smell it."

Willem turned to Sherm. "I had read this in the newspapers. Is it so?"

"Yeah, I got my nose broken a couple of times in games," said Sherm. "And my sense of smell is pretty much gone."

I asked Urdan in English how his sense of smell was, and he assured us his nose was fine.

We tasted the terrine. I melted after the first bite.

"Sir, your culinary skills are rare," said Conraad.

Willem raised his glass of Lisandran white wine. "From a

man of your girth, I'd say that was a real compliment."

Everyone (except Urdan) burst into laughter. It was totally unexpected, and technically it was a pretty rude thing to say. But the Borschic people are uncomfortable with stuffiness at the table. At heart they are beer-and-potatoes types. So when Willem made his joke, spoken in that beautiful, rich voice of his with his gentlemanly diction, it was as if the stuffiness bubble burst. Everyone relaxed, and enjoyed.

The courses went by one by one, and each one was better than the next, even the turnip salad, which is not my favorite, but Willem did some kind of creamy vinaigrette for it that was both light and rich at the same time. We poured different wines for the courses, and at dessert there was brandy with the deep, dark chocolate cake and honey drizzles. Willem was so charming, and the wine worked such magic, that I had completely forgotten about Roald until the moment he arrived.

Just as we were cutting the cake, there was another banging on the door.

It was Roald, and he had a wild look in his eye.

"Saints of the Fatherland!" he cried out to us as he appeared in the threshold of the dining room. "The Flowering Branch of Borschland has bloomed!"

No one said anything except Urdan, who leaned over to me and whispered, "Is there any more cake?"

CHAPTER 6 - WILLEM

Yes, it was I that sent the telegram to young Meester Kasmahlov. But that is beside the point.

I was not surprised to find out about the Branch, the *Bloomentwejg*, we call it in Borschland. I was surprised to hear that the government had told the press.

The government of Borschland cannot be considered the shrewdest on the face of the earth. It is very democratic as far as governments go, which means often that stupidity rules more than prudence. And with news such as this, I might have, had I been in power, kept the news of the flowering under wraps.

It is not that I have no influence on the government. I would speak to them at the proper time. At the moment, however, Borschland needed to secure a non-Borschic protector of the Branch-- and specifically, someone from North America. And as there were a grand total of three of these folk in Borschland at the time, and they were all presently congregated at 67 Nojallesanktenswej, the address of one Sherman Reinhardt and family, known to most honest cab drivers in the Greater Staff, the government could wait.

It had been a very exciting evening already, with the children and the dinner party, before Cathy's beloved Roald arrived. I made myself as useful as possible as the whole group of them gathered around the wireless set to listen to the Prime Minister give his speech about the place of Borschland in the history of the world and what a precious time it was now for all Borschlanders to unite to preserve one of the greatest miracles of all time.

It wasn't till late that night, when all had gone to bed, and Rachael was asleep, exhausted as she was, that Sherm came to my room, the guest room in the front of the house, with the window that looked out over the street.

He brought a candle in a holder, and the frown on his brows and in the curve of his mouth was most visible.

"Now tell me again," he said. "What you told me this afternoon."

"You do not have to do anything yet," I said, anticipating his first question. "It may be weeks or months before anyone finds a way to steal the *Bloomentwejg*, and certainly the outside world cannot find it because we are in a phase shift. But we must be on our guard for enemies within."

"Enemies within," Sherm said, the frown lit by the candle growing deeper.

"You mentioned that I had a collaborator in the discovery of the *Bloomentwejg*, St. Borsch. He is the one, Henrick Lojren van Borsch, after whom our nation is named. He is the one whom against whom we need to guard.

"You see, I am a Saint of Light, and St. Borsch, my rival, is a saint of Shadow. So it's more than likely he's going to show up at some point and try to steal the Branch and the petals so he can make more Shadow Saints."

Sherm drew himself up. "Shadow Saints? I thought that was a bogey man thing, for scaring children."

"Not at all. Borschland, throughout its history, has kept a balance between Saints of Shadow and Saints of Light. If ever there become more Saints of Shadow, then there will be a revolution in the country, we'll join the modern world, and there will be a big and bloody war. Because the twentieth century is the century where the wide world started saving people from disease by the millions, and started killing people in wars by the millions. Before it had been sickness that was the real destroyer of human life. But in the twentieth century it was war. So the Saints of Shadow are thinking, *We need to bring Borschland into the twentieth century so we can cure the worst diseases known to man.* But at the same time, inevitably, they will bring in the technology for genocides."

"So the Shadow Saints are evil?"

No, they are not evil. Heavens. If you learn anything about the Saints of Borschland, know that none of us are evil. And none of us are really good, either, not silver-angel-feather good. The Saints of Light stand for keeping Borschland as it is, a country that is locked in the past. The Saints of Shadow stand for bringing Borschland into the modern world. Ultimately, they are for finding out how to stop phase shifts, or at least control them, so that Borschland is always in the wide world."

"That could never happen," said Sherm, almost whispering. "Could it?"

"We have been studying it for centuries," I said. "There are theories."

"Medicine is good," Sherm said. "Take childbirth. We need help with that. How about, Borschland gets the medical stuff, but leaves the war alone?"

"It doesn't work that way. There is not one without the other. That's what it means, you know-- Shadow and Light. You can't have one without the other. It's not Darkness and Light. It's that Light, when it falls on the world, creates shadow, and there is no light without shadow, and by the same token there is no shadow without light."

Sherm shook his head. It was a lot to take in for someone who was new to Borschland. Even Cathy, seminarian that she was, wouldn't understand such things as well as the typical nine-year old child in Borschland does. It is in our, shall we say, DNA.

"So," he said. "We wait. And what about Cathy? Does she know about you, too?"

"No. And she shouldn't. Not yet. Better to keep it simple." We sat there, watching the candle flicker and flare for a moment. Then I said, "This Kasmahlov. A good player?"

"We'll see. He hasn't been in any games yet. He's young, but with promise."

"I invited him tonight because Saint Borsch-- Henrick-- will seek him out, to get him on his side. He is perfect, a young single man, open to manipulation, to become a thief of the Branch. And Henrick played ice hockey in his day, though then it was a game called *kolv*."

"Yeah, it was like golf on ice," he said, putting his finger to his forehead, then pointing at me. "Guys still go out and do it on the Borschland River, on holidays and whenever."

"So he will, so to say, speak Kasmahlov's language. And I wanted to at least delay the meeting, to help him see he belongs with you and Cathy. You are his family, not the Shadows."

"Family?"

"Yes, a very small and very important one. For just as no one can guard the *Bloomentwejg* except for you, so no one but from the wide world can steal it."

"How is that? I don't get it."

"It's a strange thing. Those who are of the Continent-- bears, foxes, everyone-- are vulnerable to something in the Branch. Smelling the flowers debilitates us, and touching it kills us. We know that because over the years, some Borschic people born in Europe tried to touch it, and we had an Australian attempt at theft about a hundred years ago that ended in the would-be thief's death. So."

"But," Sherm said, and rubbed his beard. "Don't you and Henrick both come from where-- the Netherlands-- originally? Didn't you touch it?"

"We are Dutch, and we did touch it," I said. "Both Henrick and I were born in New Amsterdam-- the Dutch colony that became New York."

"So you're saying that--"

"We are North American, and so by logical deduction,

North Americans are immune."

"But you won't handle it now," he said.

"We've been three hundred years in Borschland. Our immunity has worn off."

"I've been in Borschland five years. Won't my immunity have worn off?"

"No. We stopped handling it after twenty years. It doesn't go away that fast."

That was enough of an answer for him, it appeared. "So why is Henrick going to go for Urdan?" he said. "Why won't he go for me, or Cathy?"

"You both love Borschland as it is," I said. "You came here and fell in love and wouldn't change it. You like it this way, unsettling as it is. You are not creatures of change. I could sense it when I first approached you. If you were of the Shadow, you would have walked by me without even hearing me.

"On the other hand, young Meester Kasmahlov we do not know yet. He is young, and can be swayed. We don't even know-- I have no understanding yet-- why he came."

"I haven't talked to him about that," Sherm said.

I nodded. It was quiet, except for the crystals of snow tapping on the windows.

"Tired," Sherm said, and shut his eyes for a moment. They were the bloodshot eyes of a young father.

"I know. But just one more thing," I said. "Make sure Kasmahlov's movements are watched. Where he goes, to whom he talks. Above all, no contact with women."

"Women?"

"The easiest way to get a man to do what you want is for a woman to ask it."

"That's for sure."

"We'll see how the government reacts to the miracle. And you'll get your chance to see it."

"It."

"The *Bloomentwejg*. It is beautiful to behold. A marvel."

He held up a finger, and said, "It is true that--"

"Enough questions. Time for bed. You've had a long day and you have a surveillance to arrange."

He yawned. "You're right about the long day. And Lily will be up tomorrow morning before six."

"Don't worry about her. Get some rest."

"All right."

And that was that. I looked out the window at the phase-shifted universe, and the sliver of phase-shifted moon that goes along with it. I do not sleep much when the Borschic phase is on. That is because I sleep always when it is not.

Another story for another time.

CHAPTER 7 - SHERM

The next morning something unusual happened: sun on my face woke me up.

It isn't that the sun seldom shines in Borschland. It's that I was used to getting up earlier than it rose. Having little kids will do that to you.

I got into the habit of early rising when Rachael was pregnant with Lily, and she was on bed rest quite a bit, so I had to deal with Connie. Fun, especially after a night game, when my sore muscles were barking like dogs.

But this morning I got my face tickled by a warm ray of light, and I said, "Lily, stop," but it wasn't Lily. I checked the mantel clock over our fireplace, and it said little hand on the nine, big on the one. It was after 9 AM.

Rachael was having coffee in the kitchen and reading the newspaper.

"What's going on?" I asked.

"Willem is telling the children stories of old Borschland," she said, and took a sip of coffee.

"I can't remember the last time I slept in until nine."

Rachael turned a page. "This is what it would be like with a governess."

The papers said the whole city was on fire with

Bloomenmanuj, or Flower Fever. Everyone had been taken off their normal assignment and was covering some kind of story about it. Everyone was interested in getting a peek at the Branch itself, and plenty of idiots were saying it was a government plot to take people's minds off of whatever was going wrong in politics at the time.

They'd even called out the armed forces to guard the thing.

No one was thinking about hockey, even though training camp was starting the next day.

But I was thinking about Kasmahlov, for sure.

I had to put a tail on him, and I knew how I could do that.

But first, I had to get him to practice.

Urdan was still major jet-lagged, and after the excitement of the previous night, I wouldn't have been surprised one bit if he bugged out of the last pre-training camp skate.

But the best way to get over being jet-lagged is to skate, and Chrojstenkaamps had put me on the job to make sure he did.

I went to see Urdan at his hotel across the street from 14 Waatersdram. It brought back memories for me-- my first days in Borschland, when I got spirited by this clever taxi driver into the bed and breakfast owned by his sister-in-law. That place is famous now, and the lady is making a mint advertising it as Sherm Reinhardt Slept Here B&B.

Urdan was staying at the Hotel Sanktsimujen, an eight-story place with a restaurant and a taxi stand where we can keep an eye on the kid. The concierge said he was pretty sure Urdan was asleep, because he'd taken him rolls and coffee at 10 AM and there was no answer.

But when I knocked on the door and said it was me, it was clear he wasn't asleep, because I heard this female voice say something like *oh my saints* in Borschic and Urdan himself was like, *quiet, quiet* in English, and I wondered how the woman had gotten past the concierge.

Urdan's nineteen-year old dreamboat face appeared in the crack of the door. He had these big soulful brown eyes and a soft little bad-boy beard and his hair was thick and black and fell halfway down his neck. Very exotic for Borschland, and just itching to get messed up by a flying puck or a fist.

"Hi, Coach," Urdan said, and flashed perfect white teeth.

"Morning," I said. "After your big night last night with the dinner party and all that, I figured you'd be taking it easy."

"Yeah," he said, rubbed the back of his head. He looked at me as if it was my turn to say something.

"So who's the lady friend?"

"Nothing," he said. "Nothing, like, happened."

"The lady friend is nothing?"

He sighed. "She's not a lady friend. Just, you know, like, a friend."

"Was it a friend that you hired?" I asked. That could possibly be a very large PR nightmare, depending on how kind the newspapers were interested in being.

"No, no, hell no." He leaned toward me, cocked his head, and lowered his voice. "It wasn't like that, eh? I met her last night at the, um, lounge or whatever. She's a, she's, I think she's at the University of Borschland studying English. She speaks pretty good English. Her name's Danny."

I nodded. The "lounge" would've been the hotel bar, where they had music every night, and Urdan probably went in after he took his cab back from the dinner party. And someone might have latched on to him. But it was very strange. Good Borschic girls don't spend the night with guys they meet in bars. It just doesn't happen. No, scratch that. No Borschic girls spend the night with guys they meet in bars.

"May I come in?" I asked.

"Really?" Urdan said, and stepped back from his conspiracy whisper stance.

"Yeah, really."

I needed to find out if the friend was a prostitute. If she was, we might be able to keep things quiet, because Borschic people are discreet about that type of thing. If the lady was just someone he picked up, the papers would have a field day with it.

She was mostly dressed when I walked in. That is a feat in Borschland, because the women do wear quite a few undergarments, so if you take them off, it takes a long time to put them back on again. She was very pretty. Big mass of brown hair. Cute little nose, twinkly eyes.

"*Gut emorgenweck*," I said.

"*Gut emorgenweck*," she said, tucking in her shirt. She probably would've gotten dressed in the bathroom of the room, but there isn't a bathroom in Borschic hotel rooms. You go down the hallway to go to the bathroom, and if you want a hot bath, you go downstairs and order a hot bath in a claw-footed, cast-iron bathtub in an individual cubicle.

"This is--" I began.

"Highly unusual," she said. "I know. I am a journalist."

"What?"

"I write for the *Taglik Staff*. Women's pages. I was sent to get a story about the new North American ice hockey player."

Te Taglik Staff is a tabloid. The kind of paper that runs stories about giant whales disrupting shipping during a phase shift. And lots of celebrity news. But usually, they don't create the scandals.

"And that's what I have done," she said. "You should be reading it this afternoon. If my editor has any sense."

I tried to nod, but my jaw was dragging on the floor, and I couldn't pick it up.

"The reason," she said, then paused and took a little brush out of her purse. Borschic women are famous for their long hair and beautiful little brushes. You don't cut Borschic women's hair. If they want it short, they braid it and put it up.

She talked as she brushed. "The reason I am in his room is not what you are thinking. And neither is it the reason I have been *deshabujlee*."

Deshabujlee is the polite Borschic word for being caught with your pants down.

"When we, ah, agreed to the interview, it was very late at night. I was tired. And as we were already in his room, we both simply fell asleep."

"Fell asleep undressed?" I said, and looked over at Urdan, who had on a t-shirt, athletic shorts, and an I'm-not-busted-am-I look on his face.

"I was never undressed," she said, looking me straight in the eye, but blushing purple all the same.

"Have you a press card?" I asked.

She stopped brushing, and fished in her purse. The card said, VAN TER ROOST ANNA DANIELUJNA, TAGLIK STAFF, KORRESPONDENT. Correspondent was kind of like a stringer, one step up from running copy back and forth from editor to editor.

"Looks like you got a scoop," I said, and handed it back to her.

"Assuredly I won't write about the unusual circumstances," she said. "Meester Kasmahlov has a compelling story and life, despite his youth. I will focus on that."

"See that you do," I said. There was really nothing else to say. She hadn't done anything illegal, just potentially embarrassing.

"I will," she said, and flashed me a defiant look that was more hopeful than defiant. She knew I could look up her parents and tell on her, if I wanted to be that mean about it. It was that strict.

"Are you University of Borschland?" I asked.

"School of Journalism," she said. "My last semester."

"I see," I said, and breathed a little easier. If she was for real-- and the card looked authentic-- she probably hadn't been put up to any funny stuff by the Saints of Shadow Willem was warning against. Maybe she was just a girl out to get a story, with benefits.

Anna Danielujna van ter Roost-- Danny-- pulled on her shoes, buckled and tied them, and left, but not without first giving Urdan a look that said something like, I'll see you around, slugger.

"*Tah-loo*," I said after her. She didn't say a thing. Borschic women always make it seem like it's your fault, and they don't even have to say anything. It's just in the way they walk, the way they toss their head. I have never seen a Borschic woman even roll her eyes. They don't have to.

"Listen," said Urdan.

"Save it," I said.

"Okay, okay," he said.

"This never happened, okay?"

"What never happened?"

"Right. And one more thing."

"What's that, Coach?"

"Stop calling me Coach. I'm not your coach."

"Okay."

"Call me Sherm, got it?"

"Sherm. Okay."

"Workout. 14 Waatersdram. And eat something."

Seems like a lot longer than five years ago that I came to Borschland not knowing one thing about the country, only that I wanted my job to be skating around after a hunk of rubber. In some ways, with Cathy here now, it feels like I have always been here.

A lot has changed. Fans have gotten used to me. I still score a lot of goals, but I do other things now, behind the scenes. I have become a kind of player scout, talent evaluator, and now, with Urdan on board, I'm an unofficial translator, too. It means I get paid about 40K schillings a year, which is the highest salary in the league, but I work for it. I'll tell you that right now.

When I came to Borschland it was a perfect fit. It's one of those places where you're better off having nothing to lose, and instead of losing I gained a wife and a championship.

From there, there was nowhere to go but down. Four more seasons of skating and shooting got me some injuries (fortunately not my knee), some really bad luck at times, and a lot of hellos and goodbyes to retiring and new players. After all that time, we haven't won another championship.

We were runners up the second year, and we hit a bad patch the third year because Norbert the goalie retired and he had been so good there just wasn't a replacement for him. The fourth year we got goalie sorted out, but I had a really bad year with injuries, and the fifth year we came in second again, behind this incredibly lucky Bevinlunz team who weren't that big a deal but just won all their games versus the scrubs and got dozens more lucky bounces against the big boys than they should have.

We did win the Flowering Branch Cup last year, which is the pro-am tournament of Borschland. All sanctioned hockey clubs in the nation get a shot to play against the big boys. Of course, we had to beat Matexipar to win. All the little guys were out by the third round.

So now, this year, number six, was already starting to be the weirdest of all, with Urdan the Latvian lover, Lavishbear and the Zimrothian goalie.

Now I normally would have babysat Kasmahlov, sat him down in the hotel dining room and gotten something into him, then walked him across the street to 14 Waatersdram.

But this was the year of the *Bloomentwejg*. So I told the paparazzi outside the hotel I was going to the Bearland Embassy to talk about Lavishbear, but my real reason had to do with Kasmahlov.

I still didn't understand what was going on with this thing-- St. Noos, St. Borsch, Shadow, Light-- but I did know that the Branch was Borschland's national symbol, and if it got stolen it would crush the whole country. Whether Willem was a saint or not, he was right, he'd known the Branch had bloomed way before the rest of us had.

So I decided to follow Willem's order, and put a tail on Urdan.

After Anna Danielujna van ter Roost, it was the smart thing to do anyway.

The Bearland Intelligence and Investigation Service is a fun bunch of party animals. They gave me a run for my money once when a different government was in power. Now that my friend Junior and his party are in power, the embassy and the Service has gotten a lot friendlier with me, and I knew I could count on them if it ever came to a scrape. They were also very interested in Lavishbear making it in the league. That was a big point of pride on their part.

I was shown into the office of the deputy consul general, a grizzly named Man Greatbear. I know that's a strange name, but some bears name their kids Man the way we call people animal names, like Wolf. There's more than one Wolf in Borschland.

The office was completely different from what you'd see in Borschland. The bears like to think they are modern, so they go for white walls, concrete floors, lights hanging from the ceiling, and metal frames in their windows. Greatbear had a colorful Zimrothian rug over his concrete floor, but the chair I sat in was still one of those aluminum deals with a black leather cushion that was too wide for the average human wingspan and not soft enough for the average human rear end.

"What may I do for you, Sherm?" Man asked, in English. He was a big, calm, clear-eyed bear with a bit of gray around the ears. "More papers to sign for our Mr. Lavishbear?"

"No, this isn't about hockey," I said.

Greatbear sat back in his swivel armchair, and it squeaked.

"I need a favor," I said. "I need you to watch someone, and I need your best bear."

Greatbear nodded slowly. He did most things slowly. "Tell me more."

"I can't tell you everything right now, but it's about the Flowering Branch, and it's about the possibility of it being stolen. I know a-- I found out-- anyway, I'm trying to stop the Branch from being stolen, and there's a guy who might do it."

"Who?"

"Urdan Kasmahlov, our new player from Canada."

"How do you know he's a candidate for this theft?"

"I can't tell you that right now. I just know he is. And I can't watch him all the time, so I was hoping you could tail him. Just make sure you know who he's seeing, what he's doing."

Man made a kind of "I'm thinking it over" grunt.

"Come on, it's not like you don't know how to tail a person."

"It's not that, Sherm. It's that with this news we are after a whole new honeycomb, so to speak," said Greatbear, scratching the underside of his snout. "The Flowering Branch doesn't just concern you. It concerns the entire continent. If what they say is true about the flowers, that they confer immortality, I could name a lot of animals who would like to get their paws on it. Including our opponents in government.

"And even if the Branch is not stolen, the idea of many Borschlanders becoming immortal doesn't sit well with us. We would rather that the elixir from the blossoms not be used at all, if they can't be given to responsible bears."

"Oh," I said.

"If I surveil this Canadian," Man said, "I would expect you to report to me anything you know about plans to use the blossoms. I know you are not highly placed in the Borschic government, but here you are in my office telling me that you can't disclose your sources. That is Bearish for I have a friend."

Man Greatbear, you've got me there, I wanted to say. But I kept quiet.

"Borschland and Bearland are allies," Greatbear went on. "This doesn't have to rise to the level of an international incident. But if the Borschic authorities can be persuaded to dispose of those blooms, it would immeasurably help international peace and security. If not, Bearland does need to know, so we can take steps."

"What steps?"

The consul general of the Bearland embassy rotated his big shoulders, and the chair squeaked again. "I do need," he said, "To get this chair oiled."

"Okay," I said. "Junior's my friend, and I like Bearland. I like Lavishbear, too. He's got a great shot to make the team. But don't expect me to do something against Borschland just to help Bearland. I'm not Borschic or Bearish, but I've got a wife and kids."

"Of course, Sherm," said Man, as calmly and softly as any bear could who weighs four hundred pounds. "Just keep us posted. No harm in that."

"All right, then. We understand each other."

"I will send a bear to establish a liaison. Mattheius himself will know nothing. "

"Thanks. If we can keep Urdan out of this mess, so much the better."

"No doubt," said Man, and stood up. He was a lot taller than me, but unlike a wild grizzly, he wasn't ten feet tall. Upright Bears were smaller and they kept their claws clipped back, thank the saints.

We shook paw and hand, and I headed out to the rink. The season couldn't start fast enough.

CHAPTER 8 - CATHY

I had never seen Roald so shaken.

It was one of those things where if we were married already, we could go home and talk about it in bed. But at Sherm and Rachael's, at a dinner party, in front of the radio, he couldn't be calmed down.

He'd gone to a press conference. His editor had chosen about a dozen staffers. It was top-secret, invitation only, to papers in the area, down to the local sheets in Natatck and Rirlver across the river from Staff Borsch.

"We were downtown, in the biggest auditorium in the Ministry of Domestic Affairs, at the center of the city, where all the buildings have pillars," Roald said. "We'd all been told not to let anyone know beforehand. Or we could be arrested, my editor said, for treason against the Borschic state."

"Saints," said Conraad. "That is a serious charge."

"It is almost never made," said Lynneet.

"Eleven times in the history of Borschland," said Willem.

"So we were all terrified," Roald went on. "That's why I told you by telegram, and why I didn't say anything more about the event. Rotten luck it happened on Liluj's birthday, but I must tell you, it was historic, and I'm honored to have been there."

Roald was clearly in shock. He hadn't told one joke yet.

"They began by introducing the Minister of Domestic affairs, who thanked us all for being there, and he told us this would be the most significant thing that would happen to us in our lifetimes. He then introduced the Prime Minister."

Everyone gasped. The Prime Minister does not do press conferences as a rule. He is supposed to let others do them for him.

"What's more, next to him, was the High Archdeacon, Phillip van Eck." Here Roald nodded at Conraad. Conraad is an Archdeacon and has been the High Archdeacon before. It is a rotating office.

"Here is the bald truth, the Prime Minister said. The *Bloomentwejg* has flowered. The High Archdeacon has examined the Branch and it is authentic."

"Phillip," said Conraad to the space in front of him. "He kept it a secret from the rest of us.

"When did it happen?" Rachael asked.

"As far as we can tell, at the same time as the phase shift this morning," Roald said, his voice a hoarse whisper now. "Some scientists think that, ah, the blooming itself may have caused the shift. And that we won't shift back until the blossoms have all fallen."

We all sat there with our mouths open, except for Urdan, who couldn't understand a thing in Borschic.

"The Rijksmuseen was still closed at that hour, and the night watchmen were going off duty. A man named Gooswajk saw it first. Apparently he fainted."

"I would have, too," said Rachael.

"They told us a lot of things, things some of us scribbled down, but most of us just listened. One thing was that the fate of the nation hung in our hands. The way we reported this would be of utmost importance. They said we needed not to foment panic by telling people that the blossoms could make an elixir of immortality."

"But everyone knows that," said Rachael. "We grew up with the idea."

"They said we needed to emphasize that this is a theory only. We have no scientific evidence of anything."

"It is the only thing they can say," said Willem. "But it will be impossible to stop people from dreaming about getting a sip of the *Bloomentisande*. And soon it will be impossible for people not to believe that the government will use it for its own people. This is an opportunity to make another generation of saints."

"How many living saints are there?" Sherm asked.

"No one knows," said Conraad. "They don't make their appearances public. Some are original, and some are descendents."

Roald checked his watch and said there would be an announcement on the radio. We gathered in the parlor, Sherm clicked on the set, and the announcement was made officially by the Prime Minister. After a few hushed words by commentators, there was the national hymn, followed by religious music.

"Saints and angels pray for us," whispered Lynneet, wiping tears.

All the way through, the Borschic folk in the room had been resisting weeping. Borschic people tend not to show deep emotion. But now handkerchiefs were produced, and Conraad asked that we join in a hymn for the republic.

I knew I couldn't understand what they were feeling. It was frustrating, and yet I didn't want to be anywhere else.

Roald accompanied me back to the seminary by taxi, and what might have been a romantic little ride was a mostly silent time of looking into Roald's ashen face. I held his hand, but didn't ask him to speak, and he looked out the window at the snow and at people on street corners holding up lanterns and little Borschic flags.

The next morning it was bright and fine, and the snow that had fallen the night before melted, as it often does in Nachtober, before the real cold weather comes. Imagine my surprise when I received a note that I had a gentleman caller, who wanted to have an afternoon walk after my classes for the day were ended.

Seminary was tough for me. I entered a year after coming to Borschland, on a special dispensation from the chancellor. I could speak Borschic by then, but I didn't have a hope of passing the entrance examination. They let me in basically as a favor to Sherm. It brought good publicity to the school as well, showing that someone from the wide world could be captivated by the Borschic faith.

The Church of Borschland is a strange little thing, about as strange as a phase shift. No one expects you to be interested in it. It's not required to believe. It's there in the background and doesn't bother anyone.

But it hooked me.

I worked hard, and got better. I read constantly, figuring out the convoluted way that Borschic theologians put things, and wrote better essays. The more I read and worshipped, the more my faith deepened. I went from half-time to full-time and then overloaded a couple of terms, and I was now in position to graduate if I passed my comprehensive exams at Christmastime.

Problem was that for all the work I'd done I knew that taking a battery of exams, including an oral, in the space of five days would probably break my little hard-won fluency in Borschic. I wasn't the best student at little Sts. Francis and Clare College in Minnesota, and even though I went off and on for years, I'd never gotten my degree. School just wasn't for me back then.

But now I wanted to finish and be a deaconess in the church, spend my time worshipping, and visiting and counseling, with a chance to move up the ranks and maybe oversee a chapel of my own someday.

Of course, you didn't have to get the diploma to be in the religion. People told me constantly that I could be a subdeaconess, a layperson who was more devout than the usual Borschic citizen. I could be a subdeacon and a mom, they said, if only I would get married.

Borschland. A simpler life, and yet so complicated.

When I came back from classes that day, Willem was sitting in the common room of my dormitory, near the watchful eyes of our concierge, Marta. Marta was a subdeaconess and interested in preserving the virtue of the single female seminarians. A widow with grown children, she practically lived behind the front desk, and she knew all of us as if we were her own daughters.

But instead of the firm and unwavering stare that she usually gave to the gentlemen who braved St. Michaela's Hall, Marta was wearing a broad smile.

"Oh, Demouzeel Reinhardt," she gushed as I walked into the foyer carrying my notebooks. "You have the most charming gentleman waiting for you. He is the very incarnation of St. Noos, I don't guess," and laughed at the joke she made.

Willem stood up from the armchair in which he had been sitting. "Willem, my dear lady," he said, in that rich voice of his. "Willem is my Christian name, and all should use it."

Marta said, "He is not North American, is he? He speaks Borschic the way we used to way back before things became so modern and free." And she gave Willem a grin that said, I have lost my mind, but I am okay with that.

"I don't know, Mrs. Oorter," I said. "I don't know where he is from. We made acquaintance just last night. He is a friend of my brother's."

"Well, he is a fine man, and if he is unmarried and interested in you, you should give him your full attention."

"And I do believe you are unmarried as well, Mrs. Oorter," said Willem. "If so, I think you should be fending off your share of suitors."

Marta giggled like a girl. I'd never heard her do such a thing.

"Have a lovely walk, Demouzeel Reinhardt. It is fine out today, and with our *Bloomentwejg* flowering, I feel as if we are going into spring rather than winter."

Willem was wearing exactly what he'd had on the night before: well-worn trousers, an overcoat, a felt hat, and a scarf tied around his neck. With his cultivation and skills it was hard to think he was a homeless person.

"To what do I owe the pleasure of this meeting?" I asked in my best Borschic.

"In due time," he said. "Can we walk out onto the green, and enjoy the afternoon? It won't be so fine for a long time."

The seminary was attached to the University of Borschland, which wasn't really one campus, but different colleges arranged along a big park that was called Tujrspaark. It was like a quad that was several miles long, with lots of ponds and creeks and straight paths with huge Dutch elms shading them. A perfect place for a walk and a talk.

The talk was late in coming. Willem walked slowly, and often raised his head when we came into a patch of sunlight, closing his eyes and smiling.

"It is just good to feel the air on one's face," he said once.

After about fifteen minutes, he gave me a little conspiratorial wink, and motioned me to a bench overlooking a little lake with ducks.

"You are a bit strange, I think," I began as we sat down.

"Like all Borschic men, perhaps?" he said.

"Not like Americans," I said.

"How are American men?"

"There is a difference," I said, hitting on something just at that moment, an idea I'd never had before, but made complete sense, "between American men... and American fathers."

He smiled, and his teeth were a sweet, sweet white in the fading sunshine, not at all like a homeless person's teeth should have been.

"American dads give everything to their daughters," I said. "My father loved me. He wanted me to have everything. He broke his back providing for us, and giving me music lessons, and camps, and hockey equipment--"

"You played field hockey?"

"Ice hockey. I wanted to be an Olympian."

He nodded. "So much more for women to do in the wide world, than here. What position did you play?"

"Everything, but I liked defense most. I liked to hit, to check. I liked protecting the goal."

"Noble."

"I got on a traveling team, and I was looking towards playing in college. But my dad got sick, and I gave it up."

"Sick?"

"Cancer. Which finally, he died of."

"May he sing with angels."

"Oh, he does. He was a pretty good baritone in his day."

"But American men. Different from your father?"

"American men are kind of at a disadvantage. Because when they are young and thinking of getting married, all they have to choose from is American women, who have been spoiled so badly by their fathers. American women have very high standards. And so American men can't come up to the standards, and they're resentful about not being good enough for the women they like. So they rebel and act like children. But for those guys that do get married, and have daughters, now they have a girl who worships them. And who wouldn't want to give that girl everything?"

"And so the cycle continues."

"Yes."

We looked at the ducks, and Willem said, "You speak very well for a foreigner."

"Do you have children?"

"I do. I haven't seen them in quite some time."

"Was there some falling out?"

"I don't know that it was a falling out, my dear. It was a falling away. We are an unusual family."

"And your wife?"

"She has perished. Long since." And he looked up to the sky, the way all Borschic people do when they speak of the dead. "But let us hear of you. You are to be a deaconess."

"If I pass my exams," I said.

"Small matters," he said, and laughed quietly, as if he knew they were a big thing. "Tell me how you came to be in seminary."

"You really want to hear?"

"Without question."

"Well, I guess I was a little naive about what seminary involved. But now I'm almost to comprehensives, so I've come pretty far."

"But, at the beginning."

"I'd never been that into religion, not even when our parents were dying. They were Catholic, they sang in the choir and had a priest who came around a lot for lunch. But I didn't get it. I didn't get anything about the church.

"Shortly after I came to Borschland I was in a very bad state. Things hadn't gone well back in the States. I had a fiancée who was..." How to say jerkface in Borschic? "...not very responsible. I heard about Sherm's success here and when he got married to Rachael I came to visit. Everyone here just... carried me on their backs."

I looked Willem in the eye, and he looked back. There was so much wisdom there. What a sweet man, to listen so attentively.

"I guess I was happy to be wanted," I said.

"Of course."

"But then there was this window-- I remember this like yesterday. I was staying in Sherm's flat in Rirlver, and I looked across the street and every night someone was lighting candles in their window. And I remember I asked someone, why do they do that? Is it to conserve electricity?

"And they said, no, the candle is for hope.

"That's all they said, the candle is for hope. A little light in darkness. And this big wave of awe just swept over me, and I began to cry. Big, fat tears just rolled down. And I never cry. All through my hockey career I never cried because we lost a game. Even when my parents died, I only cried a little, even though it broke my heart.

"But this time I did. Just... water works." And a big tear popped out right then.

He gave me an intense stare, but only for a moment. He looked as if he might cry himself. Then he turned away, and I thought he must be done listening. But he was turning away to pull a handkerchief out of his pocket. "Yes," he said, and offered the handkerchief.

It was a lovely, antique piece of cloth, with little eyelets. Worn soft the way really old cloth can get. I wiped the tear. It was as good as if he had reached out with his finger and done it for me.

"And I said to myself, I want to be a part of that. I want to be the one who lights the candle for hope."

He let a little time go by; he was good at that, silences. Silly me, I wondered if he was handy around the house, too, like he was at cooking.

Finally, he said, "And the saints, what do you think about them?"

"I venerate them, ask their prayers, and try to follow their example," I said.

"How well you have been taught," he said. "But what do you really think of them?"

"I don't understand what you mean."

"I mean, do you believe in the stories? About the elixir, the *tisande*, and the saints coming back to help Borschland when it is in need?"

"Oh!" I said, louder than I wanted, and put my hand to my mouth for a second. "You're talking about the legendary saints."

"Yes, the saints of Shadow and Light."

"I haven't given them all that much thought, to tell the truth," I said. "I concentrate on the martyrs, the theological saints, the ones who provide the examples for life."

"Such as St. Rachael."

"Especially her."

"And the others?"

What was I supposed to say? I had this feeling he was fishing for a right answer, but I have never been able to give one, not beyond the fifth grade. I never think on the same wavelength as my teachers. So I just said what I believed.

"There is a part of the religion that is... well, let's say, the people's, and a part that is of the deacons. I concentrate on the deacons' side. The beauty of belief. The need of all of us for prayer. The beauty of light, life, hope. All that. The rest is... well, it's mythology, isn't it? It makes a difference for the country because our identity is shaped through it, but what more is it than just a good story?"

"Well, yes, it might be mythology, and then again it might be true, as well. You understand, don't you, that mythology can be just as true as theology? Maybe even truer?"

"But mythology by definition is factually false. Unless you're talking about the truth of the heart."

He nodded, and looked off at the ducks again, paddling, dunking their heads, shaking them.

I had the terrible feeling of having given the absolute wrong answer. And I was thinking, *Stop while you're behind. Don't make it worse.*

But that's not my style.

"Willem," I said, using his name for the first time on purpose. "I'm probably not the best person to have a theological conversation with. But I want you to know. I am a pretty good listener. I know you may have great grief in your past, but if you ever want to." Inside my head I was screaming, *Stop, stop.* But I didn't. "Anyway, I would like to get to know you better."

Willem kept looking at the ducks, and I felt as if my whole body was a big billboard that was losing its glue and the rolls of papers were just slowly falling and bunching up in a big pile.

Finally, he said, "I believe you will make a great deaconess. Perhaps an archdeaconess someday."

I got chills. It was exactly the opposite of what I was expecting. And I wished he had followed it up with, Yes, Katharujna, I will tell you my life story over a candlelit dinner tonight, but that, I knew, would be greedy.

"So," I said, after I recovered from my chills, "What was the purpose of this talk?"

"My beautiful Katharujna," he said, "you have told me all I need to know."

CHAPTER 9 - SHERM

I arrived at 14 Waatersdram after the Greatbear interview hoping to blow off some steam. I suited up for the skatearound and was pleased to see both Urdan and Lavishbear on the ice already.

I stopped in at the head coach's office, Chrojstenkaamps the immortal. He had been there forever when I got to Borschland, and he was still there, never saying much, but taking in everything.

"Reinhardt," he said, and shoved a quartered newspaper at me. "What is this?"

The byline said Anna Danielujna van ter Roost. CANADIAN CHARMER was the headline.

> Te Staff have hired on a young man from the wide world who will be turning many a Borschic lady's head. We once thought that Sherm Reinhardt was the most exotic and handsomest man on skates, but now Urdan Kasmahlov has decidedly eclipsed Reinhardt's star, married man and father that he is.

"Ouch," I said.

"Keep reading," said Chrojstenkaamps.

> The dashing Canadian, a descendant of Lipni
> Tatars, the legendary horsemen of Belarus,
> has magnetic brown eyes and a swath of rich
> brown hair that trails to mid-neck.

"Farther," Chrojstenkaamps urged, and pointed.
I skipped down.

> This correspondent is not telling why, but if
> there are those Borschic ladies who wish to
> follow in Madaam Rachael Reinhardt's
> footsteps, be very wary. Our Meester
> Kasmahlov is liable to tempt you only to
> break your heart.

"I thought you were keeping an eye on him,"
Chrojstenkaamps said. "Clearly he is developing a reputation as
a hoopfvolle. How is this possible after three days in
Borschland?"

"I am keeping an eye," I said. "That's just junk. She's
dreaming."

"We are going to send him to Oststaff," said
Chrojstenkaamps. "He will live with the cadets and follow their
routine."

On the one hand that was a terrific idea. On the other it
meant that he'd be out of my sight. I weighed the possibilities
even as I saw a bear with honey-gold fur settle down with his
paws over the practice rink boards.

"We need a sixth defenseman," I said. "You know that
Blinders isn't skating at full speed yet." Jap Blinders was a good
defenseman. Also injury-prone. "Where are we going to get
someone with his size?"

Chrojstenkaamps didn't argue, he pronounced. But as he
sat there, looking out the window at Kasmahlov taking his
sprints, I could tell he was itching to know what the kid had in
him. After all, the last North American to play for Te Staff was

a pretty good pickup, name of Reinhardt.

"No more surprise interviews," he said.

"Ergut," I said, and left the office. We would take a long look at Kasmahlov and he would take a last, longing look at Borschland beauties. If he didn't measure up on either score, he'd be shipped out to the military barracks, where, who knows, cadet life would probably do him some good.

"Victorius Sharpclaw," said the bear in a wheezy voice as I stepped onto the ice. "I got word from Greatbear he'd like eyes on your Canadian ladies' man," he said.

"Much obliged," I said.

"Greatbear also said you'd be filing reports for us," Sharpclaw wheezed. "I will take those. Just like this, casually talking. I have a photographic memory."

"Lucky for Bearland," I said.

"You understand how important this is," he said. "I have elderly forebears that could use that elixir."

I skated away, puzzled. Hadn't Willem said the *Bloomentisande* did nothing for bears and foxes?

"Hey, Coach," said Urdan as he flashed by me. He was a fast skater, and he didn't appear winded. That's what being a teenager will do for you, I guess.

Lavishbear was stretching over to the side, doing deep knee bends. "Get out there," I said. "No stick. Just sprint, behind the net, and sprint back."

Lavishbear nodded. He was lean and wiry for a bear, about as tall as I was, and his fur was honey brown. When not on the ice, he wore round spectacles that made him look like a furry scholar.

"Your eyes okay without the specs?" I asked as he came around the first time, puffing hard.

"I use the--- hhh--- for reading," he said.

When he came around again, he was doubled over and trying to get his wind.

"Do some more," I said. "We need you in shape."

"It's not that," he said. "I have an infection."

"Oh?" I said.

"Someone in the airship cabin was coughing all the way from Waterbrownbear," he explained. "My lungs are inflamed."

There were no sophisticated antibiotics in Borschland that could knock that out. Maybe at the Bearland embassy, but they weren't that advanced in medicine, either.

"Talk to the trainer about it," I said.

"I have," he said. "I would like to move to the infirmary at the embassy."

This was not starting out well. I had a playboy Canadian and a sick Upright Bear. What next?

"Pull some weights before you go," I said.

"Also, the skates are too tight. My claws--"

"The trainer."

After my workout I went home for lunch. Rachael was bursting to talk with me.

"I wrote a poem," she said. "Willem had the children all morning."

"That's wonderful, darling."

"I kept an eye on him. The children adore him. I think we should let him stay. He would be such a help. He may not cost that much. Besides..." She lowered her voice to a whisper. "I think he may be the incarnation of a saint, and if so--"

"Why is that?"

"He appeared on our doorstep out of nowhere, just after a phase shift. There are dozens of stories just like that, where the saint appears and graces you with his presence. Sometimes it's simply to test your hospitality. Sometimes it's because you are in need. It is a godsend."

"Are there ever stories of saints who come to your door and then kidnap your children?"

She laughed. "You are the silliest man, Sherman Reinhardt. I suppose that is why I love you."

Big wow. Rachael seldom uses the "L" word, though it's clear she does love me. She is very loyal. You never doubt that she is on your side, even when she is scolding you.

"*Ten sill wuj zujet,*" I said, which is like saying yes.

Rachael kissed me, and showed me her poem. She was on

cloud nine. That was excellent, because it was going to take her mind off of being pregnant-- for a little while, anyway.

CHAPTER 10 - RACHAEL

I never know what my husband thinks of my poems, and I scarcely think he himself knows. He is a man of action rather than reflection, which is good in many ways. It is a blessing.

The poem tumbled out of me in such a way as poems seldom do, and almost never have since I have become a mother. A wise person says that poems are one's children; for the past five years my children have been my poems.

Here is what I wrote:

> A little child is taught to say
> Saints of God, please thee, pray
> For me that I may grow to be
> Like a blossom on an eternal tree
>
> So much I know-- who can tell me
> Otherwise-- those children grow
> To such a size as dwarfs a little
>
> Blossom;
>
> Awesome to spy, they will grow
> As big as I, if I wait and they
> Are not clipped or blown

Away

Premature

A blossom is perfect, for a moment
Is perfect, God's elect
And finished with its purpose

And effect

And so it falls and is blown
To the moaning wind or else
Into a tea that makes

A saint

That is its fate
To give itself for others

And yet

If it had its rathers
Would it not wish?

Blossom fine

To be the saint who
Knows not dying?

It was not a poem I rushed to send somewhere, though that is my training and impulse. My poetry has always been of a rather public kind.

This, however, came from a well that had never been used to water the garden of the Borschic soul.

And I kept it that way.

I did not even read the poem to Sherm, who was so attentive to other things at the time; in fact, he did not see it until well after the *Bloomentwejg* affair was concluded.

It hid, in fact, much like the child I carried in my womb, for whom I asked the saints' prayers every day.

I have acted in a more practical manner since I have become a mother, and so, without waiting for further inspiration I devoted myself to asking Willem if he would become our pedagogue.

Strange word that was, but I could not ask him to become our governess, and the masculine form of that word is not used as a signifier of a male caretaker of children.

Truly, I wanted Willem to become something of a majordomo, which is more than a male governess. He seemed so efficient and multi-talented, I thought he might do simply as a general helper. I did wonder how it was possible that he was not already engaged in such a position, or, saints help me, as the owner of a large and profitable company, since he seemed perfectly capable of executing that. But I knew that in this world there are many people who find contentment in a simple life, for whatever reason.

So I held out hope of engaging him.

I was going to offer him a fine lunch, but when I arrived in the kitchen after finishing the poem, I found him already there, making a soup. The children were seated at the kitchen table, Connie with a great scroll of paper, creating an epic ice hockey game with colored pencils, Lily in her high chair, lining up expertly cut pieces of apple on her tray.

"Heavenly starfire!" I exclaimed. "I am overwhelmed. Both children quiet at the same time?"

"I trust your morning was blessed, Madaam?" said Willem.

"I wrote a poem," I said.

"Ah, yes," said Willem. "You are a poetess. Will you be submitting it somewhere?"

"I don't quite know yet," I said.

He had me sit at table, and Connie told me about the picture of his hockey game. "There is Daduj and there is Daduj's team and there is Willem."

"What does Willem do on the ice?" I asked.

"He keeps everyone following the rules."

"Like the referee. Should he have a black shirt, then?"

"No, Mamuj. He is not the referee. He is God."

Willem put a bowl of cream of leek soup in front of me. I looked up at him, and asked a silent question.

"Madaam, I have no idea."

Which is when I thought to myself, *should I even deign to ask this person, who is probably a saint of the fatherland, to take care of my children?*

"Willem," I said, "I would like to ask you a very silly question."

"Yes, Madaam. Is the soup all right?"

I took a sip. It was the Platonic ideal of all leek soups.

After I recovered, I said, "Just a question. You have such a way with children, and with cooking. I wonder at what other skills you have."

He wiped his hands with a dishtowel, and waited.

"So, I was thinking. If... if... by any chance..."

"Yes?"

"You would know anyone. Anyone else. Who would in any way approximate your abilities in the home. I mean to say, sir. Unless you. Because you did say you needed."

It may have been the most stammering I had ever done at one time in one place in my entire life.

"I understand distinctly, Madaam," he said. "I will give it some thought. This afternoon I have a number of errands to run, but I will return to give you my answer. Thank you very kindly."

"No, thank you kindly, sir," I said.

"May I serve the children now?" he said.

"You mean the soup? They won't eat that, sir. I apologize. They are very particular."

He dished up soup nevertheless, and the children ate it and asked for more.

I said a little prayer to the saints for Willem to come back with a yes. But then I realized that, if Willem was a saint, I had already made my prayer.

But destiny has a way of arranging things in ways one does not expect.

Willem did not come back that day. In fact, it would be a very long time again before I saw him face to face. Instead, perhaps an hour after he had left, and I was doing my level best to entertain two children and get something done on household business, I heard a knock on the door.

Connie answered it, and as soon as he did, he ran for the kitchen, where I was sitting at the table reconciling accounts, a beastly task. Lily was asleep upstairs-- at least until Connie came pelting back screaming, "It's a bear! It's a bear!"

I went to the door as quickly as I could, skirts rustling noisily.

It was indeed a bear, a she-bear in fact, who was dressed modestly as most of them are, in a rather old-style button-front dress with a lace collar, and a bonnet with a tied chinstrap. She was quite young and delicate for a bear, even underfed, perhaps.

"Good afternoon," I said, in Borschic, and quite unprepared to switch to English, which is the bears' language of instruction and what they mostly speak to each other on the streets of their nation.

"Good afternoon," she said, also in Borschic. "Am I arrived at the residence of a Madaam R.?"

She said the "R" with such a little growl that I startled, before I realized she was saying the letter, not being cross with me.

"Yes, Demouzeel Bear. This is the Reinhardt residence. What is your desire?"

"Well," she said, "I am answering your advertisement in the newspaper."

And she showed me a scrap of paper cut out from a broadsheet:

Madaam R. desires a governess for two children aged five and two years, respectively. Live in; private bedroom; board and stipend. Experienced please. Call in person at 67 Nojallesanktenswej.

"My goodness," I said. "My husband must have placed it this morning."

The she-bear considered me the way bears do, with an impassivity that comes from not showing emotions through their faces. You don't know what a bear is thinking by looking at their expressions, but by listening to their gruntings.

"My name is Melissa Shepherdbear," she said, and put out a gloved paw to shake.

"Won't you come in?" I said.

"Thank you," she said.

As Miss Shepherdbear crossed the threshold, skirts rustling just as mine did, she looked up, towards the stairs.

I turned. Lily was awake, rubbing her eyes. She had been down a grand total of forty minutes.

When she saw Miss Shepherdbear, she squealed, and ran upstairs again, pitter-pat on her bare feet.

"Goodness! I hope I have not frightened your little daughter."

Not a chance, I thought. We made a left turn into the parlor, and almost as quick, Lily was back, toting her grand she-bear doll that had been her birthday present the night before. The doll was dressed much as Miss Shepherdbear, even down to the bonnet.

Lily threw the doll at Miss Shepherdbear and then hugged her legs. "Lady bear!" she began saying.

Miss Shepherdbear took a look at the doll, then at Lily, and exclaimed, "Oh, are you saying that this doll and I are the same?"

Lily nodded her head vigorously. "My lady bear!" she cried, still hugging Miss Shepherdbear's leg.

"Liluj," I said. "You must behave. Let Miss Shepherdbear sit." And I pulled her away by the hand.

Miss Shepherdbear had a seat on the divan, and I held Lily's hand, greatly vexed that I had not offered the visitor anything to eat or drink.

"Want to see her!" said Lily, and craned away from me.

"It is perfectly all right," said Miss Shepherdbear. "I am used to it."

I let Lily go, and in an instant she was in the she-bear's lap, with her arms around her neck. That gave me the opportunity to ask if she wanted tea or coffee. She declined.

"I apologize," I said. "She is very fond of she-bears. It was her birthday, and she has just gotten this doll."

"I understand," said Miss Shepherdbear. "But I hope you won't take this-- yes, my dear, sit here nicely and we'll have a lovely talk-- you won't take this as a sign that I am at all a soft nannybear. I am very used to disciplining young ones, as far as the mistress asks."

"You are young," I said. "Have you been a nannybear long?"

"No," she said. "In fact, my experience is with cubs. I have obtained my work permit and been engaged elsewhere this past year."

"And what is it that brings you to desire this position?"

"I anticipate my situation will be ending, and I would like to obtain a new one, with a family that is fair and appreciates my services."

Miss Shepherdbear spoke Borschic flawlessly, something that is rare among foreigners, bears or not. And the fact that she was bound to speak English as well would be a great advantage in teaching the children. Sherm had not been diligent in speaking to the children in English, though we both desired that they know the language.

What was more, she was a bear. Beyond Lily's obsession, nannybears are highly prized on the Continent, for being able to keep children with loving discipline. There is something about their teeth and their growl that children respect; at the same time, their fur is the most comforting thing to have against one's skin when one has had a fall or a toy taken away. I had never had a nannybear as a child, but the friends who had them swore by them.

"Do you have references?" I asked.

"I was not able to have them drawn up before answering the advertisement, Madaam," said Miss Shepherdbear. "I thought of time being the essence, as often governess positions are filled very quickly."

"And do you know us? Do you know of the Reinhardts?"

"Your husband is an ice hockey player?" she said. "Yes, I have read the newspapers."

"And do you know that you would be in them, a celebrity

yourself?"

"If the family believe in me, and I in them, then I am prepared for anything, Madaam."

"Well," I said, my eye on Lily, who had not moved from Miss Shepherdbear's lap the entire time. "When can you start?"

"May I come this evening, Madaam? Around nine of the clock?"

"If you bring your references," I said. "I would like to see them."

It was a silly thing to say, because I was already agreeing to hire her, but I wanted to appear perhaps a bit less eager than I was.

Miss Shepherdbear said that she would bring the references, and stood up, much to Lily's chagrin. "I will see you tonight," she said, and gave a happy grunt.

A nannybear in the house. This might be even better than a saint.

CHAPTER 11 - SHERM

The first day of training camp did not start out well for Urdan Kasmahlov.

The whole team was out, including some rookies we were looking at from Oststaff. We all skated out under the bright lamps hanging from the 14 Waatersdram practice rink.

We started with a brief speech from Chrojstenkaamps-- brief is all he does-- and then endurance drills. Urdan did well on those, but then he made the mistake of picking up a hockey stick.

We'd done some blackboard work, but he wasn't ready for how defending the Borschland Hockey League actually went down.

For the first around-the-net drills, we put him with our most experienced defender, Roger Rijksmeete. Chrujstoff Anselm, Gerd Droobink and Nils Grooteluschen were the forwards. They skated in and Gerd sent a behind-the-boards pass to Nils. Urdan left the goalie, Ruud Paulus, and tried to intercept the pass, or failing that, hit Nils.

Fast as he was, he didn't get close to Nils. There is too much ice on a BHL rink.

Nils turned, avoided Urdan, who went flying by, then centered one to Chrujstoff. Chrujstoff did a neat give-and-go with Gerd under Roger's stick, finishing with a tap in by the goalie's right pad.

"One for us," said Chrujstoff, skating back to center.

Urdan cursed. So did Chrojstenkaamps.

"Coach says, stay near the goal," I yelled at him from the side. "Remember what we said in the chalk talk."

Urdan whacked the blade of his stick on the ice, and took up his position to the right of Roger.

The forwards decided to do the same thing. Gerd sent a pass around the boards to Nils. Urdan didn't take the bait at first, but then Nils came rushing at him, so he left the goalie and skated to Nils on a collision course. Nils ducked, took the puck with him, Urdan went flying by, and a couple of passes later the puck was in the net again.

This time Ruud cursed.

"That would be two nil," said Chrujstoff.

The third time, Gerd came down and raised his stick as if he was going to send it board-wide to Nils again. But Urdan was smart. He peeled back behind the goal to intercept the pass, and was waiting for it, head down, when the puck went skittering into the net for a third time. Gerd hadn't made the pass. He sent it to Chrujstoff, who sent it to Nils, who tapped it in once again.

"Off the ice," Chrojstenkaamps growled.

Urdan was soaked in sweat as he banged his blade again, this time on the boards before he hopped over to the bench.

"Watch and learn," I said, as another defender took his place.

Lavishbear was a different story. He had been a center in his own country, but we were looking at him for right wing, since he shot right-handed. Most guys in Borschland are left-handed-- not natural lefties, but most coaches teach that the top hand on the stick is the left.

After a day in the Bearland embassy infirmary, he was ready to try his hand, but he didn't have his wind, and after the first couple of goes with his linemates, he was blown. What's more, he muffed a couple of passes, letting one through him, and the other handcuffing him so bad the defenseman was able to poke check the puck away from him.

Coach sent him to the other end of the ice to do puckhandling drills.

"How's Danny?" I asked Urdan as we watched the proceedings.

"I got a telegram from her," he said. "She wants to meet me again."

"No dice," I said.

Before I left for the day, Chrojstenkaamps brought me into management offices. An easel was set up in a meeting room. On the easel was the proof for a promotional poster.

"We're going to put these up all over the city," one of the PR guys said.

On a bright white background there was the outline of a hockey stick. From the blade grew a white flower with golden petals. Above the blade, in big letters, it said TE BLOOMENSTAFF - KAMPUJONEN NUN N FVOOR ALLETIJD. "The Flowering Staff: Champions Now and Forever."

Way to put the pressure on, guys, I thought. What I said was, "You have plenty of confidence in us, I think."

One of the PR guys said, "We are the home of the *Bloomentwejg*. Te Staff is the name of the old city, and the Rijksmuseen. Surely that will give us a bit of luck to make the puck bounce our way. And the rest is up to you. Management has gotten you the players."

Of course, I thought. The teenager from Canada, the bronchitis sufferer from Bearland, and a goalie from Zimroth who hasn't shown up yet.

Chrojstenkaamps glared at the PR guy and left, which meant that the promotions meeting was over. The rest of the room cleared out, until I was left with the man who'd spoken.

"I haven't seen you before," I said. "What's your name?"

"My name is Henrick," he said, and gave me this unblinking stare that I only get from the guy opposite me just before the referee is about to drop the puck.

That pulled me up short, and I looked the dude over. Henrick was shorter than I was, but broad-shouldered, and hefty. He looked like he had played in his time, and kept in shape. He had a scar over his left eye, like a skinny capital A, maybe from running into a stick blade.

He was bald, and anywhere from forty to sixty years old. He looked too in shape to be sixty, and too wrinkled to be forty. Most older guys in Borschland do not work out. That made Henrick an oddball-- a bald guy with a flat stomach and what looked like a pretty good build, even though a black Borschic suit doesn't normally give you any impression of how ripped a guy is.

He continued to stare at me, I'm going to win this face-off, bud, didn't say anything, but broke into a little grin.

"You play in your day, Henrick?" I managed to say.

"I was a champion," said Henrick, and tapped the posterboard. "Did you ever hear of a game called *kolv*?"

"Oh my god," I said. Stupid, but I put it together. Henrick. *Kolv*. The dude was St. Borsch.

"It is very good to meet you, Sherm," he said, the grin widening into a smile. We shook hands, and of course it was more than firm on his part. I looked down at his hands. Strong, rough, big. For a three hundred year-old guy, he probably could still win all of his fistfights.

"What are you doing here?" I asked, motioning to the posterboard. "I thought you'd be out masterminding the theft of the *Bloomentwejg*."

"I am, I am," he said. He put a hand in his vest pocket, took out a watch, snapped it open and closed, put it back. "It is very important for my plan that you and the team do well this year. I am going to see to it as best I can that you do."

"What are you going to do, take right wing on our second line? We're looking for a guy to do that."

"Sherm, you are a humorous fellow and you speak Borschic very well. But you are still very North American and you don't understand our country and our history. Whatever you do, whomever you listen to, make sure you give me your ear as well, would you please? It is so important to have more than one view on any question."

"I'm listening," I said. "And I'm more Borschic than you might think. I've got a wife and kids."

"Precisely," said Henrick.

"And," I said, before he went on, "if you try to hurt them I'll bury you, saint or not."

Henrick didn't even blink. "Sherm, if you please."

"You can't do what you want without me. So leave them alone."

"Sherm."

"I don't care how old you are and whatever other super powers you have." I was going to go on, but I realized I was balling up my fists and sweating under my arm. A trickle of sweat had gone down my temple. So, whoa.

Henrick threw up a palm. "What must my dear old friend Willem have been telling you!" He took the posterboard down from the easel and looked out the window. It was clouding up again. "It is not necessarily so that you must be on his side. You have not heard me out. You do not know my love for my country."

"Well, we'll have you over for dinner sometime," I said.

"Sherm," he said, tapping the posterboard, "would you like to be able to play hockey as long as you want to, to be strong, not to worry about injuries or healing? Wouldn't you like to ensure that your child and your wife would be safe-- safe from disease, safe from miscarriage?"

Now I gave him my best face-off stare.

"Sherm, you wouldn't deny that this world runs on luck. Fortune. The deacons say Holy Luck. The people say Destiny, or Fate. You yourself benefited from such luck when you came here. So you should understand. If you are put into a position to benefit from something that was not your doing, that you didn't earn, that just fell into your lap. Something like this comes from God. Take the gift of God. Be good to your family. Give them the gift."

A little laugh came up from my throat. "I don't know.

Where I come from, God asks you to give more than get, you know? It's more blessed to give than receive, something like that. That's what I was taught about God. And anyway, what are you talking about? That you'd give me and my family some of the elixir?"

Henrick said, "We are talking about nothing at the moment. Some day we may talk about something. If you are willing."

"Well, if it's about nothing, I've got to go. I've got plenty of stuff to do, including babysitting two players who really aren't Borschic."

"They are fine skaters. Give them time."

"If you put up this poster, we won't have any. The whole city will be nuts for an undefeated season."

Henrick tapped the poster again. "We need this. We need you to be good."

"We will be good. At least I will be. I never slack off, even if you told me to do it to save my family."

"Please, dear starfire of the saints, don't mention that again. If you have anything to fear, Sherm, please know, it is more from Willem than from me." He put the poster back on the easel, wiped his thumb over the picture of the flower. "Don't be fooled. He can be quite dangerous."

"You, too, probably," I said.

The face-off stare was back. He was an intense dude, and the sweat under my arms told me I was right about him being dangerous.

"Just one more thing, Meester Reinhardt," said Henrick.

"What's that?"

"I would put Lavishbear back at center. That's his natural position. He'll be more comfortable there, and I think he'll score goals."

"We've already got three centers. Chrujstoff, Hauke, and me. That position's filled."

"But you could play right wing, could you not? You are a top-hand right stickhandler. So few of them here in Borschland. That would give you so many more options. And Chrujstoff and Hauke would not adapt as you would. They need to stay at center."

"I'm not going to play right wing. Forget it."

Henrick nodded, took out his watch again. "You'd better get home. It's late."

Right wing. *What a nut*, I thought.

Then, halfway home in the cab, I thought again.

Damn.

Maybe we should give it a try.

No way.

CHAPTER 12 - CATHY

My talk with Willem ruined my concentration. I couldn't study; my mind was racing with everything but theology. Exams were closing in-- I had all of Nachtober, Eveember, and three weeks in Detzember before the fateful week, but I still had so much to read.

Then there was the *Bloomentwejg*, about which I still didn't know that much. It hadn't bloomed in so many years, and no one was expecting it to, but it was there on my Required Topics list, History and Theological Significance of the *Bloomentwejg*. I was just, just getting okay with the theological significance of the phase shift.

It was somewhere after three o'clock the day after Willem and the ducks, and dinner in the refectory wouldn't be until seven. I was at the library, with the Theological Dictionary of the Borschic Faith opened to the entry on the *Bloomentwejg*. The room was too hot, and I was falling asleep.

What else could I do besides study? Get a cup of coffee? Nap at my desk?

Maybe a little experiential study.

I left the library, got on the SUB, the Borschic subway, and descended at Te Staff station, the oldest part of the city and the site of the government buildings and Rijksmuseen.

The Rijksmuseen, the National Museum, is where the Branch is displayed, and normally it is seen only by tourists and schoolchildren, who come from every corner of Borschland on overnight trips. Lujna Elkind, a dormmate of mine who had grown up in faraway Ejanstaff, at the mouth of the Borschland River, talked about taking a boat ride down the river when she was eleven, docking at the great city, and taking the SUB to see the Branch.

"I was so awed by everything," she told me. "But when I saw the Branch itself, I was a bit disappointed."

Now as I came rattling up the steam-powered escalator that one puts into motion by pulling a big lever at the bottom, I could see the great pillars of the Rijksmuseen across a green. But there was no lawn to be seen. The whole open space was filled with men in blue and white uniforms-- Borschland Navy- - others in grey, on horseback-- cavalry-- and finally foot soldiers with rifles slung over their backs, in forest green with brass buttons.

Across from the lawn, hundreds of people stood, just watching the men mill about. There seemed to be no particular rhyme or reason to what they were doing, except that some men were pitching tents, and others were standing guard.

A clock tower chimed 3:30 in the afternoon, clear and high, and I realized it was not nearly as loud as it might have been.

People had lined up to see the Branch, and the line snaked around the corner. A number of groups were headed by a subdeacon or deacon wearing a sash of office over his or her clothing.

It probably would've been a better idea for me to get right back on the SUB and go home, but something about it drew me in. So many people searching for meaning, awakened maybe for the first time to the idea of the spiritual, and only because of a miracle of unknown plant biology, and perhaps God, as well.

I threaded my way behind the crowds, heading for the back of the line. I had a vague thought that maybe the line would move, maybe I could get in before the Museum closed, though it was going on four o'clock and the sun had dipped below the tallest buildings.

Catty corner from the lawn with the military bivouac was a cobblestone square with trees and benches. This had been taken over by a group of people chanting. As I got close, I could hear what they were saying, but it was easier to read what was on their banners.

GEJN OOSLANDERN
BORSCHLAND FVOOR BORSCHERN
LOFLINDERN OOS

These were anti-foreigner slogans: "No Foreigners; Borschland for the Borschic; Loflins Out." And they were chanting basically the same thing.

Police and soldiers ringed the group, standing in the intersection of the street; traffic had been cut off by sawhorses, and people were crossing in front.

It seemed kind of impossible, but as I crossed that street, from the opposite side where people were standing on the sidewalk, to the Rijksmuseen side with the big line of people waiting to get in, I was recognized.

"Kathuj Reinhardt," I heard. I was in my lavender-colored seminary student outfit, which sticks out like a lavender thumb. And then, people did know my face.

"Katharujna," someone else said, loud, as if cheering.

Then: "Te Ooslaander nijkt in museen mag tej gaan." Don't let the foreigner into the museum.

I looked over at the protesting group. Their eyes had fixed on me, and they were yelling. "Ooslaandern Oos!" Foreigners Out!

Then next thing I did was probably even more stupid than staying there at all. I walked towards them, thinking I was going to reason with them.

"In the name of the saints of Borschland," I tried to begin, but it never really got out. A young man jumped over the wrought-iron chain and began to run towards me. He was sandwiched between two policemen, and never got near me, but I could see his wild eyes as he yelled, "Let me speak!" and grasped at me with his right hand.

The man's action, however, spurred the rest of the crowd-- dozens of them-- to push forward. There were plenty of soldiers and police to stop them, but it didn't matter. I froze.

"Save Katharujna!"

From behind me and to the left and right dozens of people ran into the intersection. Everyone met in the center of the street. I was jostled and knocked down. On my hands and knees, all I could see were black trousers and the occasional sweep of skirts and button-up boots. A photographer tried to set up and take a picture of me, but someone knocked him from behind and his camera went flying.

Then I heard someone singing the Borschic National Anthem, and other people took it up:

Ij sag ejn noje hemel
en ejn noj aard
en de tegenwoordig aard
war nej meer

And I saw a new heaven
And a new earth
And the old earth was passed away.

I crawled along as best I could, then someone pulled me up and set me on my feet. It was a she-bear, very young, small and skinny.

"Come on," she said in English. "We'd best be on our way."

We ran, as our skirts allowed us-- what I wouldn't have given for an ordinary pair of jeans and running shoes right then-- and I had no idea where we were going, as the she-bear was pulling me along by the hand.

It seemed as if there were people after us, because the she-bear kept saying, "Come on, come on, it's not safe," and pretty soon we were in an alleyway and then through a door and down some stairs.

The sound of machines came, and we walked into a

workshop, freezing-cold, with dozens of polar bears hard at work, swarming over the body of a giant squid. The whirring came from an enormous chiller placed in the middle of the room with a steam engine fed by stacks of peat.

"Come on," said the she-bear, and pulled at my hand, but I stopped, shivered, and looked around.

"Wait," I said. "What's going on here?"

"Don't you want to see the *Bloomentwejg*?" she said. "Isn't that why you came to the *Rijksmuseen*?"

I pointed at the polar bears.

"Oh. They are preserving the squid. Only found in the waters of the otherworld. Along with the leviathans. For the Natural History Museum."

She pulled me again, and this time I went, but with my eyes still on the bears.

We went through double doors, and the temperature normalized.

"How did you find me?" I asked. "Who are you?"

"Come with me," she said. "You'll see."

We walked down a corridor lit by little yellow globes.

"We're in the museum," she said, and stopped at some small windows near the ceiling. "Climb up."

I climbed a little stepladder to the windows. There was a perfect view of the intersection where I'd started the riot. The police seem to have restored order.

"I saw you," said the she-bear, pointing a claw at the window. "My name is Melissa Shepherdbear. And I knew I had to come get you." Now she pointed at herself. "I am a housekeeper in the museum. This is our lounge. The passageway to the polar bears' factory is a way of getting the exhibits to the museum without having to transport them above ground."

"I see," I said, though I sort of didn't.

"You're not going to be able to see the Branch by going in up there at the queue. They have been trying to figure out how to let people in. So far it's just a few at a time. The people outside, they can wait all day. They're not going in.

"On the other hand, some of us have to be in there to clean up every day. We're not allowed in behind the glass. But you can smell it. Oh, the smell of it, Cathy!"

I put up my hands. "So why are you telling me this?"

She looked up at me shyly but eagerly. "Well, I've read about you."

My very own fan.

"I heard about Sherm when I was a schoolbear and about how you came to join him, and then I had the chance to be a guest-worker here in Borschland. I've been here a year. I hope you get married to Roald. He is very dashing, for a man, at least."

"And what about you? Are you getting married soon?"

"It's not the same for bears," said Melissa, with a little soprano humph. "We are on a very strict schedule. It comes from our beastly past."

She glanced up at the window, and then spread a paw at the tables and chairs. "Wait here. At seven by the clock, after the museum closes. I'll get you a coat and a headscarf, and you can come take a peek. If you come back tomorrow they may have closed the whole thing down, depending. So stay."

We stood there for a minute, both catching our breath; then I said, "All right then, Melissa. And afterwards, I want you to come out and I'll buy you dinner. I'm very grateful for your quick thinking. Who knows what might have happened?"

"Gracious, thank you, Demouzeel Katharujna. It was a miracle, wasn't it?"

"Thank the saints," I said, and thought of Willem, a saint if there ever was one.

We talked more, doing a kind of Irish door dance for a while, so that it was already half past five when Melissa went off to fetch me a staff coat and headscarf.

I stood on the stepladder for a time, watching the crowd mill about from the ground-level windows. Then I sat at the tables and browsed the day-old newspapers that had been left. A couple of times a polar bear or a housekeeper-- always human-- walked by, but no one came into the room until

83

Melissa appeared again at around quarter of seven with the uniform, and a bucket and pail.

"Are you sure it's all right?" I asked as I buttoned the coat over my seminary dress, and hid my hair under the scarf, making sure to pin it at the nape of my neck with the pins Melissa offered.

"No one will notice. Everyone is drunk with the sight of the Branch," she said. "My supervisor is a hard woman, but last night she spent an hour gazing at the Branch, noticing nothing else. I think perhaps I may be somewhat immune to it, as I am a bear, and nature does not dazzle us the way it does you."

We walked up stairs into the main part of the museum. The lights had been dimmed, so that you could not see into the highest parts of the ceiling. Pillar shafts disappeared into the darkness.

"Have you seen the Branch?" Melissa whispered, though it seemed to echo throughout the hall.

"Of course," I said. "I got about a thousand invitations to see it when I first came to Borschland."

"It's completely different now," she said.

The ticketing area was down stairs and to the left. We turned right and went up more stairs until we came to a rotunda that had statues of the most prominent Borschic saints. Directly in front of us, on the left, was the statue of St. Noos, and on the right, St. Borsch, founders of the nation and discoverers of the original flowering tree. They were wearing traditional Dutch seafaring clothing, the long coats and boots, and the hats with the buckle on the front and a feather coming out to the side, all in bronze, and bigger than life size.

I almost unconsciously crossed myself as I went by them; they are considered holy in Borschland, and still alive and active, at least during phase shifts. I thought of them as people who pray for Borschland to the great Creator in heaven, whom most Borschic people find too remote to ever address directly. To me they were more than alive; they were examples of what kind of person I wanted to be-- adventurous, direct, perfectly themselves. The sculptors had done their best to bring this out, with the feathers that went off at jaunty angles, St. Borsch's *kolv* stick at the ready, St. Noos' feet spread apart as if ready to leap into action. But there is something dead about bronze that can't convey some feelings. I didn't think of the saints as saintly, living in some ethereal starfire. I saw them as people, human beings, people just like Melissa who embody the qualities I admire.

The idea that the saints roam among us while we are phase shifted was charming and quaint, like a lot of things in Borschland, and not something you needed to take very seriously, but you could if you wanted.

We walked down a hall with large paintings of historical Borschic events, battles and martyrdoms and weddings and the ratification of the constitution. But at the end of the hallway was the main event, the Branch. It had its own rotunda, and it was encased in glass in the center of it, a grayish-brown, smooth, crook-ended piece of wood that looked like an oversized hockey stick.

I caught my breath as we came near, for the glass case was lit up-- not by artificial light, the electric lights in here were dimmed as well-- but by the light of the Branch itself. Several police and soldiers were ranged about it, as if to guard it, but they were not looking around to see if anyone was coming. The sight of the Branch, and the light that was lighting up their faces, transfixed them.

A number of others were there: men in suits, housekeepers with buckets and pails, and several women in gorgeous evening dresses. All were watching the Branch.

And the smell. I sensed it from far off, first the suggestion only of some sweetness, as if I were passing by a gardenia bush. Then it got stronger, and for a minute was like honeysuckle, as sweet as a pancake frying. But then it changed and got wilder and spicier, more herbal. And once we were in the middle of the rotunda, you couldn't believe the scent, like nothing you'd ever smelled before, but like everything you loved. It made me hungry, because it was as strong as beef stew but as sweet as the best red wine you'd ever smelled, and at times... Well, I know you're going to laugh at me, but it even smelled like fresh-baked fruitcake.

There. I said it.

The sight may have been even more intense. You could not quite look at it, either without squinting, or sideways, for the flowers that had sprouted from the ordinary wood, only a few inches out, on grayish-green stems, had bright white petals-- four, like a dogwood-- and the centers were gold. These are the colors of the nation's flag, white, gold, and black-- and Sherm's team Te Staff also sports those colors. But they were dazzling, as if they were metal and reflecting the light from somewhere else. But they were, instead, glowing on their own, naturally, like a firefly or a phosphorescent fish that lives in the deep ocean. In the semi-darkness of the hall, it gave the spooky effect of highlighting the faces of the people watching, as if they were holding flashlights under their chins.

But even though it almost hurt to look at, I couldn't resist. I was looking at a miracle.

I don't know how long we looked, but Melissa finally pulled on my sleeve and got my attention.

"I have to get to work," she said.

"Of course," I said.

"Meet me at the Bearish restaurant The Plate at ten o'clock," she said. "Then we can have our supper."

"The Plate," I repeated, still half-looking at the Branch. Melissa gave me the address, which I promptly forgot. She led me away, down the hallway again with the famous paintings of Borschic history, and out into the saints' rotunda. It wasn't till I got there that I shook my head and realized I couldn't smell the Branch anymore. I felt the lack. It was almost as if I was addicted to the smell already.

"You can't be too long with it," said Melissa. "Something happens to one."

"But it doesn't happen to you," I said.

"I'm a bear."

"So if you drank the *Bloomentisande*, what would happen to you? Do you think you'd be immortal?"

She looked at me and didn't blink. I couldn't tell exactly what she was thinking or feeling. Bears' expressions are not as pronounced as humans'.

Then I realized Melissa was not looking at me but behind me.

CHAPTER 13 - HENRICK

First, before I relate anything that happens, we must get the record straight: the Shadow Saints are not evil.

I happen to be a man of strong opinions, as are most Shadows. We are called Shadow also because we tend to express ourselves with strong emotions. The Saints of Light are more controlled.

But you should not be deceived into thinking that because Shadows are passionate, that Lights are calm and impassive. They are not.

If you understand this, then, you might be able to understand what happened when I met Cathy Reinhardt and her she-bear companion in the Saints' rotunda of the Rijksmuseen.

The bear saw me first. Then Cathy turned, and blushed. I was in the uniform of a captain in the Borschic army. No need to tell at this point how I was able to do that, but there you have it.

"Sir," she whispered. "Excuse me."

The she-bear was inconvenient. I told her to go back to her work, and she was gone in a moment, eager no doubt to avoid being sacked for letting an unauthorized person into the Rijksmuseen after hours.

I put my finger to my mouth, and stared at Cathy, silently demanding she watch only me. The color left her cheeks as I took her hand.

"Willem?" she said.

I nodded, and said, "Katharujna," in the voice she was longing to hear. I had been watching them the other day, in the park next to the seminary.

"How did you get in here?" she asked.

I kissed her hand. "My darling, I need to ask you a favor."

"Willem?"

"You are to be a deaconess, which means you are devoted to the saints, is that not true?"

"Yes?"

Her tone told me she wasn't ready yet, she wasn't as far enthralled as she needed to be, but I didn't have time for that. Time was of the essence. "Then please obey me." I cradled her hand in mine, taking off any pressure on it, and yet leaving no doubt I was not letting go. "I want you to go back to the room where you saw the Branch, and I want you to open the glass case, and I want you to remove the tree and bring it to me."

"What? No, I can't. Who--?" Her eyes rolled back in their sockets. I was losing her.

"Katharujna," I said, still grasping her hand, now more firmly. "You can, and this is the only time this is possible. No one has figured out yet how to safeguard the Branch. They were not anticipating it ever blooming again. Before they put it in some everlocked vault, we need to liberate it."

"What are you going to do--"

"Now it is time for you to get the Branch," I said. "I have given you the courage of the saints." And I clasped her palm to my heart.

"Oh, Willem," she said, and collapsed into me, her face against my neck.

"My darling," I said, drawing away and taking both her hands. Our faces were so close, we might have kissed on the lips. "You must. For us."

I turned her palm outwards, and kissed her on the inside of

her wrist. She gasped, then sighed.

I knew she would not be unnoticed as she went to get the Branch, but with luck no one would stop her-- just follow her, as if in procession, until she came to me and I would be able to do what was necessary.

I followed at a distance, with my hand at my sidearm. I did not anticipate using it. That would be up to Fate to decide. Cathy walked slowly, bucket in one hand, mop in the other, and the purple hem of her dress trailed out from under the housekeeper's coat.

As we got close to the Branch, the smell overpowered me. It was worse than I thought it would be. So long ago, I'd smelled that smell, the smell of one's heart's desire: whatever you wanted to smell, it smelled like. It was different for everyone.

For me it was the smell of peat smoke melting snow on a cold Borschic morning next to the frozen Borschland river; it was the smell of a rabbit roasting over a low flame; it was the smell of the *Bloomentisande*, a hot, sweet smell that blows up your nostrils and into your brain and makes you see dreams of red and gold dazzle. And it was the smell of half-digested carrion, a warm, wet, stink, the breath of barbarian foxes on ice skates of carved obsidian.

All of which I smelled the first time I saw that tree from which the Branch came, that breaks your heart with its beauty.

For a moment I thought I would not be able to do it, but then the familiar strength of the *Bloomentisande* pulled me back to myself. That is what the *tisande* does, in fact-- whenever you feel you've gone beyond yourself, it takes you up in its arms and sets you back on your feet, against your will. Many the time I thought I wanted to die, but the *tisande* said no.

It was well. I didn't really want to die any of those times.

Cathy ventured forward. She believed that her beloved Willem had asked her to steal the Branch.

She walked like a spirit guest in between the various important and not so important Borschers who stood ranged about the glass case. The door to the case was ajar-- that was why the scent was so powerful-- and she walked in, unmolested. She took hold of it, attempting to grasp it where there were the least number of flowers, which was difficult to do, as there were so many. It is not heavy, and she was able to lift it off its display, two bronze rests on top of bronze posts.

She turned about, and as she did her face came back into view. She blinked languidly, like a cat taking its ease on a windowsill, and she was flushed, without a hint of panic.

No one moved towards her; no one moved at all, in fact.

With the Branch in her hands, holding it in front of her with her left hand under and forward, and her right hand controlling the other end, just like one would a hockey stick, she pointed it out the door.

The pale, delicate flowers quivered as she brought the Branch outside. The smell was now overpowering.

I unbuttoned the vest of my jacket and took out a carefully folded oilskin. In the center of the oilskin was a pair of shears. They were tooled Anvorian carbon steel, the sharpest possible shears one can buy.

Three hundred years ago, I tried to cut a branch from the original tree. I was using a Dutch East India Company-issued dagger intended mainly for hand-to-hand fighting. It was useless against the Branch, but I had never actually tried to snip off the stems that held the flowers. And the Anvorian shears-- superior by a little to the corresponding Borschic-- were much sharper than my dagger had been.

Cathy followed me up the stairs to the first landing, just in front of the statues of me and Willem. Those who had been watching the Branch had turned, but had not yet moved.

We had only a little time to try the necessary. I took up the shears, and knelt in front of the Branch. A roaring headache was coming on, and I thought to myself that I must give the shears to Cathy, to do the job. It would be difficult; so much energy had gone into persuading her that I was Willem, and that the treason she had just committed was for love.

"Hey," a gruff voice said just above me.

I looked up. Filling my field of vision was the very large

face and snout of a polar bear, with spectacles poised on his snout. Its mouth was open and its teeth were very long.

"What are you doing here?" I said.

"I'm on my dinner break," said the bear, looping his claws around the suspenders holding up his workman's trousers. "What're you doing, Cap'n?"

I looked down. The shears were on the stem, the blades glinting in the light of the flowers.

I let go of the shears and reached for my gun. Too slowly. The bear swiped at me. I felt a terrific whack to the head, and went sprawling. The gun flew out of its holster and went skittering along the marble floor.

Now for a saint to take on a polar bear in a hand-to-hand fight is something less dangerous for the saint than you might think. We are very strong, and though we are not as massive as a bear, nor is the bear as wild as his beastly cousin. I rolled, stood up, and came back at the bear with my fist cocked behind me.

I hit him straight in the jaw, and he staggered back, but my arm felt like I'd hit a wall. I felt it up to my shoulder.

He wasn't down by any means. He spit out a tooth, said, "Now that won't do at all," and, when I tried to hit him again, countered with an open paw to my face. I fell on my tailbone, and one of my own teeth jarred loose.

Meanwhile, Cathy was coming back to herself. "You're not Willem," I heard her say.

The bear stood over me, the gun was a few meters away, and Cathy was kneeling in front of the Branch. The shears lay with a stem between the blades.

"Don't touch them scissors, little human," said the Bear. "That's a crime you're going to do."

Cathy took the shears and gently lifted them away from the flower. Then she stood and faced me with the blades out.

"You're not Willem," she said, surer now, and angrier.

I looked over at the gun, still too far away, then at Cathy, with the shears, and the bear, with his claws.

So I did what I could.

CHAPTER 14 - CATHY

"To my aid! To my aid!" The man who was not Willem cried. His voice was loud and authoritative.

I did not know where I was. I had no recollection of the immediate past, except that the smell of the Branch was now a weird combination of fruitcake and Roald's aftershave, which was almost as bracing as smelling salts. The man in the Borschic captain's uniform looked familiar, but I couldn't give him a name. I just knew he wasn't Willem, and the first thing that told me was the ugly scar that went from his temple to his eyebrow.

We were on the first landing of the stairs going down to the *Bloomentwejg* exhibit. I was standing with a pair of shears in my hand, next to the Branch itself, which was lying on an oilskin. To my left stood a polar bear-- one of the giant squid restorers, no doubt.

The man who was not Willem shouted again, and the sound of booted feet echoed through the hallway. We were soon surrounded by men in uniform-- the guards who had let someone take the Branch out of its booth, lay it down on the landing, and, I began to realize as I came out of my fog, attempt to cut a flower of the Branch from its stem with the shears.

"Arrest them!" said the man. "The woman and the bear. For crimes against Borschland. Brazen arrogance to try to take the Branch!"

I looked at the polar bear. He shook his head and mouthed the word *no* in English.

The captain melted into the background, we were cuffed (somebody had handcuffs big enough for the polar bear) and hustled to the main entrance of the museum, then into the front courtyard, where we were put in a horse-drawn paddy wagon.

We faced each other, saying nothing. A guard sat with us.

Well, that's one way of getting out of studying for my exams, I thought.

The polar bear looked down and shook his head. Finally, he said to me, in English, almost grunted: "Seventy-three."

"What?" I said.

"Quiet," said the guard in Borschic.

"Remember," said the bear. "Seventy-three."

"I said quiet," said the guard again.

"Sorry," said the bear in Borschic. "My throat's sore where that coward hit me."

"You mean that patriot?" said the guard, and everyone left it at that.

When we got out of the paddy wagon at the local police precinct, the photogs were already there. They got a number of choice shots of us as we were hustled up the stairs and into the booking area. I wondered what Sherm would think of his older sister as a traitor to Borschland. I wondered if he'd believe me that, even though I'd picked up a pair of shears that were lying right next to the *Bloomentwejg*, I had no intention of clipping any flowers.

Funny, though, I did have the intention of stabbing that man in the captain's uniform. He just seemed dangerous.

The bear and I were separated, with that mysterious "seventy-three" comment still clanging in my head. The men at the police station couldn't take their eyes off me. A seminarian, involved in the theft of the *Bloomentwejg*. Impossible. And yet anything was a possible during a phase shift.

"Do I get a lawyer?" I asked one of them as they led me up steps and through corridors, then to the roof, where a small airship was moored.

"We're taking you somewhere else," said a man with a brush mustache. "We can't hold you here."

I stepped into the airship, the engine roared, the tethers were loosed, and we spiraled up, over the top of downtown Borschland. The city was lit blue and white with electricity and gaslights, and the cold breeze whipped at me and numbed my cheeks. I had no idea where we were going, and no one would speak with me. Presently we touched down on some landing area that was brightly lit with searchlights.

"Where are we?" I asked the guard who'd accompanied me on the trip.

"Oststaff," he said, and pointed.

That was what was written, O S T S T A F F, on the outbuilding in the distance, lit up now and then by the beams of the lights. Oststaff was the closest military base, and the headquarters of the Borschic Naval Air Service. It was also the location of the Borschland Military Academy and the city where Roald happened to follow and write about a hockey team.

"Let's go," said a woman who came out to meet the ship, and all the guards scattered before me. She was strikingly tall-- maybe six feet. I'd never seen a woman so tall in Borschland. She was dressed in a uniform of the *Daamenkorps*, the female wing of the Borschic military. Mostly they were nurses and secretaries, but this one had on the insignia of the St. Helejna Corps, an elite group of women reputed to be Borschic ninjas. They were named after a saint who had won a war by assassinating a key general on the other side.

"What's going on?" I said over the roar of airship engines and through clouds of steam.

"Don't worry," she said. "We're taking you someplace safe."
"Safe?"

"So the other side can't get at you," she said.

We descended into a miniature subway station-- the platform may have been 20 yards long-- and Bep pulled the lever on a four-person compartment. A steam whoosh sounded, a door opened, and we got on board.

"Where are we going?" I asked as we sat down.

"To the Academy," she said, and motioned to a bundle of clothes on the seat next to me. "This is your standard issue. You are the newest recruit of the St. Helejna Corps."

I took them, rough wool, charcoal gray with forest-green accents. The woman had the same ensemble, but somehow it seemed high fashion on her. Her blue-gray eyes, high cheekbones, and full mouth gave her the looks of a fashion model, though she was not young. Even through her perfect makeup I could tell she was over forty.

She must have noticed me staring, because she said, "My name is Demouzeel Elisabeete van Leeuwen, but please call me Bep." And she gave me her hand.

"Demouzeel van Leeuwen? Not Captain or Major of Colonel?"

"Oh, I am of a rank much higher than any name you could think of," said Bep, and winked at me.

The shuttle banged and shuddered as it came to a stop.

"Welcome," said Bep, "to your new home."

CHAPTER 15 - SHERM

NORTH AMERICAN, BEAR IN BLOOMENTWEJG HEIST, the headline on the morning *Taglik Staff* read.

Of course, I only read that headline later. I didn't have to read the papers to know something was up. The papers came to us.

Willem had not returned to the house that night. Instead, the nannybear Rachael had hired arrived at the house with her suitcase at exactly 9 PM.

"Did you put this in the newspaper?" Rachael asked, showing me a square of newsprint in the Situations section of the *Taglik Staff*, second morning edition.

"I didn't do a thing," I said.

"Maybe it was Willem," she said.

"No idea," I said.

The next morning I woke up to Connie bouncing on the bed wanting to be read to. Melissa arrived quickly after that, and took him back to bed. It was barely 6 AM. I heard voices in the street below and looked out the front window. A bunch of paparazzi and reporters were camped out under a gaslight across the street. A coffee wagon had put out a kettle of fire that was providing them early morning light and heat.

Rachael rolled over and said she felt nauseated; could I

bring her a cup of tea?

I went outside for the paper, wondering, *what is it now?* We'd obviously gone to bed too early the night before.

When I opened the door, they all surged across the street, notebooks and cameras in hand.

"Sherm, do you have any comment on your sister being arrested?" someone shouted.

"Did you know about the conspiracy, or did she keep it a secret from you?" someone else said.

I put up my hands, the paper in one of them, and said, "You boys have gone straight off your heads."

Then out of the crowd someone else came up in a wool suit and carefully tied tie. "Mr. Reinhardt, I'm sorry to bother you," he said. "Detective Wolfenstejn, Borschland National Police. Do you have a moment to talk?"

"I've got to get my wife a cup of tea," I said.

"It won't take long," said the detective. "Just need to get a statement."

I led him into the kitchen, but not before he slipped on Connie's wooden puck. It went flying, and he ended up on his keister.

"You all right?" I said, as Lily ran to be picked up. Wolfenstejn shook his leg, tested it.

"I'm hungry now, Daduj," she said.

"*Ergut, Lilujbeest,*" I said.

"Do you know that your sister has been taken into custody?" asked Wolfenstejn.

"You want tea, too?" I asked.

"No, thanks. The coffee wagon." He pointed. "But..."

"I had no idea until you said it, Detective," I said. "It sounds a bit ridiculous, don't you think?"

"It does, except that she was found next to the Branch with an oilskin laid out on the floor under it, and a pair of Anvorian carbon steel shears in her hands."

"Anvorian," I said, striking a match for the gas and putting a full kettle of water over the blue flame.

"That's correct," he said, and fished a small notebook and

stub of pencil from his coat pocket. "She appeared to be in the process of cutting the flowers from the Branch."

"Did she succeed?"

Lily danced around me, saying she was hungry. Rachael liked to make her an elaborate porridge that was supposed to help her gain weight, but I cut a piece of bread, buttered it, and gave it to her to eat standing up.

"That would be impossible. The Branch cannot be cut by man-made materials. Or at least that is the belief."

"Well then, no harm done, no penalty won," I said, quoting what every Borschic hockey announcer said when someone got away with a hook or a trip on the ice.

"I'm sorry, Mr. Reinhardt. I wish it were that simple. She attempted to steal the Branch. That is a capital offense. It's treason."

I shook my head. "Cathy didn't try to steal the Branch. She may have been guilty of trying to get a look at the thing. She's religious. She's a seminarian."

"Well, they had a devil of a time getting it back into its case," said Wolfenstejn, and put his pencil to his notebook. "Tell me, Meester Reinhardt, did you have knowledge of this conspiracy? How much did Demouzeel Reinhardt tell you?"

"Nothing," I said. The teakettle began to whistle. "It's ridiculous. There's nothing to it. Wrong place at the wrong time."

"You deny any knowledge of the plot?" Wolfenstejn said, and tapped on his notebook with his pencil.

"There isn't any plot."

"If you don't answer the question..."

"Deny. I had no knowledge. Because there was nothing to be known."

"All right. And just one more thing."

The kettle whistled louder. I turned off the flame.

"Do you know of anyone who might have put her up to this? A friend, an acquaintance, anyone she might have met?"

Just for a second I saw Willem in Wolfenstejn, just enough that I must have dropped my poker face.

"I thank you, Mr. Reinhardt, and apologize for the intrusion. Do you have plans to travel, sir?"

"Are you a saint?" I said.

Now he dropped his poker face, and shook his head, but not to say no. It was more like *Don't blow my cover.*

"We're going to Oststaff in a week to play the cadets in an exhibition game," I said. "Are you Shadow or Light?"

"We may have more questions," he said.

I pulled the kettle off the fire and buttered another slice of bread for Connie, who had arrived in the meantime. I pointed down at the kids. "With these two hanging on my legs, I'm not going anywhere, believe me."

Wolfenstejn nodded gravely. "You might want to consider hiring a governess," he said.

I almost said, *We have*, and I realized that Melissa was not with the children.

Wolfenstejn shook my hand. "Willem will be in touch," he said, and left.

Melissa hurried downstairs as soon as the front door shut.

"Children, children," she said. "Come back to bed. I am sorry, Mr. Reinhardt. I had to... attend to..."

"Sure," I said. "And it's Sherm, by the way."

She gave me a grateful grunt, and herded the kids away.

"Thank the saints for Melissa," Rachael said, sitting up in bed and blowing on the mug of tea I'd brought her.

"Yeah," I said. "How much is she getting a month?"

Rachael either didn't hear or didn't want to say. Instead she said, "Did we shift back?" and sipped the tea. She had her hair in a braid, with a few strays curling out from her temple and the nape of her neck. Even sick, she was gorgeous.

"Not that I know of." I opened the paper and saw the big headline. I debated for a second whether I should let Rachael see it, but she already had.

"Steal the Branch? Kathuj?"

"Don't get--"

But she had already taken the paper and was reading the first paragraphs. Rachael is a reader, first and foremost.

Catharine Rowena Reinhardt, thirty-two years, nine months of age, was taken into custody at the ninth municipality of the Detachment of Staff Police, then quickly spirited away by Borschland naval airship to a national detention facility. She will be arraigned for theft of national treasures, sedition, and fomenting of anarchy.

"Anarchy!" Rachael crackled the paper in her fists. "*Unglaaberlickt!*"

"She'll be let off. There's no way they're going to pursue this."

"But what if they do?"

"We'll use the saints to spring her."

"Perhaps Willem has gone to rescue her even now."

"I don't know," I said, thinking again of Wolfenstejn. "But there's nothing we can do about it. We've got training camp today and a practice game in three days. So I've got to attend to that."

"And talk to an attorney about Kathuj. There might be something my father could do."

"Visit her," I said. "But we'll see what else there is. Like bail."

"Bail? Bail? For the likes of national treasure snatching? You're dreaming."

I was dreaming. That day, I got a telegram to appear to a magistrate as Cathy's next of kin and be briefed on what was going on with her. She had been taken to a secure, undisclosed location, for her safety. There would be no bail. Because Cathy was a foreign national, it was almost certain she'd try to flee-- to somewhere else on Continent, and then off Continent when the shift returned us home. The official charges were violation and attempted theft of national treasures, sedition, the fomenting of anarchy, and conspiracy to overthrow the lawful government of the Borschic people.

The evidence was clear: they'd found her fingerprints on the Branch itself, and on the pair of shears Wolfenstejn mentioned. The fact that the Branch was safe, nothing was cut from it, made no difference. She'd intended to steal and cut, and that was enough.

She was going to be hanged.

There was only one clue missing: who was the captain who alerted the guards to Cathy's actions? The man had disappeared shortly after Cathy's arrest.

I had a good idea of who that might be, and I wasn't happy about it. But it didn't make sense that Willem would want Cathy to steal the flowers, unless he just wanted the flowers somewhere safer than the museum.

After all, if someone like Cathy could just waltz in and take the Branch, it certainly wasn't well guarded. Willem had never said he wanted us to move the Branch, just protect it.

I went on to practice. In addition to the mob of paparazzi that followed me from the courthouse, a group of protestors had set up across the street from 14 Waatersdram and were being held behind sawhorses by the police. They were the typical crowd, the ones that wanted foreigners out of Borschland. But this time they had something real to be mad about, and that's what they were.

"Out of Borschland, Reinhardt!"

"Bears out!"

"Protect the Branch!"

I didn't wait to hear all their chants. As I was ducking in the doorway, I heard a smack on the wall just above me, and felt a spray of something sticky on my temple. I looked up and saw a stain of pulp and juice. Somebody'd chucked an apple at me, and they hadn't missed by much.

In the past you could chalk this up to fans from opposing teams, but no one had ever dared to heckle me on my home turf. When I felt the apple on my face, I almost turned to the crowd. Borschland wasn't my native land, but it was my family's home. They weren't going to take that away from me.

But popping a fan would've made things even worse, except for the newspapers, of course. They would sell a lot of papers just by publishing a picture of the apple. But imagine if they got to publish an edition with the front-page headline

REINHARDT ARRESTED FOR ASSAULT, FACE BROKEN BY ANGRY MOB.

Inside, the guys were all there and dressing. Normally if something was happening in my life, they didn't hesitate to cheese me off, but this time they were quiet.

"*Waass te huupe?*" I asked. What's going on? "Somebody's mom served them a bad beef stew?"

Chrujstoff spoke up. "Thought you wouldn't be here. Don't you have to defend your sister?"

"Where's the bear?" I asked. "Sick?"

"Sending him back to Paradise," said somebody else. Paradise was a Borschic term for Bearland, the place of legendary sunshine. "For his own good."

Urdan wasn't there either." And Kasmahlov?"

"Oststaff."

"Look, Sherm," said Oovie. He was the oldest guy on the team and a good friend. "We know Kathuj didn't do it."

"Who says she didn't?" someone piped up. He was a defenseman, and always getting beat to a loose puck. I hated that about him.

"Hey," said Oovie, not loud, but firm. "We know she didn't do it."

"But the evidence," said the defenseman, and a few others chimed in a yes, but more guys shushed them.

"We had a team meeting," Oovie went on. "And we voted. We don't think she did it."

"But it wasn't unanimous," said the defenseman.

"We can't field a team three men down," I said.

"Cramps said we'd take some guys from Oststaff," said Chrujstoff. "He's already been in here. He told us to send you in to him when we were done talking."

"I just don't think--"

"We voted," Oovie said. "And Cramps agrees. And so does management. We're on your side. But we couldn't protect you if you went on ice, maybe not even in our home place. Sherm, it's a tough thing. But you've got to leave the team."

"My God," I said, and a big empty sinkhole opened up in

my gut. Not play. That wasn't even close to being on my radar. It was the reason Rachael and I were saving our cash, because we know I couldn't play forever. But I never had the idea I wouldn't play.

Everybody was stone quiet. That was the worst part; everyone agreed, whether they were on my side or not.

"Well, you guys know best," I said.

"Good luck, Reinhardt," said the defenseman.

"Hold on," said Oovie. He came over to me, hesitated. He was going to shake my hand, but instead he hugged me. "Good luck, Reinhardt."

They all hugged me, even the defenseman. That really meant something. Borschic men don't hug each other as a rule, even after big goals. You might get a group hug after a game winner, but individual hugs? Forget it.

"I feel like I'm at my own funeral," I said after we'd finished.

No one cracked a smile.

"Well, win it all, boys. I'm counting on you."

"Yeah," said Chrujstoff. "As soon as we get those cadets up here, we'll be scoring a dozen a game."

That was about as light-hearted as it was going to get. They were staring down a four-man deficit, including their captain, and I-- well, I had to admit it-- may have been done with hockey in Borschland.

"*Tah-loo*," I said, the Borschic way of saying I'll see you soon.

In the office above the practice rink, Cramps and I watched the workout for a few minutes. He didn't say anything, just shook his head slowly.

A knock came on the door.

"Staamfuuler," said Cramps.

It was Henrick, St. Borsch.

Henrick stood there, and I turned to Cramps. He shook my hand. "Good luck, Reinhardt," he said.

Henrick and I went to the same room where I'd looked at the poster before. Same window, same sky, just a little chillier outside. The room felt shadowy, as if a bulb was out overhead. I looked up. All the hanging lamps shone pale white.

"So what's going on?" I asked.

"I told you not to trust Willem," he said. "Saints can be very persuasive. He clearly convinced Kathuj she was doing something for the good of the nation. For the good of the faith."

"How do I know it wasn't you? The papers said there was a captain from the army. That he disappeared after Cathy was arrested. Didn't even get his name."

"Ah," he said. "Yes, that's the problem, isn't it? A mysterious captain. Some saint, no doubt."

"Like you."

"Kathuj doesn't even know me. Why would she commit treason for me?"

I had no answer for that one.

"It doesn't matter who persuaded or compelled her to do it. We must not let the Branch remain unused, as if it were some relic. We can learn much from it. We Shadows are for science. We are for taking a sample from the *Bloomentwejg*--"

"Even though no known blade can cut it."

"We haven't tried everything. And the petals. How do they work? We need to determine who to give the *tisande*. For the progress of the nation. And we don't have much time before the blooms fall and the opportunity is lost for hundreds of years."

"So that means Willem-- or you-- still have to get one of us to steal the thing. Someone from North America, where you were born. The government--"

"--will not let anyone touch it," said Henrick. "Believe me. They are too stubborn. But we can find a way. And then we can get you back on the ice, and your sister out of jail. Reinhardt, you do know in what kind of trouble you are, don't you?"

"Yeah. Yeah, Borsch. I know."

"It's Henrick."

"How about Hank?"

I was pretty sure he wanted to punch me, but he held it together. "Weather the storm as best you can," he said. "You should not talk to the press. Have your groceries delivered. No more trips to Schmeecks."

"That was on my list to cross off anyway."

"We can hire you a governess through whom you can get orders. We can make this work."

Why was everyone talking about a governess all of a sudden? I said, "We've hired somebody already. Yesterday."

"Let her go."

"That's not happening. I'm not going in with the Shadows. I'm not stealing the Branch."

"Remember our last talk? About Rachael, and the expected child? Now it's about your sister. And your livelihood. Don't let everything slip away, Sherm."

He had me there. The room felt very cold. I could feel myself oozing into a very big carton of deep yogurt.

Henrick put out his hand to shake with me, and I looked into his eyes. He stared at me, I stared back.

"No blinking," I said.

"You're being stupid," said Henrick, and turned away to the window. "You have a strong spirit. That's why we need you. You're the only one for this job."

"Get Urdan to do it."

"He's too young," Henrick said, and the frustration in his voice sounded like that might have been the only true thing that he'd said to me so far.

"No agreements, Hank. Not until you give me some reason to trust you."

He turned back towards me, big dramatic eyes. "Sherm, you don't have a lot of time. You don't have a lot of leverage."

"You don't have a lot of foreigners to pick from."

He shook his head. "Don't count on Willem."

"I'm not."

"Don't let your sister hang."

"I won't."

"See that you don't."

He went to get some papers for me to sign. Suspended, with pay. As soon as he was gone, my muscles released, and I felt like I'd been through three periods of hard checking. I wanted to go home and go to bed. But I couldn't. Henrick was dead right. I had to make some quick decisions. Or Sherman Ignatius Reinhardt and family were finished in Borschland.

CHAPTER 16 - CATHY

The morning after my arrest, I woke in my room in the *Daamenkorps* barracks. It was a little birdcage: the window had a sash for opening, but there were bars on the outside. There was a good view of a parade ground and an airship landing area. Fog and low clouds obscured the horizon. No one was out. I felt the windowpane. It was cold to the touch. Winter was coming fast.

The room was plain-- dark wood paneling, bare linoleum floor. My bed, a nightstand with a candleholder, and a chair and table with another candleholder on it. No electric light on or visible; the only light came from the barred window.

I went to the door. There was a bolt, which I threw back. The hinges creaked-- loud in the morning silence-- and I opened it. The hallway was cold and dark except for a single bulb at the end. I followed the hallway to the bulb, where I tried the door. It opened, and on the other side was a woman standing guard in a Daamenkorps uniform.

"*Gut emorgenweck*," I said.

She nodded and I walked past her, wondering how far I would get. I went downstairs to a front room like a lobby, where another wofman sat at a desk reading a newspaper.

As I walked by, the woman said, "Demouzeel van Leeuwen

will meet you for breakfast. Be back in half an hour, no more."

The air outside was damp and freezing. Other buildings with entrances like mine ringed a green with a flagpole in the middle. Could I escape? Just keep walking? Maybe, but where to?

Back inside, I said to the woman at the desk, "Too cold for a walk."

"Yes, and you without a coat," she said, not looking up from her newspaper. It was open to a big photograph of the *Bloomentwejg*.

I looked over to my right. There was a dining hall, nearly empty, but with an enticing coffee smell.

The woman said, "There is a bath at the other end of your hallway. Wash up. Demouzeel van Leeuwen will come for you when she is ready."

It sounded like the thing to do.

In the bathroom, there was a tub and a washstand with a hot water tap and soap and a hairbrush. I would've liked a bath, but the fact that the tap was connected to the washstand meant the tub was supposed to be used seldom.

I washed my face instead, brushed my hair, and got dressed in the Daamenkorps uniform left on the table.

Demouzeel van Leeuwen was prompt. She knocked on my door, and we went downstairs into the dining room and had coffee and toast, jam, ham and cheese.

"Feeling all right?" she asked.

"Yes, I suppose," I said. "But I still don't understand why I'm here. If I'm to be accused of some crime, shouldn't I be awaiting a bail hearing rather than impersonating a cadet?"

"You don't want to be out on bail. Too dangerous. Anyway, they wouldn't let you out. And even in a jail, you'd be in grave danger."

"Why?"

"Because the entire nation thinks you were trying to steal our national treasure. I don't know that the Borschic authorities can protect you from someone who wants to put an end to the fomenter of anarchy."

Anarchy. It was a word I had hardly ever heard.

"You know I never did-- never tried-- to do anything."

"Oh, we know. That's why we want to protect you."

"We? You mean the *Daamenkorps*?"

"We. The Shadow saints."

Immediately I saw the face of Willem, telling me that sometimes mythology is truer than theology.

"You may not remember me. You did not grow up with the stories. I am St. Bep."

"St. Elisabeete? The legendary matchmaker of the Borschic saints?"

"The very one."

"So the saints-- the mythological ones-- are real?"

"And some of us are beautiful," she said, and gave me a perfect little charming wink.

"And the stories about the Shadow Saints, and the Saints of Light..."

"Are also true." She sipped her coffee. She left a lipstick stain on the rim. *Saints are real*, I thought, *and even use makeup.*

"And the *Bloomentwejg*--"

"Katharujna," said Bep, and plucked a bit of lint from her sleeve. "We need to apologize to you. The Shadows. Henrick. St. Borsch. Was rash to ask you to take the Branch."

"St. Borsch?"

"Yes. He saw an opportunity and took it. That is his way. But he got you into rather a *schuunmoute*." She meant a mess, a stew.

"Well, you are opposed to the Saints of Light. You must be very busy."

"In the case of the *Bloomentwejg*, yes, we are working at cross purposes at the moment. We both are working for the good of the country, but we have different ideas on how to accomplish that."

"So how do I know which side is the good guys? Who should win?" I didn't say "good guys" in Borschic. I asked, who are the morally good ones, the *duugsaamen*, the virtuous ones.

"No one is *duugsaam* all the time," said Bep, and she swept her hand across the table, as if sweeping the question away. "But enough of saints. Let's talk about you. We have great plans for you. We feel very lucky to have you."

"Why, don't you have enough women to fill up these dorms?"

"Don't be silly. We have great need of you. We want you to coach our women's hockey team."

"What?"

"There are not many teams on the Continent, but every three years there is an international tournament, and it is taking place in Loflinland-- in Bijfhaaf, their capital, so it's close by. It's called the Ladies All Nations Continental Ice Hockey Cup. The Women's College of the University of Borschland has had a team for some years, and they will be at this tournament. And we, the *Daamenkorps*, would like to start a team of our own. After all, Oststaff and the University of Borschland are traditional rivals in the men's game. So why not a woman's team?"

"That surprises me you don't have a team. I thought Borschland had the best hockey and the best hockey coaches."

Well, we are behind in our women's game. Anvoria is the best at women's sports. Bearland doesn't count because they have a tradition of she-bear competitions that are quite frightening. Many she-bears in Bearland are actively attempting to have these competitions banned, because they take away from the sense of civilization that the bears have fought so hard to win for themselves."

"Uh huh."

"We are going to say that you are from Anvoria. Your name will be Karolujna Kretschmer. We will dress you differently and do your hair differently and no one will know that you are Katharujna Reinhardt."

Oh, good name, I thought. *Very alliterative.* But I said out loud, "And you're doing all this just because you like me."

"We are looking out for your welfare, Kathuj. And if we say that you are Karolujna Kretschmer from Anvoria, then you can live a normal life, and travel with the team."

"Normal."

"As normal as possible. We need to see the Branch situation resolved. Once it is, and we, the Shadows, have done what is best for Borschland with it, then you will be freed, and can go back to seminary, marry Roald, or be whatever you like."

"Marry Roald." I laughed. "Is Roald going to marry a fomenter of anarchy?"

"Kathuj, my dearest twinkling of the starfire. You forget. I am St. Bep. I can talk to him if you like. I am very persuasive."

"Wow. I feel so taken care of."

"You should," she said, and pointed at me with a shiny fingernail. "Because you are. It was wrong of you to follow that bear into the museum. I should say, I understand your curiosity. But that was a foolish thing to do. Anything could've happened. You could've been shot. When in fact you were simply manipulated by your love for--"

She put her finger to her chin, and looked down at it.

"My love?"

Bep changed the subject. "Tell me, whatever happened to that she-bear who helped you?"

"You mean the polar bear? He wasn't with me."

She laughed, a tinkling little laugh, like a society matron, and the life came back into her eyes. "Please don't lie, my dear. I know there was a she-bear with you in addition to the polar bear."

"And how do you know that?"

She didn't laugh this time. Wheels were turning in her mind, I could tell. "A topic for another day, Kathuj. I mean, Karolujna. We have practice this morning beginning at eleven of the clock. Your assistant, Meester Fleemisch, will fetch you at the proper time. I must be on my way. We have great doings in this country, darling."

And that was the end of the breakfast with St. Elisabeete, who preferred to be called Bep.

When I got to the rink, which was outdoors, several of the

guys on the Oststaff team were finishing up a morning skate. Bep was there, and pointed Urdan out to me.

"That is Urdan Kasmahlov. He is a Lipni Tatar. He will have many great loves."

But can he clear a puck on the penalty kill? I wanted to ask, but I stayed quiet, and had a look at the women who were sitting in the bleachers, wearing long dresses and tightly-laced skates, and holding hockey sticks. Over their carefully pinned-up hair they wore helmets with little iron facemasks. Ribbons that tied at the chin and made a bow held the lids in place. A man was sitting next to them with his hands in his lap.

Bep motioned to him, and he walked over to us. "This is Fleemisch, your assistant," said Bep.

We shook hands, or I should say my hand got lost in his. Fleemisch was bald and had big ears, googly eyes and bad teeth. Quasimodo as water boy.

Bep said, "Now, Demouzeel Kretschmer, I leave you to your team," and she turned with a swish of her skirts.

The first thing I said to Fleemisch was, "Can we do something about the dresses? This isn't a fashion show."

Fleemisch blushed, something he did a lot, I learned. "This is the way we do it in Borschland," he said. "Proper ladies wear dresses and skirts. Men wear breeches."

"You don't have to speak so slowly," I said. "I understand Borschic."

"Oh," said Fleemisch, and blushed again. "Demouzeel van Leeuwen said you were from Anvoria."

One of the women lifted her skirts and showed her socks and shin pads. "Don't worry, Coach," she said. We all have these."

And they all lifted their skirts, as if on cue. Fleemisch's ears turned purple. They were ladies, but they were also *Daamenkorps*, a bit different from the rest of Borschic womanhood.

"Well, let's get out on the ice," I said.

They clomped on, and skated out. I had them skate in a circle around the rink to see what we were working with. Lots of fluttering skirts, lovely lines. Fleemisch went and got a bucket of pucks. I asked which one was the goalie. One named Greetje piped up. I told her to kit up and get cozy with the crease.

"Now let's shoot some pucks," I said. I lined them up at the blue line, and had one of them feed pucks to the others just above the circles.

They were very polite. The passes were very slow, and the shots were very elegant. It was like playing shuffleboard.

"Can't anyone shoot harder than that?" I yelled.

"We don't usually shoot from so far out," someone said.

I threw a look at Fleemisch, who blushed again.

I guess I shouldn't have been surprised.

At the end, I sat the ladies down and we had a talk.

"How many of you have played hockey before?"

"I played field hockey," said one of them who was named Philuumeena.

"Yes," a number of others said. "We played field hockey."

"Hockey on ice is a bit different, I think," said someone else.

"Have any of you ever played ice hockey?"

No one moved. They didn't even look at each other.

"We have all skated," someone said. "Everyone in Borschland skates."

Now there were nods.

"So you're saying, are you, that this is a brand-new team?"

"Yes," said one of them. "That is a wonderful way to put it. We are brand-new."

So ended practice number one.

We had lunch in the cafeteria, and I sat with Fleemisch and looked at a photo album he brought and got names with faces. After a half hour or so, the women scattered to their various duties in the *Daamenkorps*.

Fleemisch stayed with me till Bep reappeared. She led me to an impossibly gorgeous, wood-paneled library filled with blue-uniformed cadets, and walked me to a study carrel, a cell about six feet square, with a smoked-glass window with carved stone dragons coiling around its frame.

"To review, for your exams," she said.

All of my materials were there.

I spent the afternoon following the curves of the dragons, watching the sun drop through the clouds like a little pat of melting butter. A woman came at about three o'clock with a cup of tea. When the sun began to set, the same woman led me back to my room.

All I had written in my notebook was WILLEM.

There, a table had been set for two, and there was a big candelabrum with two unlit tapers.

A note on the table said I would have a caller at six of the clock.

I went into the bathroom. On the washstand there was a mirror and cosmetics. A bath had been drawn, steaming and deep. I took my time in it.

When I came back to my room, a dress had been laid out for me. It was lovely, lace, with pearl beading, and an off-the-shoulder neckline. A Vinasolan woman came in and put up my hair.

Then a waitress entered and lit the candles in silence. It was dark by now, and the candles made an intimate globe of light about the table.

At six o'clock exactly, the door opened, and Roald appeared in a gray suit, with a little bowler hat.

He smiled. "How beautiful you are, my little criminal," he said.

"At least you can still joke," I said.

He took my hand, and kissed my wrist. I wanted so much right then just to lose myself in his arms. All the skin-hunger of the past four years in Borschland came rushing to the surface.

But there was decorum to be followed.

We sat, and the waitress came with Borschic champagne and a cold lobster appetizer.

I said, "What's going on? Are you doing a story about me?"

"No, I'm here very strictly off the record. My editor doesn't even know I'm here."

"Why not? What's going on?"

"I had an anonymous telegram. Be here at this time, at this place, if you would like to see Katharujna. Do not tell anyone. We will find out, and you won't see her."

"Did you tell anyone?"

"I am so glad you are safe. Are you?"

"Yes, it's almost as if I'm not accused of anything. Except that I don't know what would happen if I just walked off base."

"Have you talked to anyone? A lawyer?"

"No one."

"That's against the law. You have the right to defend yourself."

"They are telling me it's for my own good right now. That the whole nation is out to get me, and we have to let things cool down."

"That's false. Many people are on your side, and Sherm has retained representation that is fighting for you even as we speak."

"That's good. Is there any word as to when I might be set free?"

"None as yet. They are waiting for the captain who discovered you to come forward."

"What? What do you mean?"

"The man who accused you has disappeared. In order to know rightly what happened, the authorities need his testimony."

"Well, it makes sense that he isn't coming forward. He is St. Borsch."

"Saint?"

"I know, I know. It seems incredible. But a lady who calls herself St. Bep is the one holding me here. And she apologized for St. Borsch's actions. You know I would never steal the Branch on my own. Somehow he charmed me, manipulated me. I don't remember picking up the Branch or taking it. I just remember I was kneeling there in front of it."

"Manipulating. Manipulating." Roald was thinking hard.

The waitress came back and gave us our fish, a mountain trout with sautéed potatoes and pink roe. She opened a bottle of dry cider and poured a glass for both of us.

Roald said, "If we can make a positive identification that it was St. Borsch-- St. Henrick van Borsch-- then you would be immediately exonerated. Was there anything about him that you remember? Any kind of identification, scar, or something?"

"There was a scar," I said, recalling the triangle above his eyebrow. "But..." And then it came back to me, what the polar bear said in the paddy wagon.

"Yes?"

"There was a number. A number I was supposed to remember."

"What was it?"

"Seventy-three. The number seventy-three."

"Was that the company he was from?"

"It may have been. I just know I had to remember it."

"Katharujna," he said. "Seventy-three is a famous brigade of the Army of Borschland. Everyone knows it. It's the saints' brigade."

"Really?"

"The Seventy-third brigade, first Borschic division, is never filled with recruits because it is our ghost army. We always feel the seventy-third is with us in spirit when we go into battle. No one has the number seventy-three on their uniform-- unless it is a saint."

"Is there a saint with a triangular scar over his left eyebrow?"

"Yes, there is-- Saint Henrick van Borsch."

I thought of the moment I came to myself, in the Rijksmuseen, and seeing this man Henrick, and how I felt such a longing, and a disappointment, that he wasn't Willem.

"St. Borsch was trying to steal the Branch," Roald said. "But he cannot by himself, because anyone born on the Continent cannot touch the Branch or we die."

"Bep told me they were with the Shadow Saints," I said.

"And what about the Saints of Light? Are they involved as well?" Roald asked.

"Doubtless. But I don't know of any. Unless." Willem, a saint? It made perfect sense. Willem van Noos, the statue in the Rijksmuseen.

"And the whole point is, which of them gets the Branch. For the *tisande* of immortality. All those old stories."

I looked up at him. A look had come into his eye, a look that would have been welcome at any other time.

"Yes?"

He leaned over and kissed me, first on the cheek, then lightly on the lips. Then he cradled the back of my neck with his hand and used a thumb to lift my chin up to his. And we locked in a very deep, long kiss.

After he caught his breath, he said, "When you are free, we shall be married. This is your ring." And he took out a little black velvet box.

"Where-- where did you learn to kiss like that?"

"All Borschic men know how. We just don't do it every day."

I opened the box, and the ring blazed like a power plant. Baguette diamonds in a circle with a big, gorgeous ruby in the middle. Rubies are Borschland's national gem.

"Oh, it's like a sun," I whispered.

"Or a flower of the *Bloomentwejg*," he said. "It is my grandmother's. It is said to have been made by Kikerertwen, the lover of St. Bep."

"It's too much," I said. "This can't be for me."

"But it is."

I thought of Willem again. Such a good, wise man. Older. Distinguished. Wise. Yet sexy. And a saint? How stupid was I being?

And so at the very moment I was being asked to enter an important Borschic family, the Greningens, and be a celebrity for the rest of my life, I thought instead about the good, quiet life that Willem and I could have, if only he weren't immortal.

If only I could just see him again-- to make sure.

"You will be my bride, Katharujna," said Roald.

"*Ten sill wuj zujet,*" I whispered to him, and looked away.

He sat up straight. "We will see?" he said. "Not yes?"

"Oh," I said. "Well. Probably yes."

"What do you mean, probably yes? I have given you my solemn promise. We kissed."

"I don't know. You act as if it's fated. You didn't even really ask me, Roald. You just assumed."

"I thought you wanted me to ask. Friends have been telling me for months that you wanted me to."

"And so, why didn't you?"

"I was waiting for the right time."

"And now that I'm in prison, I guess it is."

"I want you to know that I will stand by you, come what may."

"Well, Roald. That isn't the best time to be making a lifetime decision."

"But I am sure now."

"Well, I am not."

"Why is that?"

I looked hard at him, and he looked hard at me. It was one of those times when you are looking so close at a person's eyes you can see the little twitches.

"Anyway," I said, "What are you doing promising to marry someone who stole the *Bloomentwejg*? Aren't you better off without me?"

"What are you trying to play at? This isn't a game, it's a promise."

"I just want you to know, maybe I'm not the right one for you."

"What, is there someone else?"

I hesitated just enough that he drew back, and went pale.

"I can't believe this," he whispered.

Oh, the drama. "Roald, listen. Maybe Bep is just manipulating you. Maybe you'll feel differently afterwards."

"I don't think that--"

"Listen. Go back to Sherm and tell him about the seventy-third brigade. He'll tell his lawyers and maybe we can get me free based on that. We can't be thinking about ourselves right now. If the Shadow Saints are trying to steal the Branch, they must be our opponents. Someone has to stop them."

He kept on staring at me, with an expression that said I'd betrayed him.

"Will you go back and tell Sherm, at least? For me. Whatever happens. Please."

"I will never rest till I find out who is the other suitor who is pursuing you."

"Roald. Please."

He shook his head, and his eyes went down. "Is it that Canadian?" He asked.

"That's ridiculous. Get a hold of yourself." And I laughed, despite myself.

He was startled. Now his eyes turned puppy dog, irresistible.

The door opened. It was St. Bep, with the dessert course.

"Saints alive," she said. "Have I caused trouble, here?"

Roald stood up, put on his hat, bowed to me, bowed to St. Bep, and left.

"Pity," said Bep. "This is chocolate mousse. And I have good news."

"Good news," I said. A tear rolled down my eye.

"What, are you worried about that scribbler? I told him this was his chance. What did the wretch do?

"He proposed."

"He proposed? He proposed? Holy starfire, what did you say?"

"*Ten sill wuj zujet.*" And another tear rolled from my other eye.

"Heavens, girl. You make things so complicated. Whatever could you be thinking?"

"I just need to think things over, that's all. I need time."

"You need time. You need time. You have had time. Roald told me he's kept you waiting many months."

"I know. But now that he's asked, I just don't know."

"Of course you know. But you are afraid of something."

"I'm not afraid."

"A woman who is presented with a proposal from a man with prospects such as Meester Greningen does not temporize unless...."

I looked up at her through a film of tears.

"...Unless there is someone else. Is there?"

"Not really."

"Not really. Oh, but this mystery suitor is obviously more suitable than the scion of the first family of Borschic journalists."

"Well, I have to know that that road is closed before I...."

"This wouldn't have anything to do with a lovely man named Willem, would it?"

I looked away, and my eyes welled up again.

Bep took my hand, and our eyes met. "That road is closed, Katharujna," she said.

"I don't know."

"It's closed."

"I have to find out."

"Oh, you will. You will find *Te Hart* and you will find *Te Harteleed.*" *Your heart's desire, and your heart's pain*, she meant.

I laid my head in my hands.

"But now for the good news, my unhappy child who should be rejoicing. We have scheduled a skirmish with the *Daamensveltinstitut*. The University of Borschland team. Next Wednesday. You have quite the challenge, Demouzeel. To put together a team in one week."

CHAPTER 17 - SHERM

The first day after Cathy's arrest we spent indoors, with Melissa on the assist. The next morning, Roald visited the house and told us he'd had a secret meeting with Cathy, and had some information.

We went downtown to my lawyers', and Roald told them about "seventy-three," the Borschic saints' brigade. I sent a note to Wolfenstejn, and he got a statement from the polar bear, who confirmed it. Seventy-three meant there would be no prosecution: a saint was behind the theft and would never come forward to testify.

"Just like that? On the say-so of two of the accused?" I asked Roald.

"We know there was a mysterious captain. Now it makes sense."

At the end of the fourth day, Cathy's lawyers made the argument that the case could not be pursued if the only eyewitness to the crime was a saint.

And with that seed of doubt planted in Borschland's head, I went back to the team.

It was a big circus. There were people on our side-- lots. We got hundreds of telegrams pledging support. There were people on the other side. Foreigners out. People who had never accepted me. So it became something that sold a lot of papers. And the mystery captain became all that anyone talked about.

I was reinstated on the day we played a practice game with the Oststaff cadets. We took a special subway train, with crowds lining the way as we walked downstairs to catch it.

The rink was absolutely packed, and Urdan was in the starting lineup, right defenseman. He'd gotten better at judging distances and helped the cadets keep the score reasonable.

I didn't get a lot of ice time because I was out of shape, but I did get to speak to Urdan a couple of times in front of the net.

"How you holding up?" I asked.

"Okay," he said, and blocked a shot off his shin. It went into the boards and the wings went after it.

"Anyone talk to you about the Branch?"

"Branch?"

Then we shot it in, I tried to tip it, failed, and the cadets cleared. When I saw Urdan again, it was clear he didn't even know about the Branch at all. No one was speaking English to him; they were giving him a cadet hazing experience.

"You get any news from anyone at all?"

"A lady from a newspaper. Said she was a friend of Danny's. And did I want to see her again. Said she could make it happen. Said cadet life was tough and everyone needs a break."

And that was that, till the third period. We were ahead something like 6-1, and everyone was taking it pretty easy by then.

I stood at center while the cadets had a little spin around the goal, and Urdan stood with me.

"Listen," I said. "You need to be careful. I'm just going to tell you one thing. If you decide to say yes to that lady from the newspaper, remember that they're going to ask you to do something in return. So if they do, try to make sure I know. Okay?"

"Okay."

"This is big. A lot bigger than you getting a job playing hockey in this league. It could mean the difference between a big war, and peace."

"Okay. Well, as long as we're in a phase shift, no one can get us, right?"

"What do you mean?"

"I mean, no one outside can come in, right?"

"Outside. You mean outside the Continent. Yeah, so?"

"Just. That's all. That's all I wanted to know."

The action changed, the puck came out to me, and that was the last I talked with Urdan.

I had had no contact with Man Greatbear since the Branch thing came down; all the bears in Borschland were keeping low profiles, including Lavishbear, who was still nursing bronchitis anyway.

But Cathy wasn't released. I never got a straight answer from anyone about that. The papers quoted her as saying she would spend the rest of the year reviewing for her exam. But the following Tuesday after the Oststaff practice game I got a message from "Staamfuuler" that I was going to have a talk with Karolujna Kretschmer, the Anvorian coach of the new *Daamenkorps* ice-hockey team. They airshipped her and her team over to watch our practice, and she wore a wig. We took no questions, because you could've told she was from Minnesota and not Anvoria as soon as she opened her mouth. Then she and I got fifteen minutes before she had to go back to Oststaff.

"So, how's wearing a wig?" I asked.

"Oh, not bad," she said. "Food's good."

"And you're fulfilling a lifelong dream. Didn't you say you wanted to coach?"

She laughed. She had given up hockey when Dad got sick. We'd already lost Mom to a heart attack only a year before. I never knew if it mattered that much to her. She never said.

"You should be out. This should be over," I said.

"Technically the investigation is still on," she said. "And they want to protect me from the *Ooslaandern-Oos* crowd. But it's a good way of making sure I can't be used by the Lights."

"That just stinks."

"Have you seen Willem?" she asked. "I wonder what he thinks of all this."

For a second I thought I should tell Cath about Willem, but the standing order was no leaks, not to anyone.

"Listen," I said, "If there's anything I can do."

"I'd like to see Willem," she said, and looked away.

"You can't focus on him."

"Sherm," she said, "I know the Branch is a big deal. It doesn't seem right that we're the most important people for keeping it safe."

"And Urdan."

"Yeah, and Urdan. But we're Borschic now, and it's okay. I'm going to do what I have to do."

"I know you will."

"So listen. When we get on the other side of this, let's have a pizza. Just the two of us. Until then, don't worry about me. I'll get through, and so will you."

"There's no pizza in Borschland, Cath."

"We'll open a restaurant."

Best idea of the year.

The season began with Lavishbear still shelved, Urdan on Oststaff, and me distracted with the Branch. The good news was that our Zimrothian goalie, Cemreth Cefreth, joined us about three hours before we had our first game, versus Tarlunz at their place.

Cramps stuck Cefreth in there, because Ruud Paulus had gotten injured, and the third one, Groothammer, was almost like not playing a goalie at all.

So it sort of made sense we lost, and the score made sense, 8-2, which was the most goals we had given up to Tarlunz in twenty-seven years. I remember that number because about a dozen reporters repeated it to me afterwards when each one had to ask the very same question even though the guy before him had just asked it.

"Did you know that's the most goals Te Staff has given up

to Tarlunz in twenty-seven years?"

"Now, I do. Thank you for telling me."

"But what about the honor of the Staff team?"

"We are all ashamed of this result and intend to do better."

"Thank you, Sherm."

At least they thanked me.

Game number 2 was versus Holtzlund down at their place, and the bear made the trip and even played a few minutes at right wing, but did not contribute to the 1-1 tie we gave away after leading 1-0 for most of the game. Holtzlund is never very good, and their offense was bad, but Cefreth still had to play well to keep it a one-goal game.

On the train the next morning after that game, Willem showed up again. This time he was disguised as a train conductor, and he gave me the high sign as he was walking through our car announcing the late breakfast service.

I went and looked for him, and he was sitting at a table with a cup of tea in the dining car, dressed like an ordinary citizen.

"How do you do that?" I asked when I sat down.

"With a bit of planning and help, it's not difficult at all," he said. "Remember, I have been hiding in plain sight for centuries."

"So what's going on?" I asked. The authorities had stopped up the Rijksmuseen, but good, with soldiers the past couple of weeks, and no one from the public was seeing the Branch. "Cath's been asking about you. I need to know what to say."

"Say nothing to Katharujna," said Willem. "'Let the Shadows spend their energy on her. You are the important one."

I was going to say I didn't agree with that, but there wasn't really any point.

"The government have fashioned a duplicate Branch," Willem went on. "It doesn't smell or look the same, but they can say that they have ordered glass from somewhere that stops the scent from escaping, and they can keep people far away, and the lighting low. That way we can have an exhibit, and the people's heart to see it will be satisfied. In the meantime, we need to find a safe place for it. It is ultimately vulnerable in the Rijksmuseen."

"Why is that?"

"The Shadows control the army. Individually, each man in the military is committed to protecting the Branch, but if they are commanded to let the Branch go, they will do it. Because they will believe it is best for the country.

"So I have a plan, and I need your help with it."

We were following the Borschland River back to Staff Borsch, the same track I'd taken when I first came to the country. The river was on the right, reflecting early-morning sunlight. The city of Meechen was a half-hour away, Staff Borsch an hour and a half.

"I would like to hide the Branch," said Willem, "and I would like you to guard it. We can do this by having you carry it around in your equipment bag."

"What?"

"Quietly," he said, palms down. He took a sip of tea, looked out at the river, and said, "We can disguise the Branch as a hockey stick. In fact, you can use it as your hockey stick if you see fit. That way it would always be with you."

The waiter came by and asked if I wanted breakfast. Willem gave a quick shake of his head, and I ordered coffee.

"The *Bloomentwejg* actually began its life as a hockey stick-- a *kolv* stick of Henrick van Borsch. It was transformed into the *Bloomentwejg* by being planted in the place where we found the holy tree of Borschland."

"So it isn't a branch of the holy tree?"

"No, it isn't. That is what is popularly believed, and what we wanted everyone to believe. But it is Henrick's *kolv* stick. It is the size and the shape of a stick, and it has a bend to it at the end with a blade. It isn't as wieldy as a modern stick, but to play hockey with it, well, I think it would be..."

"Except for all the flowers on the Branch, this is making perfect sense," I said.

"Yes, that's very sticky isn't it?" He emphasized sticky, as if he was making a joke.

"Sticky."

"Yes. Like tape."

"Tape."

"Yes. Tape."

The waiter brought my coffee.

"You don't mean."

Willem leaned forward and whispered, "Tape the stick. Tape the flowers down on the stick."

I sipped the coffee. It still tasted like coffee, so I figured I was still in the same parallel universe, and not in another one where they taped magic hockey sticks.

"You do know," I said, "that hockey players don't tape the entire stick. Only the handle and the blade."

"Habits change, practices change. Sometimes by the action of one trailblazer."

"And you really think this is going to work?"

"I don't know. But we must try it at least. The government has already given me its permission."

"The government, but not the military."

Willem gave me an exasperated look. "The government is in charge of the military."

"Unless there's a phase shift, and Henrick is in command."

"Will you try this or won't you?"

"Of course I'll try it." Emphasis on the try. "What do you think? That I don't want to save Borschland?"

Willem sat back, looked out the window again, and toasted me with his tea. "You have changed your tune since that first day on St. Noos Oval."

"Well," I said, toasting him back, "only a saint can make a *terrujn* that good."

CHAPTER 18 - CATHY

A week and a snowfall later, we were ready to take on the Women's Ice Hockey Club of the University of Borschland.

Ready as we could be, that is. We had a semblance of three lines and five defensemen. The goalie, Greetje, was pretty good at stopping the shots that we sent her way. Not that we shot that hard or accurately.

Philbuja was our star center. She could skate well, and had a nose for the goal. The best defenders were Haanelore and Jaane, big hulking girls who were okay with taking pucks off their shins. They would not be able to stay with fast skaters, turn on a dime, or help out on offense. But you work with what you have.

We were to play on the same rink that the University of Borschland men's team used, a pond sunk into a concrete depression, with a civilized oval of benches ringing it. Instead of glass to hold the puck in when it was lifted, there was an ornate metal screen, gorgeous metal work with UB in the center of each panel. It wasn't a screen you wanted to get checked into, that was for sure.

"It is wonderful metalwork," said Fleemisch, out of the blue. "It is very pliable. If a player skates into it, it bends. Then after the game one can hammer it back into place."

No one had bothered to sweep the snow off the benches. It didn't matter. About no one was there except us and the other team.

The University of Borschland team wore lovely white skirts and shirtwaists with black belts and tasteful armbands with a big crimson B on the side. Their white skates were highly polished and the color of the laces matched the "B." They were slim and tall and very prim, whereas we, with our military issue charcoal grey, mostly looked like big blobs out there.

I would have said we had a good team for hitting. We were big and eager and had a lot of energy. But the Borschic game isn't the same as the American.

They played keep away with us the entire first period, making precise passes and avoiding us when we tried to get near. We hadn't learned a lot of fine technique about poke-checking yet. The women were used to field hockey sticks, which are quite a bit shorter. So they did a lot of chasing about, and the students made a very gentile goal about halfway through the period, and we were behind 1-0.

Between periods I gave a little poke-checking tutorial, but the second period went about like the first, and with about 2 minutes to go-- I had Fleemisch check his pocket watch, because the scoreboard clock was not being used-- the students went up 2-0, and by that time their goalie had touched the puck about three times the entire game.

Around the start of the third period, some drunken guys appeared at the top of the stands and began singing university songs. By that point frustration had set in. And I got a bit more frustrated than I should have.

So I said to Philbuja, "Go out there next shift and the next time you get a chance, I want you to whack the puck as hard as you can at the goalie. I don't care how far away you are. I don't care how high it goes over the top of that screen. Just wake that goalie up."

She nodded, and went out there, and they lost a draw, and the puck came quietly into our zone. The students played it a bit, acting bored, and finally Noora got the point of using her stick, and flicked it out to Philbuja, who was just above their blue line, as a good Borschic center should be, waiting for the puck to come out.

She turned, wound up, and whacked a slapshot that went flying into their zone on a wicked line. I had no idea she was so strong.

The goalie was standing up, and by her reaction to the shot, had to have been somewhere in la-la land. She actually put her hands over her head and bailed out of the goal, and the shot hit the top of the crossbar and went in.

The puck went skittering out of the goal, and was back at their blue line in about a half a second.

The goalie looked around her. Philbuja put up her hands in triumph. Their defenseman picked up the puck and pushed it towards center.

"Goal!" I yelled. "Goal!" and pointed.

The referee did not give a signal. There was no linesman, just one referee, and he must not have seen the puck.

He finally blew his whistle, a squirrely little tweet, and skated up to the scorekeeper, who was sitting between the benches.

"Penalty," he said. "To the gray. Lifting the puck."

"What? That was a goal. That was a goal. That was unbelievable. What are you talking about?"

"Two minutes to the gray," he repeated. "And please if you would lower your voice, Madaam."

"Lower my voice? I'll lower you," I said, and had begun to climb over the boards with my fists clenched.

I felt a hand pull me by the collar. It was Fleemisch. Strong dude.

"Please, Demouzeel Kretschmer."

"What?"

"The rule is," said Fleemisch, "that there shall be no striking of the puck so as to raise it above the knees. Doing so intentionally will result in a minor penalty, and doing so accidentally will result in a face-off in the offending team's offensive zone. The intention of the rule is to prevent facial injuries to the players."

That's amazing," I said. "Do you have the rulebook memorized?"

He blushed. "I have most elements of the rulebook at memory, Demouzeel."

I pulled my shirt forward. "All right, then. All right. You don't have to horse collar me."

"It were not to our advantage to have our coach banished from the bench," he said. He could have been an international diplomat, he was so tactful.

"That's true."

"What's more," he added, "I think that referee would've gotten far the worse of that bout of fisticuffs. I was looking out for him as well."

I smiled at him, and he blushed to the tips of his ears.

We played like maniacs after that. We broke up their passes and skated into their zone and whacked the puck on goal-- at heights all under the knees, by the way-- and had them on the run for the rest of the game. We scored another goal that was allowed, and were behind only 2-1 when Philbuja had a chance to tie it with a point-blank shot, and whiffed.

I pulled the goalie with about a minute to go, and students got a hold of it and were skating out of the zone when Haanelore caught up with them and flattened the puck holder. They were awarded a penalty shot and scored it. The final was 3-1.

And at the end, I looked up to the top of the seating bowl, to the little ticket house where I'd seen the drunken university students. They weren't there anymore, but someone else was.

He was wearing a bowler that shielded his eyes, and a long, elegant topcoat, but his face, the way he carried himself was unmistakable.

Willem.

I must've flinched or something as I stared, because he looked down at me, tipped his hat, turned and went. And I felt a big wave of *Te Harteleed*.

When I turned around, Fleemisch was standing there with

my coat. "What is it, Demouzeel?" he asked.

"Nothing," I said. "I just saw someone I thought I recognized."

"That is the way of the world, Demouzeel," he said. "All those we see we know."

As I walked up the stairs to the locker rooms on the opposite side from the ticket house, I realized what Fleemisch had said was a theological principle of the Borschic religion, and it was part of a Borschic prayer said over and over in regular services: no human being is a stranger to us, for we are all of one image, one heart, one Creator.

"It is all right, Coach," said Philbuja after the game. "That was the best fun I've had so far."

The others agreed. "The chalk head goalie ran from that puck as if she'd seen a mouse."

Chalk head was what they called students.

Fleemisch then spoke up, hoarsely and angrily. "Never do that again. Do you understand me?"

Everyone looked around at each other, wide-eyed.

Then Fleemisch said, in a much meeker tone, "It is illegal."

I said, "Fleemisch is right that you need to follow the rules of the game. This time, Philbuja was carrying out a direct order from me. Understand?"

They understood.

Fleemisch nodded, then apologized to me privately. "I was out of order," he said. "I regret it mightily."

"That's perfectly all right, Fleemisch."

"It's just that we shouldn't attract attention to ourselves," he said.

"Why is that?"

He wouldn't give me a straight answer, just mumbling something about propriety.

"Well, we've got to do something. That tournament in Bijfhaaf is coming up, and I want to make a good showing."

"It is all right if we don't," he said. "We are just beginners."

"Fleemisch, why didn't they make you the coach instead of me? I probably would've been a good assistant."

Fleemisch said, "*Prejts uu zischtsonderzinn,*" which means, literally, you are talking blessed nonsense. It was a very polite way of telling me I was an idiot.

I asked Bep the same question, and she said, "Is he making trouble? I will speak with him."

"No, please don't," I said. "He's odd. But I feel like we need him."

"Oh, you do, darling," said Bep. "Of this you can be sure."

CHAPTER 19 - SHERM

Before I got the real Branch in my equipment bag, Willem suggested I tape all my sticks all the way, to get people used to the idea. He'd keep an eye on the Branch in the Museum. Then at the proper time, I'd get the Branch-- take it myself, said Willem-- and we'd tape it. No one in the government would know when or where we made the switch, and the Shadows would be thrown off the scent.

"The petals should begin falling within six months," said Willem. "Certainly by the end of the hockey season."

"But what if Henrick finds out it's disguised?"

"It doesn't matter. Katharujna will not take it from you, and we are watching Kasmahlov."

"Better watch him well."

When the team first got wind of what I was doing, they thought I had gone off the deep end. I told them I was doing it to change up our luck. That, they understood. Borschic people are all about luck, fate, and destiny.

When I announced that I would be taping my stick completely, it started a big stir in the league. Was it legal? Yes, it was. Tape companies called. Would you endorse our tape? No, I wouldn't.

The photogs took about a hundred pictures of me taping

my sticks, which I special-ordered to be longer than my usual ones.

The scribblers asked me the same questions over and over again. I always said I was doing it to change my luck.

The general public took it in stride. It just isn't done that you tape an entire hockey stick, but if Sherm Reinhardt does it, there must be a good reason. Kids began asking their folks for rolls of tape, and pretty soon two or three kids would be on a pond using fully taped sticks.

The season heated up. We lost at Bjaward, won at home versus Onatten, then tied Domaatische at their place. Cefreth solidified some, but we were still giving up too many goals, and I heard that Kasmahlov had become a monster over in Oststaff. He'd turned twenty; the team was undefeated and had given up an average of less than a goal a game.

The pattern was for us to eke out wins like 2-1 and 3-2 against lesser teams and then lose big, giving up 4, 5, 6 or more goals, to the better ones. We lost to Matexipar 9 to 1, another record number of goals. By the time Willem had worked out his plan for the Branch, we were lucky to be near the middle of the standings at 3 wins, 4 losses, and 2 ties.

Henrick was nowhere to be found, but I thought about him often. In fact, after the blah results of November, I figured we had nothing to lose in following his strategy.

"It's time to let the bear play center," I said. "Put him on the first line with me and Oovie. I'll play right wing."

Cramps nodded. We hadn't scored more than 3 goals in the last 5 games, and we had to do something.

"One other thing," said Cramps. "We're buying the Canadian's contract. He'll play versus Wrischer."

We looked like geniuses. Wrischer is never any good, but this year they were particularly bad. Lavishbear scored two goals, Kasmahlov dominated around the goal, and we won five to zero.

So now we were at five hundred and headed into a tough road game at Bevinlunz, the league leader. The day before we got on the train to go there, a telegram showed up at my house with the anonymous message

BRIEFING NINTH DISTRICT POLICE HQ 3 OF CLOCK TODAY

Ninth District Police Headquarters was actually a code we'd set up beforehand. I was supposed to take a taxi at 3 PM from my house, and guess who the driver was going to be?

"Where we headed?" I said to Willem as I stepped up into the cab.

"14 Waatersdram. Say hello to Mr. Reinhardt."

Another guy sat on the seat opposite, dressed like me.

We went into the museum by a back entrance, and Willem carried a little shoulder bag full of adhesive tape in it.

Adhesive tape in Borschland is not as advanced as it is in North America, but it's perfectly fine tape. It is a cotton tape with a rubber adhesive that comes from Bearland. It doesn't last as long as tape back home, and it's really gummy, so you run the risk when you tape your stick up, of getting the puck stuck to the blade. This happens after you have many layers of tape on there and the gumminess kind of bleeds out of the tape.

Some players love the gumminess. They feel like it gives them an edge, like they can hold onto possession better and be trickier with their puck work. I'm not one of them. I buy sticks made of very hard wood and I tape the butt end of the handle so that the gumminess gives me a better grip and I can pick up the stick from the ice easier because it's leaning on the butt end rather than flush to the ice. Then I do a very light layer of tape on the blade to protect it some from the wetness of the ice.

One other thing: it stinks to high heaven.

Willem said, "How is it going with the taped dummy sticks?"

"Not bad. I even got a couple of guys to do it themselves. And apparently a bunch of little kids are doing it. I'm sure their parents are going to send me the tape bills."

"All to the good," said Willem.

"By the way," I said, as we walked past huge statues of Willem and Henrick. Not amazing likenesses of either of them.

"If I use the stick in games, is there a chance I'll break it?"

Willem shook his head. "Not one iota of a chance," he said.

"And the smell? Won't it come through the tape?"

"We won't know until we try it. And you will be the one to try."

"What if I mess up the flowers with the tape? What if I rip them?"

Willem gave me a don't-be-stupid look. "I don't know of anything that is stronger than the *Bloomentwejg* flowers. While the Branch is blooming, there is nothing more beautiful, gentler, and yet more resilient."

"Okay, well, I was just checking."

"I know. I know you are a patriot, Sherm."

Funny how that word sounded coming from a Borschic saint.

I smelled the Branch as we walked down the stairs into the main rotunda, but I couldn't much tell what all the fuss was. It was pleasant-- smelled a little like summer back in Minnesota. But there was too much junk in my sinuses to tell exactly.

The sight was incredible. Like there were fireflies hovering all over it.

I took the Branch in my hands. It felt like a hockey stick-- heavier, for sure, longer, and not as balanced as a true stick made for the purpose. But that didn't matter. I couldn't believe the energy coming off of it. Just holding it in my hands, I felt like I was immortal. Like I couldn't be stopped. I couldn't wait to get on the ice with it.

"It's longer than a regular stick," I said.

"But still regulation," said Willem. "The rules are flexible."

Willem looked on as I took the tape and began wrapping. The tape was extra-wide, and very gummy, and when it came in contact with the flowers they adhered. I wound the tape around the Branch, as tight as I could so that the flowers would be as flush to the stick as possible. It took a long time, because I had to make sure the tape was flat against the flower and that the flower and the stem were as straight and flat as they could be against the stick.

When the tape stuck to itself Willem cut that section off with scissors. He was sweating, and breathing through his mouth.

"*Alles ergut?*" I asked him.

"It's the scent," he said. "Hard to fight it. Keep working."

"I don't smell it so much. Smells like something I can't place."

"You are perfect for the job. It is doubtful Katharujna or Urdan could hold it for long without being overcome."

We worked, and finally got one layer of tape over the stick. The flowers were as flush as we could get them. It was lucky, or smart of Willem to think of it, that the flowers were so delicate. They didn't snap back or push the tape off the stick. At least they weren't doing it right away.

"We will have to retape often," Willem whispered, a drop of sweat trickling into his mouth. "Now again."

The second layer was easier. We were taping tape, and it was only a matter of keeping it tight. We put a third layer on, then retaped the handle and the blade. I picked it up again.

All in all, it took about three and a half hours to do, and I couldn't smell the flowers anymore, and only barely the medicine smell of the tape.

"Can you smell it?" I asked, standing and stretching.

"Yes," he said, and wiped his forehead with a handkerchief. "But you can get away with it."

"It's awkward," I said, standing up and putting the blade of it parallel with the floor.

"But?"

"You're saying I can use it in a game. You want me to use it."

"You have to keep it with you at all times. You are the guardian. And I will be your head of security."

"Sounds like a plan."

By the time I came into practice the next day the tape had loosened and the grip was mushy. I wondered if I was going to have to retape every day-- and I mean cut all the tape off and pull it off of the flowers, which could be messy and take a long time.

I put another layer of tape on the handle, and that helped some, but it was still strange starting out. That energy, though-- the feeling that there was something crawling on my hand when I had it-- was still there. And as I got used to it, the grip tightened a bit, and I thought of those flowers underneath-- how could they survive? Wouldn't they be mush?

That night I cut off some of the tape from the middle of the Branch, and the flowers came away from the tape almost as if nothing had happened to them. The scent came back again, too, and not even a scent but a kind of warmth, like when you stand near a fireplace. I did a tight tape job back, put the Branch into my gear bag, and got on the train for Bevinlunz.

Bevinlunz is one of the oldest cities in Borschland. It is on the coast, around a harbor that has an island near it-- Itasca, which is a sacred place to the Loflins, the native people of Borschland. Today, Itasca is a beach resort and a place with a lot of vacation homes. But there are forests on the top of the island where no one goes; it's a national park, and the thought is that Loflins slip in there by boat at night, especially during the summer, to do ancient rituals.

The hockey team of Bevinlunz is not bad. They've won some championships, and they have rich owners who keep the team stocked with good players. They are always a good game.

The old city is built on a series of terraces carved into the low bluffs and cliffs that ring the harbor. Surrounding it, the new city spreads out to the east and north. The rail line follows the river that empties into the harbor, through a narrow valley called Te Deel. The river feeds the hockey rink, which seats almost ten thousand and is the biggest seating bowl in the country. And even though Bevinlunz isn't the biggest city, they sell it out, especially for us. The fans do love their "Buffies," which sounds lame when they are in last place but totally cool when they're champions.

Te Rijngk ter Deel is a horseshoe with a tall half-bowl of seats built into the chalk hills, and the other half-bowl rising by a steel superstructure above the river. Water is fed into the rink from the river, and then frozen by artificial means. The rink is a lot like Te Staff's, except that Te Staff has not built anything on the river side of the rink, allowing it to stay as it always was, a sandbar with standing room for the workers of the city who are not able to make it into the 6,800 person grandstand.

This year Bevinlunz was still cruising on their fluke championship win of last year. They added a couple of good players over the offseason and had been crushing people throughout the first part of the year. They were at the top of the table, 6 wins, 1 loss, and 3 ties, better than Meechen, Matexipar, and us.

This is it, I told the boys. If we can win this one, we can win the championship. No one's better than Bevinlunz on home ice.

I don't know that anyone in the room believed we could win. When you are 4-4-2 and your best center has been a bear who's always sick and your previously best center hasn't been playing well because of legal troubles, well, who could blame them? But we are Te Staff. That name means something.

Lavishbear started at first line center, with me at right wing, and Oovie at left.

"Reinhardt," said Groomengill, the Bevinlunz left wing with platinum blonde hair. "The bear's sick. He has a runny nose, Reinhardt."

I didn't even look at the guy.

In another league, Groomengill would probably be injured more, because his body would pay for in checks and fists what his mouth spent in goon talk. But in Borschland payback is subtler. Guys don't get checked as much, and fights are seldom. So you have to get back by playing well, and getting in the odd elbow here or there.

Lavishbear growled when the referee held the puck up for the draw, and that unnerved their center, Wijk. So Lavishbear won the draw, and we attacked their zone. I went behind the goal, took a pass, flipped it into the crease, and Lavishbear whacked one that banged off the top of the goal, over the glass, and into the crowd. The reverberation of that CLING on the goal could be heard throughout the stadium.

On the ensuing face-off, Groomengill didn't say anything, and when he showed up on a later shift, he wasn't saying much, because he was huffing and puffing from having to help back on defense. So much for the talk.

I didn't feel a thing. I had my wind, and I could see the whole rink. Coach let us go longer on our shifts, just stretching us a little, because we had it: the chemistry, the energy. The puck seemed to float on my blade, and it made perfect sense when, after Lavishbear had tried four times to bust through the goalie, Eevembersprek, I deked to center while at right point and shot instead. Eevembersprek was cheating towards the bear and let it go under his left pad.

Next time I skated up to Groomengill, he said, "You're quite a right wing, Sherm. It must be the taped stick."

"Look but don't touch," I said, as Lavishbear won the draw and we were off and skating again.

I would love to say it was an easy game from there on out, but it's tough to beat the Buffies at their place. Anyway, the game turned out not to be the most important thing.

We were up 4-3 and working hard, with about five minutes left in the game. I came back to the bench from a shift, thirsty as hell, and called for water. I look out of the corner of my eye, and there's Henrick, standing behind the Buffy bench, dressed like an assistant coach. *Oh, no, what's up*, I think.

On the very next shift, this goon, Bouschaum, who almost never plays because he is so slow, begins to shadow me. I try to keep my head on a swivel looking for this dude, but the puck goes in low and behind the net, and I've got to dig it out.

So Bouschaum goes in, forgets the puck, and levels me, a cross check into my lower back. He sandwiches me against the boards, and I drop the Branch.

Immediately the referees toot up the penalty. I'm trying to peel myself off the boards. I panic as I realize I don't have my stick in my hands anymore. But I've gotten my bell rung, and I'm seeing stars.

I turn around, and there's Urdan.

"You okay, Coach? Here's your stick."

And he hands it to me.

That night, Urdan collapsed at dinner. Fainted straight out. Rushed to the hospital. I went with him, to translate, if necessary.

Willem was in the hospital, dressed as a doctor.

"What's going on?" I hissed at him.

"We just saw his papers. Urdan wasn't born in North America. He was born in Belarus. He came to Canada when he was five."

"Oh, God."

"Henrick knew. I'm sure he did. I'm sure he was testing the boy. Just in case there was some immunity."

"What's going to happen? Is that it? Is he gone?"

"He isn't Borschic," Willem said. "He could get better."

"What about the elixir?"

"The *tisande* heals everything. But it may also make him a saint. It depends on how much is needed for the cure."

"Well, that's the end of using the Branch in games."

A real doctor approached, and Willem faded into the woodwork. Later on a received a telegram that said, USE IT. JUST BE CAREFUL.

I never held on to a stick like that before or since. We won all our games, including one on the road against a tough Bjaward team, and just like that we were in second place at 8-4-2, with one game left in the first half.

Bevinlunz stumbled. They went 1-2-1 including their loss to us, making them 7-4-3. Only Meechen was above us at 8-3-3.

And Urdan held on.

Eighteen days after Urdan touched the Branch, we visited him in the hospital again. We were in town for the Flowering Branch Cup-- the tournament we'd won the year before. We were playing Itasca, a team based on the island across the bay from Bevinlunz. It was supposed to be a cakewalk, an easy draw before the round of sixteen.

After the Bjaward game on Wednesday night, Detzember 15, we stayed over in our hotel and trained to Bevinlunz

Thursday morning, a five-hour ride, in order to see Urdan in the hospital and then do a public appearance.

The event was a trip to the Itasca National Park, to see the native shrine there and the chapel that had been built next to it. A deacon was coming along to pray for Urdan.

Willem got the bright idea to have me ask for the sticks to be blessed, too. Otherwise I would've had to carry the Branch along or beg off from the trip for no good reason.

In the hospital, Urdan's face looked as small as a baby's. He was wrapped in covers. His eyes were glassy. When he turned towards the window, you could see the reflection of the gray sky in them.

"Hey, bro, how you holding up?" I asked.

He smiled. "Hey, Coach." It wasn't more than a whisper.

Oovie said, "Tell him, the deacons are praying for him."

I started, but Urdan shook his head. "Listen, if I don't make it," he said.

"You're going to make it."

"Tell my parents. Okay? Once we're out of the phase shift."

"Urdan, you're going to make it."

"And one other thing."

"Yeah?"

"Tell Danny I love her."

"What'd he say?" someone said.

"Says he's going to kick Bouschaum's ass once he gets better."

We took horse carriages out of town along a road paved with flat stones. The way was uphill, and switchbacked. It was foggy and gray the way the Borschland coast gets in winter.

After about a half-hour, we came to the gate of the park. The paved road ended, and the path inside wasn't big enough for a carriage. There was a stone wall about five feet high that stretched out of sight on either side of the gate, topped by the evergreen branches of Borschic beech trees.

Our guide, who happened to be a Loflin, said, "This is the holiest place of the Loflin people. The people of Borschland have granted this place to remain as it was in Loflin times."

He unlatched the gate, which was bigger than a regular door, with wrought-iron bars. We walked. There was no snow on the path, but a lot was piled up in the woods. The trees were mixed beech and fir, and some of the trunks of the beech had markings on them-- Nils was here, year 223-- but also, stuff that looked like it must have been the Loflin script.

Chrujstoff joked, "Look out for a Loflin ambush, guys," and a couple of people laughed.

But after the first half-mile or so, the talking stopped. It was spooky. The trees were really big, but when the wind came up they bent and creaked, and the wind whistled. Birds had high-tailed it out of there for the winter, so no chirping. It was mostly our boots on the hard ground, the wind, a camera lash from a photographer, and the voice of the Loflin guide.

"In a few minutes, we will come to the clearing where the Chapel of St. Rachael is built. As you know, St. Rachael was a friend of the Loflins who died tragically as a result of an unexpected disease while visiting the Loflins during a religious ceremony."

For a sec I wondered which side St. Rachael would've been on, Light or Shadow, and then I thought, *there should be something else*. Only two sides of anything is crazy stupid.

The chapel was the size of a cottage, maybe a two-bedroom house, made of stone, with a slate roof. No cross on top. Borschic folk tend not to put crosses in prominent places.

"Are we going inside?" Lavishbear said.

"Don't know," I said.

The guide ranged us around the entrance. He stood on the steps going up. There was a stone table in front, with a basin in it filled with leaves and frozen water.

"That's the Loflin altar," whispered one of the guys to me. The photogs encouraged us to pose in front of the altar and lay our sticks on top of it.

When the flash bulbs stopped popping, it was completely still for a sec, and then a whirring sound came from somewhere, like a motor. I thought of my dad's diesel generator in the basement of our house. I looked around. It didn't stop. It seemed to be coming from everywhere.

The guide looked up. "No surprise," he said.

"Airship," said one of the photogs.

We all looked up. The belly of a good-sized blimp, with a gondola strapped to it, was overshadowing us. From above came a bunch of ropes. And down the ropes came a bunch of furry-tailed creatures with caps and overcoats.

"Foxes!" somebody said.

The foxes-- maybe a dozen-- zipped down the ropes on harnesses that made a zinging sound. And as they landed they drew guns.

"No moving," hissed one of them. "Hands being up."

We all put up our hands.

They collected the hockey sticks on the altar, put them into a kind of stretcher, wrapped them, and tied them with rope. Then the sound of a mechanized pulley came from above, and the sticks flew into the air.

All except for one.

Oovie said, "God of the saints!"

Chrujstoff said, "They're stealing our sticks?"

Then a fox motioned to me with his gun. "To pick up your stick," he said.

I picked up the Branch, and one of the foxes came in front of me, while the others trained their guns on me. He strapped me with a harness, and he himself tied his harness to me, so that we were kind of buddy-tied.

We went up first, but they caught up with us quickly. They were small and light-- the tallest may have been five six, and I was six feet and at my playing weight of 185 pounds. So by the time they were all in the gondola of the airship, my fox and I were still dangling about twenty feet from the ship and a hundred feet in the air.

Then I heard a whining sound, followed by an explosion and a puff of smoke off to our right.

We swung back and forth, and the crane started pulling us in on the double.

I looked over my shoulder. A big airship, its balloon silver with a gold and black chevron, was hovering maybe a half mile from us.

"The Borschland Navy," I said to the fox, as if he couldn't tell himself.

We were almost in the gondola of the fox airship when another round came from the Borschic airship. This one was ear-splitting, and the gondola shook back and forth. I heard ping-zip, ping-zip and looked up. There were little rips in the fox's balloon. If that was a warning shot, they must have missed. It was okay that there were holes in the outside balloon, though. Airships in Borschland have nested balloons, four or five sometimes, and you have to shoot through every one to sink them. If you just fire close and rip through one balloon, only a little of the gas is lost.

I didn't know how many balloons ours had, though.

One of the biggest foxes met me as we clambered over the side of the gondola. He put a gun to my head.

"Standing up," he said. "Facing that Navy ship."

I did. I saw the airship with its front-mounted cannon, and a couple of pink faces in crow's nest-like protrusions, behind telescopes. I don't know if they knew who I was, but through that telescope I'm sure they could see the big pistol with the long barrel pointed at my head.

Someone took a megaphone and called an ahoy to the airship. We were now over the ocean and headed fast away from the island.

"Kill the Reinhardt!" One fox shouted. "Going away and leaving us alone!"

It was unlikely the Borschic ship heard. The wind was loud in my ears.

Still, they didn't fire another volley from the cannon.

"Stopping to follow!" said the fox into the megaphone.

"Heave to," came a voice from the Navy ship. "We will fire to hole all balloons."

Then we went into a cloud.

Fog is pretty frequent on the north coast of Borschland, but it's low. If you go into a fogbank you risk smashing into something like the side of a hill. The foxes didn't mind, though. Between the side of a hill and a Borschic airship cannon, they would take the fog.

The barrel of the gun went away from my head. The fox poked me in the back with a claw. I turned.

"Reinhardt," said a voice I knew. "So glad to have you along."

CHAPTER 20 - SHERM

"Busby!"

There he was, dressed up as an airship captain, looking undersized in a long coat, jaunty shoulder belt and holster, with a bunch of other tools hanging from it. He was wearing boots that went up over his knee, and a soft skullcap helmet with goggles. Recognizable from before, when he was just the special assistant to the head coach of Te Staff, but a lot more ridiculous.

"Sherm. You're looking well."

"You look so..." I said. I couldn't describe it without insulting him, and he had a big gun in that holster.

"Air pirate?" he said. He took the Branch from me. "Okay. I don't mind that. If it gets me what I want."

"I thought you were in prison," I said.

"I was," he said. "For a little while, anyway."

"What happened?"

"I'm sure we'll have a lot of time to catch up, Reinhardt," said Busby. "But first let's get this valuable cargo stowed."

He disappeared with the Branch, another off-Continent person who could handle it.

A Loflin stepped forward. You could tell by his green eyes, pale skin, and black hair. He was a lot taller than Busby, and younger-- in his twenties, as far as I could tell. His outfit was black leather, with the same soft helmet and goggles.

Seriously? I thought. But when you're in an airship in the fog, you go with it.

"Call me Newton," he said, and stuck out a black-gloved hand. He spoke English, and almost without an accent.

"As in fig?"

"As in the scientist, hosehead," said Busby, who had returned. "Sort of an ironic reference. Newton discovered gravity, but it was there all the time. Same thing with the idea of freeing the Loflins."

"Clever. Funny, I haven't heard of you," I said.

"Gravity will be reversed," said Newton. "And the Branch is our lever."

Busby rolled his eyes. "He means there's going to be a revolution."

"Well, you can try that," I said. "But the Branch isn't going to be any lever. You need to give it back. You stole it."

"That isn't happening," said Busby. "The *tisande* from the flowers is going to be very valuable for us."

"If you get away with it. I don't think you will."

Newton said, "Should we turn around, then? I think he's right."

Busby cursed. "I'm trying to get him to talk straight. It's not easy."

"Straight talk is crooked," said Newton.

That made Busby think of something. He looked down at his wrist. It looked like an oversized watch, maybe a compass of some type. He said something to Newton, and Newton barked orders in Loflin. The fox assault crew leapt into action, too.

"Let's get down below," said Busby. "I don't know how far this fog goes, and those balloon pigeons with the fancy popgun are bound to be after us. In fact, the whole barmy nation is probably after us, if they know your twig is the Branch."

We went down the spine of the gondola, which probably about as wide as a two-lane street in Staff Borsch, and made of polished wood and brass. The sides went up only about seven feet, and there were numerous brass struts that connected to the balloon superstructure.

Down below was a room in the stern of the ship with a big porthole, two sleeping couches built into the wall on each side, and a table in the middle with four chairs. We sat in the chairs.

"Warmer down here," I said.

"Hopefully we'll be home soon," said Busby. "No more rocking and swinging."

"How'd you find out about the Branch?"

"Guy named Henrick," said Busby. "Probably the guy in the Borschland Navy ship back there."

I shook my head. I guess it'd make sense he'd find out where the Branch was. He just needed another off-Continent person to steal it for him.

"We will untape the Branch," said Newton. "And wait for the petals to fall. My people know about the Branch. They have known about it for a lot longer time than the Borschers. It is really ours."

"There will be enough of the elixir and money for everyone to have exactly what they want," said Busby.

"Money," I said, turning to Busby. "That's your whole thing, isn't it?"

"A man's got to eat," said Busby.

"They give you food in prison."

"Hey, I served time for what I did in Canada. They let me out on parole; it was on the up and up. Then they were arguing with Borschland over sending me here for trial. It took a long time for anything to be done, because it had to be through telegram. So in the meantime, I kind of disappeared.

"At first I thought I would hang about in Australia, but then I got a hankering to be in Borschland again. I don't know; the place sort of grows on you.

"I hired on as crew with an Australian yacht that was bound for the Kerguelen Islands and eventually South Africa. Once we were underway I convinced them to visit the Continent, and we met up with Foxian pirates before long.

"I made friends with those guys, and eventually turned up in Loflinland. All legal, by the way. Loflinland is a sovereign state."

"Except that you're wanted in Borschland for kidnapping and racketeering, and you parole-jumped in Canada."

"Yeah, Except for that."

He made it sound like he was saying, *Except for that parking ticket.*

"I met Newton," Busby went on. "He was Bearish educated and wants to visit North America. One of the Loflinders' princes, eh. But most of them are not interested in taking over Borschland. He was considered crazy for his ideas. As if sitting in that fogbank eating potatoes is anything like a life."

Newton nodded. I could tell he liked Busby, thought he was cool with his holster and goggles and friendship with Foxian pirates. He didn't know that Buzz was pretty much just a rink rat, like me.

"But we didn't have much except this airship, something Newton and his friends had built with his parents' money. We were sitting in a bar in Bijfhaaf one night soon after the phase shift, and out of the blue this Borscher comes up to us and asks if we want to join a conspiracy.

"The Bearland government, the foxes and the Loflins, he said, are going to drive out the Anvorians and Borschers, and we can all take our land back.

"At first we just thought he was crazy. What Borscher wants anyone to take over his country? But he gave us money to start an army, and he sent us telegrams keeping us updated about the Branch. That's what he wanted to do, steal the Branch. He'd gotten wind there was a North American in Loflinland. You're Canadian, he said. You can handle the Branch without getting zapped. He said if we stole the Branch, he'd cut us in on the elixir. We'd be supermen, and we could start our war against Borschland. The bears have the technology. It wouldn't take a long time, he said. Just steal the Branch."

I sighed, and looked out the porthole.

We were over treetops, Borschic beech, like on Itasca. The fog was less, and no other ships were in sight, and no towns, either. But you still couldn't see beyond half a dozen treetops.

Busby said, "Pretty soon Newton and I came to an understanding. Who needs this guy? He'd given us enough money to start our outfit. We could just take the Branch and keep all the *tisande* for ourselves. So when he sent word that the Branch was probably in your custody, disguised as a hockey stick, and that you were going to be on Itasca, we put our plan into action."

"You can't have thought it was going to be that easy."

"Well, it was that easy. We got away, didn't we?"

"For now. I met that guy, Henrick. He's a saint, by the way."

Busby didn't have anything to say back immediately, but Newton threw up his hands and gave me a wide-eyed stare. Oh, great starfire," he said. "A saint! He knows everything, and we are caught."

Busby glared at him.

"I meant, the great idiot knows nothing. Our base is secret."

I said, "He basically controls the Borschic military. They will find you."

"Who says he's a saint?" said Busby. "He's probably just an old nutter, and that ship was a random Coast Guarder in the wrong place at the wrong time. We have the Branch, and this *tisande* is going to make us invincible. We're going to take back Borschland and split it half and half with the foxes. And Reinhardt, there's no reason you can't join us. Pitch in with the winners. A bit of *tisande*, you'd be playing forever with the new Bijfhaaf team that would win the championship for years to come."

Bijfhaaf was the capital of Loflinland. A second division team at best. "There'll be hockey in the new Borschland?"

"Why not? The Loflins are mad for it, but they don't have the money to build a team that can compete. Te Staff has the hereditary claim on the championship, after all."

"That is not true," said Newton. "There is no hereditary claim."

Busby said under his breath to me in English, "And yet he doesn't get sarcasm. I don't understand that."

I couldn't decide who was more stupid, Newton or Busby. They clearly didn't know what they were doing. Busby was the king of schemes that didn't work. He'd tried to make a lot of money once before, kidnapping me and putting his life savings on a game he thought Te Staff would lose because I wasn't there.

To give him credit, it almost worked.

But now I was in this dunce's custody. He and his sub-dunce had long-barreled revolvers hanging from their hips, and we had a cannon-equipped airship after us, probably with Henrick van Borsch captaining it and who knows what kind of super powers at his disposal. I needed to find a way to get the Branch back to safety before we were all blown to bits.

Except that it was absolutely true that Henrick van Borsch needed some off-Continent hero ultimately to pick up that piece of wood and deal with it if he wanted the *tisande*. He couldn't kill both Busby and me. Unless Urdan was in that ship with him.

A knock came on the door.

"What?" Busby barked.

"We're out of the fog," came a voice.

A big pool of sunlight rayed through the porthole. And then shadow.

Busby looked out and cursed. "How could it?" he said.

Newton went even paler than normal. "You mean?"

"That airship's on top of us."

CHAPTER 21 - SHERM

"Abandon ship!" screamed Newton.

"Shut up, you idiot!" Busby roared.

"All right, all right! All hands to battle stations!" screamed Newton.

Here we go, I thought. *All dunces to dunce stations.*

"Go on," said Busby to Newton. "We can do this. Just like we trained."

He left.

"Just like we trained?" I said to Busby.

"Shut up. Whatever."

"Where's the Branch?"

"Safe," said Busby, unholstering his gun.

"Listen, I can take it. I can handle it. I can hide it. Just lower me down. They don't have to see me."

"I'm not going to let you take the Branch."

"Where can I go? Down there it's forest and swamp, right? You think Borschers are going to find me? I don't think so. But Loflinders? Sure. They know that country. Catch up with me later."

Busby looked me in the eye. Or as close to it as he could, poor bastard. "We're going together," he said.

It was the right move. If it meant a pitched battle between

the Borschland Navy and Buzz's foxes and Loflin irregulars, guess who was going to win? Especially with Henrick in command. So taking our chances in the swamps in winter sounded better than being killed or captured right away.

Pop pop pop went handguns. Clang went the brass struts above us. The Borschers were too close to shoot Newton's craft out of the sky. They wanted to take it over and find the Branch.

Newton came back down the stairs. "They're throwing grappling hooks."

"They're sitting ducks," said Busby. "Fire as they come across decks."

Newton hesitated, but went back up the stairs. Then he tumbled back down, tangled up with a fox.

"He's shot!" screamed Newton.

"Get back up there," said Busby. "I'll be there in a minute." Then he said to me, "Loflins are taught that if they use gunpowder, they go to phase shift hell when they die. Tough to get them off that superstition."

Pop pop pop poppity pop. I would say that I was scared, but the whole thing was too surreal for that. Busby opened a hatch in the floor. There was a crawlspace that led to the engine area. We scrambled along a catwalk, past a guy that must have been the engineer.

"Everything's okay," said Busby. "Steady as she goes."

We went through a door and into the crew's quarters. A couple of foxes were standing at stairs, guns drawn.

"Get up there," said Busby, motioning toward the stairs with his gun.

Their ears went back, but they went up the stairs.

Busby opened a locker with a key on a string around his neck. All the sticks were there. Busby took out the taped Branch. Then he opened another hatch below us. Cold air came up and the sight of beech trees, with snow underneath. Busby uncoiled a rope that was tied next to the locker and let it out through the hole.

"No harness," he said. "No time to rig it up. I hope you

know how to shinny."

"I hope you know how to," I said.

He stuck the Branch behind him, into his pants and out of the top of his long coat. "You first," he said. "I want to see you."

I shook my head, but obeying him was the only thing I could do. I didn't want Henrick to get the Branch, which is what was going to happen if we stayed on the ship.

The air was freezing. Fortunately I was bundled up pretty good and wearing gloves for the trip to the national park, so the rope didn't bite into my hands right away. But when I got about ten feet down and the rope began to sway in the wind, my hands ached from the force of trying to hang on.

I looked up. Busby was trying to shinny down, but something was stopping him.

"What's going on? Let's go!"

"Damn it! I'm hooked."

"What the--?"

"The freaking blade is hooked on the hatch."

"Pull yourself up! Unhook it!"

"I'm not Superman, you dick!"

He was right. Shinnying down a rope was not so hard. Going back up, without upper body strength, was a lot harder.

I hung in the air, my hands and wrists starting to burn. The rope was thin, and there were no knots for my legs to rest on.

"Just pull yourself up six inches!" I screamed. "You can do it, Buzz!"

"I'm trying."

Dude. Forty years old and hadn't lifted a weight in a decade or more, the arms are probably not going to pull up the belly.

Then there was a bang. My ears rang; sour gunpowder smell filled my nostrils and smoke flashed by me. The ship yawed over and I lost my grip for a second. I clutched for the rope and looked down. Treetops were about three feet below us, and the rope was tangling in branches. The ship was losing altitude.

"Got it!" Busby said. "Oh my god, I got it."

The rope began to tremble, and the ship yawed over again. I looked up. The Borschic ship was tight against the Loflin one. It looked like a mama whale and a baby. Smoke was coming from the Loflin ship.

I flew down that rope as fast as I could, and Busby wasn't far behind. Pretty soon we were deep in the branches, and I screamed I was going for a trunk. I let go of the rope. The tree I chose was not strong enough and it bowed down like a Christmas tree branch with a 185-pound ornament. Fortunately it didn't snap, and I let go and fell towards another tree that looked like it had a bigger trunk.

Who was I kidding? I didn't even come close to catching that trunk. I smacked through about ten branches and held on to the last for dear life. Ahead of me, I heard an oww and a curse. Busby had made it to the ground.

The ships passed by us. The light above was dim. It was clear, but it was late afternoon and going to be dark soon.

"You okay?"

All I heard was cursing. The dunce was alive, for sure. Was he okay? Maybe not so much.

I went hand over hand to the trunk of my tree, felt for a branch below, and stood on it, panting. I was all over sweat, which wasn't good for spending a night in the woods in winter. We had the Branch, but odds were someone was going to pry it from our cold, dead hands.

I clambered down to the lowest branch, jumped, and fell into snow. That was good, because if not I probably would've sprained my ankle.

"Busby!"

"Over here."

I trudged over. The snow wasn't deep. The trees had kept out most of it. He was sitting in the snow on his side. His coat had ripped, and the Branch was sticking out.

"Can you walk?"

"Get it out. Get it out."

I pulled at the Branch. On the top end, the one where we'd made a knob with tape, the tape had torn away and a flower had popped out.

"What's it like? My back. How does it look?"

He clutched at his back, exactly where he couldn't touch. I took off the coat and pulled out his shirt. In the dim light, I could see the Branch had run a deep gouge in his back. It was red and raw, and there was one part that was a star of pulp and blood.

"The flower cut into your back," I said.

"What? That's impossible."

"It's a flower-shaped hole in your back, dude."

"It hurts like hell," he said.

"It's not good," I said. "Can you walk?"

I tucked his shirt back in. There was nothing we could do about the wound, just hope it closed up. The smell of the Branch was starting to come strong from the flower that was free. We would need to retape if we wanted it to hold. Otherwise, flowers and broken tape in a couple of hours.

"Oh son of a bitch, that stings," he said, as I helped him upright.

"Where's your gun?" I said, looking down at his empty holster.

He looked around. No gun.

"Reinhardt."

"Hey, you know what? You're lucky to be alive. How far did you fall?"

"Not that far. I held on to a branch, but it snapped. Just, come on, Reinhardt. Sherm."

"Don't freak, Buzz. We're in this together. And a long way from safe. They'll be looking for us before long. It's just a matter of when they discover the Branch is gone."

"Maybe we should signal them," Busby said. "It might be better than freezing to death out here tonight."

"You freeze. I've got a coat. And gloves."

"Holy hell, Sherm."

"Shut up. We need to get away from here. Make tracks. As far as I'm concerned, north for the coast. You've got that fancy wristwatch, don't you? Tell us where north is."

159

He looked down at the dial on his wrist, tapped it. "It's this way," he said, and pointed.

"How far to the coast, you think? Are we in Loflinland?"

"Twenty miles, tops, and who knows where the border is. I know we're beyond the hills and close to the Oondujn Peat Bog; that's why the fog ended. We need to get back to the top of the hills, and then downhill to the sea. Probably we're going to find some kind of logging road before this, though."

"Are we close to the so-called secret base?"

"No. That's another ten miles that way, closer to the swamps, the river basin." And he waved off vaguely in the opposite direction.

"Okay."

We walked the direction Buzz said, and it was fairly easy going. The snow wasn't deep, so we didn't sink into it, but at the same time it filled in all the holes and covered the exposed roots and rocks, and made a kind of pavement. No more than a half-hour in to the hike, it was fully dark.

"We're going downhill," I said. "We need to stop. Go back the other way."

"No," said Busby. "It may be a little ridge that we're going down, but we'll be going up again soon."

He was right. After we negotiated through a hollow, we were going up again.

After about an hour, I was ready to call it quits. I hadn't eaten since lunch, hadn't even had a mouthful of water. I picked up snow in my hand and put it in my mouth. It melted, but didn't give much water, and my mouth was frozen.

"Buzz, we need to have a plan for the night. We can't just keep walking."

"I don't know."

"What don't you know?"

"I don't know if we should stop walking."

"Why?"

"If we stop walking we'll freeze to death."

"Stop."

He turned. He had a weird light in his eye.

"What's going on, Buzz?"

He fell forward as if he'd been stabbed. Another flower had stuck into his back.

I pulled it out. The first wound was purple but had closed up. The second was red and bloody like the first one.

I checked his pulse. He was alive.

The flowers gave a glow, so I pulled on the tape and freed others. The smell seemed stronger, and there were little shiny trickles of nectar on the petals. I didn't feel cold at all, and I wondered for a second if I was freezing to death, but somehow it didn't matter. I pulled the rest of the tape from the Branch, and the flowers and the smell of them seemed to warm me.

I lay down on my coat. I didn't feel the snow underneath me. I slept.

CHAPTER 22 - SHERM

It was still dark when I woke, but there was a glow coming from somewhere, like moonlight.

I held up my head. Busby was still unconscious, in a fetal position next to me. The flowers, fully popped out again, were glowing, and nectar was running on the petals, and even with my busted nose the smell came through.

I wasn't smelling flowers, though, as much as memories. Every new breath, I smelled something different, but after a while it settled on the kitchen of our house back in Minnesota, the deep coffee and frying pan smell that you never forget. It smelled like 5 AM on those mornings when you've got that skate before school and it's about 20 below outside but your dad is up and ready to go and he's warming up the car, and your mom is fixing something quick for you to hold in your hand with a napkin and eat on the way to practice.

I was cold and stiff, but not numb. The Branch didn't give off any heat that I could feel, but being next to it must have kept me alive.

"Buzz, you awake?" I whispered. I was thirsty, and scraped up some more snow. It chilled me to melt it in my mouth, but I felt a little better from it.

No answer from Busby. I looked up through the trees and

saw a little black sky. I hoped that the glow of the Branch wouldn't give us away to Henrick.

"Buzz," I said again, and finally he came to.

He let me look at his back, where the flowers had gouged into him, and there seemed to be no infection and no sign of a cut, just a big purple mark like a deep bruise.

"Feels like somebody slammed me into the boards with his stick high," he said.

I said, "We need to get to water. There's got to be a creek around here somewhere."

I picked up the Branch. Without the tape on it, the vibration from it was even stronger. I stood up straight, stretched, got some of the kinks out, and began walking again.

We came to a pretty wide stream that was frozen hard on the sides, but not so much in the middle. That water was cold but so good. Between holding the Branch and the drink of water, I felt almost okay.

"If we follow this down, we're likely to get to the coast. Isn't that true?"

"If we've gotten over the ridge. But according to my compass, this flows east, not south. God, my back hurts really bad."

"It just looks like it's bruised, which is funny. It was a big cut last night."

We made our way down along the streambed, as best we could, around big stands of bare, thorny bush and clumps of dry grass. There were places we could walk on the ice, though the surface would crack as we went along it.

We'd picked our way for what seemed like a long time, and the sky above was mixed gray and blue, when Busby stopped and said, "Just a sec."

I stopped and looked him over. He had dark circles under his eyes. He'd never been Mr. Wonderful, looks-wise, but now he looked a bit like the guy on the desert island in the cartoons, the one where the joke is a whole case of soup washes up and he doesn't have a can opener. All he needed was a little more beard on him.

Busby sat down with the base of his spine against a tree trunk. "Listen, Sherm," he said. "Let me have the Branch. It's clearly giving you strength. You don't want me to die, do you?

I thought about it. Really, I did. And he was right; I did feel better holding it.

"Forget about it, dude."

"Come on. Just for a little while. I promise I won't do anything. What could I do, anyway?"

I didn't know what he could do with it. But being the hosehead he was, he could probably figure something out.

"Listen, let's not go any farther today. Let's try to make a fire."

"Why?"

"I don't know. I'm cold."

"We can't make a fire. You have matches?"

"No. Wait a minute." He went through his pockets and brought out a coin. "Think we could use this to make a spark or something?

"Buzz, please. Keep walking, okay?"

"I don't think I can."

"You can. You have to think you can."

Then I saw this little blue engine in my mind's eye and my mom's blue eyes and I lost track of where I was for a sec and almost fainted. My stomach was so empty, it was heavy, like a rock.

"You can't walk either," he said.

"Yes, I can. Think I can," I said.

This was bad. If we made a fire and I fell asleep, we might burn the forest down. I could see that, Buzz making off with the Branch and me burned to death in a forest fire.

I leaned up against a tree trunk. It was all I could do not to slide down it and sit down.

Buzz lifted himself on one knee. "Just a couple of minutes. A blow."

"If I sit down I won't get back up again."

"Sherm." He put his hand out to me.

"What do you--"

"Let me touch it. While I had it, I could feel the energy coming from it. I know it's helping you."

Busby was right. The energy from the Branch may have been the only thing keeping me upright at the moment. "Listen," I said. "You can't have the Branch."

"But can I touch it? My back really hurts, Sherm. I can't do anything." He turned his back to me and opened his torn jacket so I could see his bruised back.

"Okay, okay," I said. "I'll make you a deal. You can touch it once. Then you're going to get up and do a half-mile or whatever. And if it helps, I'll let you touch it again. It's probably not going to make any difference, just touching it, but one of us has to stay strong, and you know I don't trust you."

It was dumb. Very dumb. I held out the Branch like I was holding it as a hockey stick, blade side towards Busby, but holding it pretty lightly because with all the flowers there was no place for my whole hand to rest.

Busby didn't treat it with the same care. He snatched it with both hands, rammed the Branch into the underside of my chin, and knocked me on my back.

Wow, that was a different feeling.

I clawed at the wood but he snatched it away. As I coughed and gurgled, he stood up with the Branch in his hands. He looked a lot less desperate now. There was a lot more color in his cheeks now. Did the Branch just transfer power that quickly?

"I don't know what it is," Busby said, rotating his arms and neck, "but whatever happened when the flowers stabbed me-- I feel a lot better. Still hurts like hell, but there was something in there."

"Gghh," I gurgled. I tasted blood where I'd bit my tongue.

"So now I'm heading out. You can try to follow if you want, but I have a feeling you won't be able to keep up. By the way, we aren't going towards the coast. We're going back to Newton's base, deeper into the forest. A compass is a nice thing to know how to use. We should be found by some of his men pretty soon. And then all we have to do is wait for the flowers to drop on the Branch."

Great, I thought. *Just great.*

"Sherm, you're a good guy. Always were. So thanks. I feel good enough, I could probably kill you with my bare hands. But I think the winter and the woods will do it quick enough. See you, buddy."

He was gone really quickly. I followed for a little bit, but he was out of sight in a couple of minutes. And I was left with no Branch, the winter, and the woods.

CHAPTER 23 - CATHY

Sherm and I were trading headline news.

HOCKEY STAR REINHARDT KIDNAPPED BY FOXES screamed the paper. It was pretty freaky. Everyone was ready to see foxes in the dark alleyways of Staff Borsch.

When I heard the news, I was at a blessing service for the team two days prior to hopping on the train to Bijfhaaf for the international women's hockey tournament. In the ensuing time since that first game with the University of Borschland, we'd played them again, twice, and we'd hosted a team from the Queen Maeve Royal College of the Celtlands, who had piled it on, winning 7-0. But UB couldn't touch us. We tied them 1-1 and then won 1-0 with Greetje having the game of her life in goal.

We were in the Chapel of St. Noos, which is only about five minutes away from Sherm and Rachael's house. Bep took us to be blessed before our tournament. The chapel is famous for blessing hockey players because it is the closest historic church building to the Rijngk, Staff Borsch's home ice.

It was a gorgeous place, stone and stained glass, circular instead of long and narrow, so that no one could sit very far from the front. Candles were lit in every corner, on little perches and niches, on candlestands, and hanging from the ceiling. You could smell nothing but beeswax and burning wicks. It was unheated, but it didn't matter. The hundreds of candles seemed to transform the cold into something holy.

Not that we took our coats off.

The deacons and deaconesses kept warm in layers and layers of vestments, crimson, gold, white.

We knelt below the altar table with an elaborate candle-holder, red glass, gold frame (18 karats, Bep told us), with the Christ candle burning in it and consecrated communion wafers next to it in a silver box. Communion was once a year, on Maundy Thursday.

The prayers took a long time, so long that my knees turned numb and I began to nod off. A sting of holy water on my forehead, thrown from a little broom the deacons were dipping in a bowl, woke me up, and I saw Willem's face above mine.

"Bless you, daughter," he said, putting his hand on my head. The other deacons were resting hands on the other players as well. He leaned over and whispered into my ear. "Quiet. Don't move or talk. I will be your confessor."

Willem meant that after the blessing, if anyone wished, they could go to confessional booths lining the walls. Confessions are normal in Borschland, and are used more for talking out problems than listing sins. Call it a Borschic therapy session.

A single candle in a holder on a small table illuminated our booth; there was no partition between the deacon and the confessor, just two lovely carved wood chairs. I had gotten my candlelight, but not my dinner.

Willem started by telling me he was a saint, one of the most famous saints of them all, St. Willem van Noos, the discoverer of the *Bloomentwejg* and maker of the first *Bloomentisande*.

"I'm sorry I couldn't be as honest as I wished. But Borschland is in grave danger. My dear, I need you. Sherm has disappeared and so has the Branch."

I was in the presence of real living history, but I couldn't shake the feeling that I was in high school and a boy was breaking up with me.

"You couldn't tell me before," I said. "But you did want to

get my opinion on the so-called mythological saints."

"Forgive me," he said. "I was going to tell you. But you tried to steal the Branch, and the Shadows snatched you up."

"I didn't try to steal the Branch," I said hotly. "Henrick..." I couldn't find the word in Borschic. I wanted to say hypnotize.

"I am not blaming you for--"

"I wanted to see it. That's all I wanted."

"That is all right. Everyone wants to see it."

I began to roll my eyes, then realized it was the exact same thing I used to do with my dad. Dad.

And I understood. That was it. That was the last time I ever thought of Willem romantically.

"Katharujna," he said.

I looked at him, and he probably took it for contempt. It wasn't. It was just looking, not worshipping.

"Willem," I said, "What can I do to help Sherm?"

He explained about the Branch, that Henrick had gotten me to move the Branch because I was from North America. He said that Henrick had tried to get Kasmahlov to touch it, but he hadn't been born in Canada, and had gotten sick.

He told me about the taping plan, the idea of hiding the Branch in plain sight, and that Henrick must have found out about it, bided his time and waited for a good opportunity.

"It was a good plan," I said. "Sherm was brave."

"Understand. I had no intelligence about an airship manned by foxes, or that such foxes knew that the Branch was among the hockey sticks of the Staff team. But Henrick clearly knew. His air frigate, one step down from the largest flyer the Navy has, was unauthorized to be patrolling in the airspace above Itasca Island.

"The communiqué from Navy Central Command was that Henrick's frigate, the *Starfire*, neutralized the craft that was not part of the Loflin Civil Defense Force, and killed or captured all aboard except for its captain, one Weeritz Nuurleck, also known as Newton.

"As the craft attacked by the *Starfire* was set ablaze and its boiler exploded, the Navy was not sure whether Nuurleck was blown to bits or made some escape. It was stupid of Henrick to open fire on them, to board them, and so on. But his philosophy is to shoot first and let the rest sort itself out.

"I just have to believe that the Nuurleck and our Sherm had made their getaway before their craft blew up."

I looked up at the candle and said a little Borschic prayer for Sherm.

May all be well, dear Creator
May all manner of things be well

Willem went on. "We tried to search. Night intervened before any other airships found their way to the battle site. The ground was thickly forested, and we turned up nothing.

"So, with the Branch and Sherm truly missing, we saints decided it was time to unite. Set apart our differences and find the Branch. That is the most important thing. The *tisande* is secondary to keeping the symbol of our country intact.

"So we are now down to you, my dear. Which means you must come along in search of the Branch."

"Is there anyone else who could have taken it?"

"Do you know of any other North Americans here?"

I had to admit I didn't. We were very rare.

"It is a convenient thing that you are going to the tournament in Loflinland. That will be your cover. If we find Sherm and the Branch safe and sound, then you need not be involved. If Sherm is hurt, or out of commission--"

"Out of commission." It was all I could do not to sob or scream.

"We will pray not. But if he is, then you must come in to transport the Branch. We will take you and the team by airship to Bijfhaaf, and the airship will coordinate our search. Sherm must be somewhere in Loflinland."

We stood up. I felt as if he should shake my hand or something, but he didn't. He bowed. He knew he'd done me wrong. He knew I was being kind to him.

And he knew I would do anything to help my brother.

I was allowed meetings with Roald, and Rachael.

Roald was busy. He was going to Bijfhaaf to cover the Flowering Branch Cup game that Oststaff was playing with Bijfhaaf on the evening before the first day of our tournament, and he had the exclusive assignment of reporting everything from the game that weekend. He had plans for a feature about Loflin hockey, how it was developing, how they would pick kids off the streets of Bijfhaaf to play in their academy.

"Oststaff was pretty good while they had Urdan," he told me. "They were able to beat Lojren in the second round, which they haven't done in almost twenty years. Now they have a pretty clear road to the fourth round. Bijfhaaf isn't close to our level. They are twelfth in the table out of fourteen teams."

It was good to know that Roald could talk hockey in such a dire time for the nation. Of course, he had no idea that the Branch was missing. And he seemed to have no recollection of our fight, either. But maybe he wasn't speaking about that out of respect for Sherm.

"I'll see you there," I said, to give him an opening to talk about us. "Maybe we can have a glass of weshnak." Weshnak is Loflin spirits, made from a local bitter herb. It's one of the nastiest things I've ever tasted.

Not a chance. "I will be reporting and writing the entire time. And you'll be coaching hard."

I gave him my best longing look, and hated myself when he didn't notice.

"And I'm sorry about Sherm. He has to turn up. He always does, all saints' prayers with him."

All saints' prayers with you was a way of saying *fingers crossed.*

"All saints' prayers with him," I repeated, but inside I screamed, Willem better find Sherm. Alive. Safe, sound, and with or without the Branch.

When I saw Rachael, she seemed to be completely calm and to have everything planned out.

"We are taking the next train to Bijfhaaf," she said. "The children and I, and Melissa."

"That's ridiculous. You need to stay here," I said. "Wait a

minute. Melissa? What Melissa?"

"Melissa, our nannybear."

I was about to say something, then stopped. My Melissa had disappeared. Had she reappeared at Sherm's house? Sherm had told me a few stories about Bearish spies. They had the funniest way of getting their paws into everything.

"Let me ask you a question. It may seem strange, but did this Melissa suggest that you go to Bijfhaaf?"

"We discussed it, yes."

"Was she in favor of it?"

"She certainly made me more confident that I could do it with the children if she were there."

"But you're pregnant."

"Nevertheless, we are going."

"We do not know that he is going to turn up in Bijfhaaf."

"But he was lost over Loflinland. We do know that."

"He was lost somewhere near the border."

"There is no need to split hairs, Kathuj. We will be in Loflinland. The Loflin government has already invited us."

"Saints of the fatherland. Have you thought they might mean that ironically?"

"I don't care. I am taking the invitation."

"Maybe you should go to Limpael. It's near the border, and it's bound to be safer. You know there are plenty of foxes in Loflinland, too. They allow them to live there."

Rachael tossed her hand, pish-tosh. "The foxes can all go to fox purgatory or Bijfhaaf, as they wish. But Limpael? We are not going to that forsaken bit of sand dune. I went there once for a leg of the Flowering Branch Cup. Their team was a bunch of foul-smelling fishermen."

"Bijfhaaf isn't much better."

"Bijfhaaf is a lovely little place with frozen canals instead of streets. You can skate to the greengrocer and back again."

That was true. Built on the delta of the River Paas, Bijfhaaf was often called the Venice of the Continent. I had never visited, but it was a favorite subject of the travel pages in the newspaper.

"Do you truly believe this will be good for the children?"

"It doesn't matter. They need to be there when their father is found and brought back."

Then Rachael set her mouth. Sometimes you can get her change her mind, but when she sets her mouth, that's it. She's an only child, and she's used to getting her way.

I sighed.

"Well, I will see you in Bijfhaaf. We have a tournament."

"It is ridiculous that they have disguised you like this. And I am being told nothing, except that saints are involved."

Both Bep and Willem had warned me not to tell Rachael any details. But I did allow one dig against Willem. "To think, St. Noos, taking dinner in our house, but we never knew! How dishonest."

But Rachael shook her head. "That is the way of saints, sister. I knew, how I knew!" Her face shined. "They say you can always tell when a saint has visited you, even though you never really know until afterwards. And I knew. He made a *terrujn* like I have never tasted before. And the *drejanthus*. So traditional. No one knows how to use that herb anymore."

Bep the timekeeper appeared, and Rachael left, on her way to Bijfhaaf on a noon train.

"Did Henrick really put Urdan up to taking the stick?"

She sniffed. "He promised him that young journalist. It was not much of a payment."

"Why not?"

"Because they are already madly in love, my dear," she said. "And it doesn't take a saint to recognize that."

CHAPTER 24 - RACHAEL

I suppose it was *apfelkoffeld*, a favorite Borschic word for "insane," for me to cart along my two children and a nanny with me to Bijfhaaf, home of the Loflins and who knows how many outlaw foxes.

But I felt quite sure I was doing the right thing. There was no way I was going to leave my children to go await Sherm in Bijfhaaf, and there was no way I was going to perch, unmoving, like some gargoyle on a chapel while my son broke windows with his practice puck.

Melissa made it simpler. She was a very organized she-bear, very levelheaded, and she oversaw the packing for the children, so that we could travel as lightly as possible while still having some comforts. Each child, for example, was allowed one favorite toy and one favorite sleep charm. What a racket they put up when they realized they could not take their whole rooms with them!

But Melissa was adamant. And in the end, they chose what was dearest to them. Lily took her she-bear and a blanket, and Connie, bless him, took his wooden hockey puck.

We took the Staff Borsch-Bevinlunz Limited on the morning of 16 Detzember, at 10 AM. I recall it was cloudy and windy, but there was no snow forecast, which is a blessing, because a blizzard tends to slow down the Borschic Rail Service.

We had reserved a first-class cabin, and the government agreed to station an agent at the door of the car to keep out the journalists and photographers, who occupied the second-class car next to us.

At Bevinlunz we (and the hangers-on) detrained and waited in the first-class lounge for our local to Bijfhaaf. There are no expresses or limiteds to Bijfhaaf. The north coast of Borschland is quite a rudimentary area. You stop in places like Limpael and the Loflin border town of Hijluj Moruu before getting to Bijfhaaf, and then the train limps on, back into Borschland, to the far northeast edge of the nation, to a town called Ejanstaff and the delta of the Borschland River. From there, if you wish, you can take a train ferry across the water and transfer in the town of Krosstop to a Vinasolan train, for express service to Altium Decenni, the capital of Vinasola, which is even colder and more wind-swept than Bijfhaaf.

But the Vinasolans have the very best baths. I will give them that.

The train to Bijfhaaf was late; that was no surprise, and it was no surprise that we got the first notice of boarding when we had finally been served our lunch. Melissa had been for purchasing lunch from a cart, and Connie had been encouraged in the idea that he might get a chocolate mousse wrapped in a waffle for lunch, as this is one of the many things they have for sale from carts in the Bevinlunz-Kikerertwen Station.

I insisted we sit down, however, and behave like civilized people.

So it was that we ate like day tourists to the Sajbell beaches, once our lunch was boxed up and sent along with us, and we finally got to the platform with the engineer tooting the horn most importantly and a brace of conductors scolding us for almost missing the train, and the journalists all lined up yelling questions and taking pictures.

The newspapers, no doubt, ran a headline that afternoon:

MADAAM REINHARDT TARDY TO BIJFHAAF LOCAL SERVICE, LUNCH ON LAPS RESULTS IN STAINS, TEARS.

But as we crawled along, and the afternoon advanced, I still had no doubt we were doing the right thing.

That is, until Melissa piped up.

"Madaam," she said, after the children had finally fallen asleep on the benches across from us. "I must tell you."

"What?" I asked. Melissa had an urgent tone to her voice, something altogether unexpected.

"We will need to detrain before Limpael," she said.

I asked her why.

"There will be a delay," she said. "A significant one."

"How do you know?"

"I can't tell you. But in order for all to go smoothly, I need you to follow my orders exactly."

I put my hand to my throat-- too much like my mother, I'm afraid. She is an excitable woman, and I style myself as a bit more adventurous than her, but I am more like her than I wish to admit.

"Orders?" I said. "Whatever can you mean, Melissa?"

"I'm sorry, Madaam. No questions," she said with a little tiny growl in her throat.

"None at all?" I said.

"None," she said.

"This is very abrupt," I said. "I would counsel you to be gentle with my children. The authorities will be dealing with you most severely if not, I can assure you."

She continued looking out the window. Her face was in silhouette, the light behind her soft yellow, as the setting sun showed its face under the clouds. It was quiet: all I could hear was the click-clack of the train wheels, and Connie breathing through his mouth. He had a stuffy nose, and my handkerchiefs were almost all used up.

She turned her snout to me. "Madaam, do you trust me?"

"Trust?"

"Yes. You said you wanted to be reunited with Meester

Reinhardt, correct?"

"Correct."

"If you follow my orders, and we successfully carry out the plan my superiors have made, by this evening your whole family will be together again."

I was speechless and stupefied. I looked over at my sleeping children and asked the saints to protect them, beyond what I could do myself.

"*Alleskeet ergut*, Madaam," Melissa whispered, and went back to looking out the window.

Alleskeet ergut. I nodded, all the while wondering where a nannybear might conceal a handgun.

It was around sunset-- four in the afternoon-- when the train ground to a halt, and a conductor came through saying that there would be a delay.

"What is it, Meester?" I asked.

"Line out, Madaam," he said.

"Line out. Line out. Whatever is that supposed to mean?"

"It means that the track has been displaced."

"How long will it be?"

"No way to know, Madaam."

"What is the next station stop, please?"

"We have just crossed over into Loflinland. Hijluj Moruu is next."

The children stirred. As soon as the conductor was gone, Melissa said, "We are leaving the carriage. We must keep the children as quiet as possible. Nothing that would make a journalist prick up his ears."

"Did your government blow up the tracks ahead? Is that what happened?"

"Please, no questions."

We got the luggage down from the rack, and Melissa said to Connie, "Do you want to see a beautiful boat?"

He rubbed his eyes and nodded. What he was imagining I couldn't guess.

"Want to see a boat," said Lily, who was habitually grouchy after waking from a nap.

"Here is your bear," said Melissa. "And here is your blanket. We are going to leave the carriage now, children, and take a boat to see your father. But the only thing is that we must be very quiet."

"Issa," said Lily and hugged her blanket and she-bear to her. "Issa" was what she was calling her doll and her nanny. I picked her up and held her in one arm, and carried my valise and Liluj's bag on the other side.

Connie took Melissa's hand and carried his own bag. Melissa took her valise. We picked our way to the end of the car, opposite of the journalists.

A conductor was sitting in a chair, reading a sporting newspaper.

Melissa said, "We are changing compartments. The one we're in has lost its heat."

The conductor jerked upright. "I'm so sorry, Demouzeel Bear. I am... I apologize. I will find the service engineer at once."

"We will take this compartment," said Melissa.

There was only one other set of passengers in our car, so the conductor nodded and asked if we needed help with our baggage.

Melissa shooed him away to find the service engineer.

I thought of screaming, "The bear is an impostor! Arrest her!" But it might have put the children in danger. I had no idea if she were armed. And she had promised to bring us to Sherm, which was the whole point of our journey.

Trust won out.

Melissa tried the door to the carriage, found it bolted, and began to worry it.

"Thirsty," said Lily.

"Quiet, sweetheart," I whispered to her. "We must be quiet."

"Need to pee," said Connie. "Want to go bathroom."

Melissa had gotten the door open. "Take him," she said.

I was grateful to get Lily off my belly. I handed her to Melissa, and took Connie to the front of the carriage, where there was a water closet. He went in and took what seemed like a very long time.

"Thirsty, Mamuj," said Lily from down the corridor.

"Just a minute, my dear," I called.

Finally Connie came out.

"Did you wash your hands, son?"

He looked up at me with wide eyes, no doubt wondering whether he should lie.

"Come on," said Melissa. "Bother it, let's go." She had put the luggage in our new compartment, but the children still had their toys and charms.

"We can't bring the luggage," Melissa explained. "And they will keep it for us."

She opened the carriage door. The sea breeze whipped at my face and cut through my coat. My nose felt as if it was going to fall off.

"Cold!" said Connie.

Melissa jumped down. I handed her the children. There was a smell of burning peat, and the stones in the rail bed clattered as the children kicked them. It was almost completely dark. The sunset was a thin line, hardly illuminating the back of the train. To its right, sand dunes topped with sea grass, and presumably the sea beyond.

"The boat is there," Melissa said, pointing at the dunes.

Connie tried to go by himself down the embankment, slipped on shingle, and went sprawling.

Melissa gasped and looked back at the train. If Connie yelled in pain, that would be the end of her plan, for the conductor must be returning with the service man soon. No doubt he had already alerted the scribblers that our compartment had lost its heat.

Connie, however, styles himself a hockey player like his beloved father, and hockey players never cry when they fall.

When I got to the bottom of the embankment, he was wiping tears, but he said, "*Alleskeet ergut*, Mamuj."

"What a brave boy!" I cried, and swept him up in my arms.

There was a way through the dunes in deep sand. I half-expected to see foxes with revolvers around every corner.

"Where are we going, Mamuj?" Connie asked.

"To the boat," said Melissa. "A beautiful boat that goes as fast as a locomotive."

We emerged from the dunes onto a flat, desolate beach; the wind whipped itself into a gale. The last of the light illuminated crashing wave tops and flat sand as far as the eye could see. It was as if the whole world was horizon.

"How far?" I asked.

But Melissa could not hear me over the screaming of the wind.

Darkness soon covered us, and both Connie and Lily began to whimper. Lily was not saying she was thirsty anymore.

"Come on," said Melissa.

Presently, a twinkling light appeared on the horizon. It got bigger quickly.

There were bears, and a motor launch, the hull of which had made a big crease in the sand.

"Quickly," said one of the bears in English.

"Well done," said another to Melissa.

"Lieutenant Honeybarrel," said one to me. "Thank you for coming."

I wanted to tell him I had little choice.

Connie was happy about getting into the beautiful boat, but Lily clung to me and her she-bear and blanket. The other bears, dressed snout to toe in foul-weather gear, pushed the boat into the surf, and waves crashed over the prow, but in a few seconds the powerful gasoline motor had gotten us over the break line and into open water.

The sound of the engine and the vibration of the boat were all I could sense for a while, as they extinguished their running lights.

"Are we going to see Daddy?" asked Connie.

"Yes, darling," I said, though I had no idea whether we were.

It seemed a long time before we were being winched up along the side of a Bearish warship.

"Man Greatbear," said a grizzly with important-looking mortarboards on his shoulders when we emerged on deck. "Let's get these children out of this wind. If you let a breath of wind up their noses, they will be sick for three weeks."

We walked through a rabbit warren of decks and corridors, and finally went into a kind of lounge with a table and chairs.

"Welcome aboard the BSS *Integrity*," said Greatbear. "We are a helicopter carrier class four."

"That is very comforting. Are you now going to explain to me the situation?" I asked. "Before I need to put these children to bed?"

"What is their bedtime?" Greatbear asked.

"The stroke of seven," I said.

"Well, as it is quarter of now, I don't see a problem with that. Shepherdbear."

Melissa saluted.

"C-17, Officer's Deck. Have the steward bring up some cakes and tea."

"Yes, commander."

"And Shepherdbear."

"Yes, commander?"

"Well done."

"Thank you, commander."

And both children went with Melissa, for she was their nannybear.

Greatbear and I sat for a while in the lounge, and he explained.

"The government of Bearland is vitally interested in the Branch, as you might think. And the last we knew, Sherman Reinhardt was in possession of it. He was the only North American near it, in any case. And whoever kidnapped him had to use him to move it. So we are quite sure that he is still alive and that he has the Branch. Now it is simply a matter of finding him.

"We would like you to come along on the search. If necessary, we want you to let him know that our intentions are friendly. If he should happen to think that he must guard the

Branch and not let bears get their hands on it. Which is not what we want. We are not interested in the theft of sovereign Borschic property.

"We would like Sherm, as a national of Borschland, willingly to hold the Branch with our protection until it sheds its petals. Which should not be very long. The *tisande* made from the petals is potentially among the most volatile and destabilizing substances on the continent. Our government's position is that it is better not to have it be made at all."

As he paused in speaking, I guessed it was my turn. He looked at me with that peculiar emotionless expression of bears, cocking his head a bit, his eyes a-twinkle.

"You are saying-- you are saying--" I could hardly get the words out. "--That my Sherm has possession of the Branch? But I thought it was in the Rijksmuseen."

"Appearances deceive. All signs point to his using it as a hockey stick this season, disguised under tape."

"That is why he taped his entire stick and went through all that mess and bother? He has been guarding it under hockey tape for the last six weeks?"

"Yes, he has. An ingenious plan, by the way, to preserve it from theft."

"Theft. Which is what you are proposing today, to me, is it not, Commander?"

"We are not stealing the Branch. We will conceal Sherm of his free will. No one knows where he is. When the time comes, and all the petals are shed, we will introduce him back into Borschland."

"And the petals?"

"Will be disposed of."

"My country and your country will be at war over this."

"Not if Sherm-- and you-- agree to keep our secret. He can say the petals were lost in the woods, from a great wind, in a blizzard. Anything. They will have to believe him."

"So you'd want him to lie."

"For the good of the Continent, yes."

"For what you perceive as the good of the Continent."

"Yes, if you insist, Madaam."

I didn't know what to think. I am not one of those nationalists that used to have such a wonderful time writing telegrams to Sherm telling him to leave Borschland. I know that our nation does not have all the answers, nor all the virtue and none of the vice.

But the Branch-- and its petals-- was ours.

"I cannot condone such a scheme," I said. "And I will not."

"Yet I ask that you endure it," he said. "It is not an evil plan. Bears do not benefit from the elixir."

That was true, although they could always sell it to those who could.

We stared at each other. There was no panic in his eyes. Much the opposite: he seemed supremely confident.

I sighed. "When are we going on this search?"

It seemed to me the first and most important thing was collecting Sherm. After that we could reckon with the Bearish theft of the petals, as we were able.

"We are waiting till after midnight, when it will be less possible for the Borschic authorities to notice our helicopter."

"You are going to just fly into Borschland?"

"We are going through Loflin airspace first, Madaam. But yes, there may be a Borschic element to this rescue."

"And I am going, am I?"

"Yes, you are."

"And my children?"

"They must go as well, which is why it is good for them to sleep now."

"We are really just bait for Sherm, are we not, Commander Greatbear? So that he will willingly come to you, and be reunited with us?"

"I prefer to call you friends of Bearland. And patriots of Borschland."

"You know, we can have you sacked," I said. "We are personal friends of Lucius Black Jr. He is very highly placed in the government."

"Secretary Black signed off on this mission," said

Greatbear. "It is very risky. I can't tell you how much. But the Secretary personally vouched for the courage of the Reinhardt family."

It was a clumsy attempt at flattery. Still, it was better than nothing. "Well," I said, "I should like never to see Miss Shepherdbear again. She deceived and frightened us."

"Lieutenant Shepherdbear will also be along. I don't know that the children will be manageable without her. And she is a trained commando. She regrets having to do what she did, but I assure you, it was all with the best intentions."

A wave of dizziness swept over me.

"Madaam Reinhardt?"

I put my head to my temple. The room was spinning about.

"We will have a physician in immediately. But Mrs. Reinhardt."

"Yes?"

"We must ask you to be brave."

It was the last thing I heard before I passed out.

CHAPTER 25 - SHERM

I tried to follow Busby, but I hadn't been at it long when I found out someone had been following us.

The someone came up behind me, snatched my hand, held it behind my back with a grip like heavy pliers, and put his other hand in front of my mouth.

Then he said, "Quiet. Not a word. Till he gets far enough away."

A couple of painful minutes later, he let me go. I turned around, and got a big surprise. The guy who'd just held me in a vise-lock was short, bandy-legged, and barrel-chested, with a salt-and-pepper beard. But his arms were like Popeye's.

"Sorry," he said. "Had to make sure you wouldn't cry out."

His face was smeared with black camouflage goo. He was dressed in gray pants and jacket, and a gray stocking cap with a green tassel. A leather belt circled his waist, and another was slung over his shoulder. On his left sleeve he wore a circular metal shield, about as big as a dinner plate, with tiny incisions on it that could have been pictures, designs, or words. I couldn't tell in the light.

"Hello," he said, and shook my hand. "I am Grundel Mittelmascht. You may know me as Sankt Bogg."

Sankt Bogg. One of Connie's favorites. Back in the old days

there was a saint who spent a lot of time smoking out Loflins who were kidnapping Borschers back then. His real name was Grundel Mittelmascht, and he was a grandson of St. Borsch, and the church called him Sankt Mittelmascht, but the people just called him Sankt Bogg, or the Swamp Saint.

"Here is some food. We need to pursue that man. I would have done it myself, but I need you to handle the *Bloomentwejg*. The smell of it, incredible, isn't it? I've never seen it this way. I've smelled things I haven't smelled in centuries."

He gave me five or six strips of jerky, and they tasted like the best food I had ever had. He looked down at the ground.

"Won't be hard to follow," he said. "Snow gives good tracks."

"Thanks--"

"Call me Grundel. And you are Sherm, are you not?"

"You know me?"

"Of course I do. I don't get newspapers where I live, but I get news. I am a big partisan of the Domaatische team, and I was very disappointed to hear of your great success. Te Staff have had plenty of success. Now they need to spread it around to other teams."

I ate the jerky as we walked, him in front. He reminded me some of Willem, though he was shorter and fatter. Though his stride was a lot shorter than mine, I had a hard time keeping up. He huffed and puffed, an old red-faced man in incredible shape, wearing a stocking cap with a little tassel on it that bounced up and down as he went.

"This Busby has gone away quite swiftly," said Grundel.

"He had to. He took the Branch," I said.

"That's not all of it. He moves like a saint. Has the Branch begun to shed its petals?"

"Not that I know of. But he fell on the Branch, and got stabbed by a flower. The wound miraculously closed up, and now he has super powers."

"Ah. Some of the pollen in the flowers went under his skin."

"Is that good?"

"It's part of the *tisande*. So it might make him immortal. Or it might kill him. You never know. We never tried to gouge ourselves with the flowers before."

We walked some more, and the only sound was our shoes grinding on the thin snow.

"Was I what you were expecting?" Grundel said after a while.

"I don't know. I thought you'd be taller."

"We didn't grow as tall back then."

"And did you do all those things that the storybooks say? Rescue captured Borschlanders and round up Loflins and trap them in snares meant for animals?"

"I did a lot of things in my day; I don't remember a lot of them anymore. When you sleep in the woods for hundreds of years, your mind goes a bit."

"Well," I said, "are you a saint of Light or Shadow? I need to know because I'm on the Light side, so you may not want to help me."

"I am neither Light nor Shadow," he said. "I am a grandson of St. Henrick van Borsch, but I never wished to be a part of their conflicts. I guess you could call me a Twilight Saint." And he laughed.

Before long we had come to a place with recently-cut trees. There was the smell of sawdust, and axed tree limbs were scattered on the ground. The cloud cover limited the light coming through, but it was a lot brighter than being in woods. I estimated it must be somewhere mid-afternoon, maybe 2 PM.

Grundel put his hand up, crouched, and pointed first ahead of him, then to his left. We peeled off and put our backs to beech trees. He pulled a crossbow from behind his back, propped the front side against the ground, and put his foot on it. Then he cranked it up and put a bolt-- like a big dart-- in the slot. The guy's forearms were huge. Like he could hit a softball 600 feet.

He then peeked around the tree, and sighted. When he pulled the trigger, there was a chunk sound, and a whine, and then an oww.

We walked out into the cleared area. A man was on his back with the dart sticking out of his thigh.

"Is he dead?"

"No, but he will not be happy when he wakes up. The poison on the bolt overwhelmed his liver function momentarily and he is in shock. It will wear off, but he will be sick in bed for a few days."

"So you don't use guns?"

"I don't wish to. They're loud and the powder smells bad and once you shoot, everyone knows where you are. When I was hunting Loflin insurgents in my youth I began with guns like everyone else. Loud and terrifying, and inaccurate. One shot and these men would scatter into the woods. Then I remembered something." He tapped his temple. "My ancestors had been beekeepers in Bavaria, and they had many hives spread out in the woods. They carried crossbows in case they had to defend the hives against bears-- beastly ones, of course. There is no other kind in Bavaria."

"Naturally."

"So I thought, *ah ha*. What better forest weapon than a crossbow?"

"Why didn't you shoot Busby before he made off with the Branch?"

"Well, I dozed."

"What?"

"I dozed. I'm not as young as I used to be." He smiled so that the wrinkles around his eyes crinkled up. Grandpa with a crossbow. "No, Sherm, this is not a bad thing, that he has taken the Branch. It makes us still the hunters. If we had the Branch the others would be hunting us. And I did want to see the base again. It's a quaint little place. Young, idealistic men trying to be ironic."

"You've been here before?"

"Since the phase shift, I've been all through the forest. I like to see what's going on. And for a good while there, they would make roaring fires, smoke everywhere. They cut down trees, built houses, spent a lot of time arguing. They thought they were secret because it is a long way out here. And I'm sure the Loflin government is not sending out airships to patrol the woods. It doesn't have the money for such nonsense."

We had walked to the other end of the timber clearing. There was a definite path between the trees.

"Quiet, now," said Grundel. "They are more wary than they used to be, and now Busby has brought home their prize."

He replaced the crossbow on his back and pulled his tassel cap lower on his forehead. In a couple of seconds he was about fifty feet ahead of me, duck-walking from tree to tree, just off the path, completely silent. He looked back, and motioned to me to catch up with him. I couldn't duck-walk like him, so I kind of commando-crawled and got a lot of snow on my coat and made a lot of noise, I guess.

So much noise that we attracted two Loflin guards with guns drawn.

They'd seen me but not Grundel, who was flat on the ground behind a scraggly, bare bush. For a second I thought he was giving me away on purpose, but as he lay there he winked at me, and waved me to go farther back in the woods. I commando-crawled back to another tree and propped myself up next to it.

"Who's there?" someone said, in Borschic.

There was a whine, a thunk, and an *oww*. Then another soon after the first.

"Let's go," said Grundel when I reached his side. "They'll miss these very quickly."

We crawled up to a house that looked to be roughly cut boards nailed against a plank frame. No windows, and just a small opening for a door.

"In here," he said.

There were mattresses and heavy blankets, and a mess of clothing and personal items. In one corner of the room, a big sheet of metal hung from heavy straps to a wooden frame. The frame had a little pouch nailed to it, which was holding metal and wooden dowels.

"These boys are drummers," said Grundel. "The Loflins are

very avid musicians."

I stared at the metal sheet, carved with swirls and stars, while Grundel put his eye to a knothole in one of the boards. "We're safe for the moment. The headquarters is in the center of the camp, and Busby is probably already there, arguing with the Loflins about what to do."

"What do we do?"

"Sit and stay for a minute. The authorities, in whatever form they come, will be on the scene soon. You don't lose the *Bloomentwejg* and not put your best people on the case. My grandfather is already in the vicinity, no doubt, but the Light saints won't be far behind. The thing is, Henrick may not have any outlanders with him and won't be able to take the Branch anywhere. He needs you for that."

"He probably has both Cathy and Urdan," I said.

"And he doesn't know about Busby. Just thinks they are using you to transport the Branch. The other North Americans certainly may be accompanying, but he won't want to put them in danger just yet. He has to neutralize the opposition first."

"I forgot to ask. What do you want in this?"

"I want to make sure we all die," he said.

"What?!"

"That was not put perfectly well. Here is what I mean. The saints who have contacted you may have told you many stories about their political philosophy. But the main thing for them is the *tisande*. We are reasonably sure that if we don't get any more, we will depart from this earth at the next phase shift and never return to life."

"How do you know that?"

"We are not perfectly sure. But we spoke with foxes and bears and Loflinders long ago who all agreed. They knew about the tree before, and had sworn themselves off of it because of the conflicts when it bloomed. They told us that we would die."

"Maybe the Loflins are just being ironic."

"They do not lie, they just say the opposite of what they mean sometimes. If you know what the opposite of something is, then you know what they mean. If they say you will live forever and you never need any more *tisande*, we know that they mean that you do need it."

"Don't you want to live forever?"

"No, Sherman, none of us wish to live forever. Our bodies tell us to do so; they tell us to seek the *tisande*, because the body wishes to survive. I, however, have mastered my body over these long, long, centuries in the wild and the cold and the bog, and I know we are all ready to go over and join the rest of the saints."

"So your plan is..."

"Sherm, once we get the Branch, we are going to retire into the woods and wait for the flowers to shed. Then you will bring the Branch back, put it into the Rijksmuseen again, and perhaps one day it will bloom again and Borschland will be wise enough to let the flowers be."

"Henrick told me that he could get me and my family some of the *tisande*. He offered me the guarantee that I would always be strong and could play hockey as long as I like. And he said he would give some to my wife so she could have children and not have the possibility of dying in childbirth. Is that true? Could we just have a little and not become saints?"

"Yes," said Grundel. "Many have done this. A drop makes you well from an illness, a sip makes you strong for a lifetime, and a draught makes you a saint. Which is why some, like Busby, would like to sell it. Unfortunately, all those who drink the *tisande* in any way are bound to the Continent for as long as they live. If you try to leave, you die. Saints, of course, are bound to the phase shift, and live only when Borschland is in the other world."

"So is Busby bound to the Continent?"

"I would expect he is."

"Is he invincible now?"

"You couldn't beat him in a fistfight, and he could make a very good ice hockey player."

"But if you shot him with a crossbow bolt--"

"Would slow him down for a bit. An hour? Maybe more."

D.W. FRAUENFELDER

"What about a bullet?"

"Not fatal in most places. He will heal very fast."

"But, say, if you shot him in the head."

"I didn't say in all places. But don't speak of killing Busby. He already has sealed his fate, a miserable one. He already was greedy and narrow and unjustly angry with others instead of himself. Now he will simply become more of that as he realizes he has power."

Grundel put his face to the knothole again. "He's coming."

I looked through another knothole. There was Busby, with a gun, on his way towards us. A group of Loflins was following him.

Grundel's voice went to a whisper. "Down, there, by the threshold. When I give you the signal, you must run like you never have before. Loflinders cannot guard the Branch. They are helpless as to its perfume. They cannot pick it up."

So we began the biggest game of Capture the Flag I'd ever known. I hunkered down at the threshold, and put my hands above my head. As if that would stop a bullet.

"Stop," said Grundel to Busby. "Stop, or I will make it painful for you."

Busby had stopped. No more grinding of boots in snow.

"Who are you?" Busby called.

"My name is Grundel Mittelmascht. Some people call me Sankt Bogg."

There was a gasp from the Loflin contingent.

"The Swamp Saint," said Busby. "I guess where there's a Branch there's a saint, eh?" He motioned to his people. "Surround him. Bring him out."

The Loflins didn't move.

"Come on, what are you waiting for? You can kill the man who killed so many of your people long ago and penned you up in this little god-forsaken reserve. Don't you want revenge on the saint?"

"Yes," said one of the Loflins, "we want bloody revenge."

"I am not afraid to die," said another.

"His poisonous crossbow bolts are like the bite of a fly."

Busby rolled his eyes. "Oh my god. Don't start."

"There is more than one way to capture a foe," said the first.

During this exchange, Grundel had moved some things around, maybe hid. I don't know. I wasn't looking at him.

"You heard them," said Grundel. "They're a bit petrified of the legendary Grundel Mittelmascht."

"Well, I'm not. And I won't hesitate to shoot you through that board. I'll kill you, Swamp Saint."

"You're welcome to *try*. No guarantees of succeeding."

Busby cocked the pistol and fired. One of the boards splintered, and there was a ping and a whiz.

"What the--?"

"Try again."

"You put up some kind of shield."

"It is a metal shield, yes."

Busby fired again. Again the splinter, the ping, and whiz.

I stayed down with my hand over my head.

Busby fired four more times. Four more of the same.

"You are out of bullets, Meester."

"I can reload."

"Before you reload I'll shoot you, and you don't want that. Your Loflin friends assure you of such a thing."

One of the Loflins said, "Such pain would be the proper subject for a very short poem."

"You see? So let's do this another way. I challenge you, Busby, to a duel. Hand to hand. The winner takes the Branch away, no questions asked. In fact, I will hide you in the woods when Henrick and the saints come to get the Branch. I will even help you to make the *tisande*, provided you win the duel."

Busby lowered his gun. "What do you mean, hand to hand?"

"A wrestling match. The Loflins know about it. Strength versus strength. The one who throws the other nine times is the winner."

"But you're a saint. Don't you have super-strength?"

"I might. But I also might be a very old man in need of

more *tisande*, and this is the only way to get it."

"Oh, I see. If you win, you get the Branch. And if you lose, you show me how to make the *tisande*, and I give you some. You get it both ways."

"Slant it as you wish. I make you this offer."

"How do I know you'll keep your promise?""

"A Borschic saint never lies."

The Loflins laughed.

Grundel made a psst sound. I turned, and he gave me a quick nod.

Action time. I flew out of the shelter's opening, pivoted on my hand and made a u-turn, and lit out for the headquarters.

Busby turned. "Reinhardt?!"

There was an *arrgh* and a *what's that* and I heard a *click click*. Busby didn't have any more bullets in his gun, so he must have snatched a gun from a Loflin. An unloaded one.

"Get him!" shouted Busby. "He's going to try--"

There was the sound of a board snapping. I looked back as I dodged one of the guards. Grundel had smashed his way out of the shelter and was on top of Busby.

There were at least a dozen guys between the headquarters and me, but it wasn't exactly like Capture the Flag at camp. In that game, you only have to touch the enemy to make them go to prison. Here, they had to knock me down and sit on top of me.

The Loflins were tall, but not very coordinated. It was easy to dodge most of them, and when one came close enough to wrap his arms, I rammed him and knocked him over.

"Bunch of poets," I began to say, and then I ran into a brick wall. I looked up. A humongous dude was standing over me.

My ears were ringing; it was quite the body check. But I hadn't spent twenty years playing hockey to stay on the ground and let a big defenseman get in his shots. As he leaned over me I caught one of his arms and used it as a lever to get up. Then I gave him an upper cut, which straightened him, and then a shot to the belly, or maybe somewhere a little lower. I wouldn't say it would've been legal in boxing, but I needed to get away.

He bent over double, clutching at me, and I took off running again. I bounced off another guard, and was right at the entrance to the headquarters, which was an actual building and not rough planks nailed together. I ran up the steps and wrenched open the door.

Inside, there was a glow, and an overpowering scent of kitchen and early morning and coffee and something else: now there was Rachael's perfume, and the smell of the kids' baby food, and the sweetness of Lily's birthday cake.

"Wow," I said, and stopped dead. The Branch was laid over a chair, all its flowers brightly blooming, glowing, almost pulsating. A couple of Loflin women were there, sitting by it with little camp stoves going and water boiling in pots.

"Are they dropping-- the petals?" I said, to the women, and to no one.

I came closer-- I wanted to snatch the thing up and run, but my knees were jelly-- and the Loflin women, old, pale, gray-haired, with piercing eyes, stared at me.

Outside, the Loflin rebels were making a huge racket. Busby and Grundel were having their Loflin wrestling match.

I moved towards the Branch. One of the women put up her hand. I wasn't stealing, but she made me believe I was.

"This is Borschland's," I said, and picked it up. As I did, one of the petals fell off. Just fluttered to the ground like a snowflake.

The women gasped. One of them, the one who had put up her hand, fell to the ground over it and snatched it in her hand. She put it up to her mouth, her green, cat eyes locked on mine, and swallowed it.

I didn't wait to see if she became the Incredible Hulk. I took the Branch in both hands and ran out of there. Good thing, because Busby was on top of Grundel and wailing on him while the Loflins were hanging around like hockey refs waiting for the guys to get tired out. I did what came naturally-- smacked Busby with the blade end of the Branch. That was enough to get his hands off of Grundel, and a couple more petals went flying off.

Then Grundel smoked Busby in the ribs with a big shot. I could hear a snapping. Busby crumpled up on the ground, and Grundel lurched upright with a big groan.

"Come on," he said, out of breath. And he motioned us back to the house where we'd hid.

I ran. The Loflins didn't pursue. They were too busy picking up petals. Six or eight had gone to the ground, and they were white like the snow and very small, so they were hard to find.

Grundel was chugging right behind me. He stopped inside to pick up his crossbow, but then we were away. Busby was yelling at the Loflins, so it was clear the broken rib wasn't that big of a deal, but at least he wasn't following us. Yet.

"We're losing petals," I said.

"I know, and leaving a trail," said Grundel. "But that's all to the good. I wish I could strip all the petals now and throw them in a peat bog. But they come off of their own accord. We've only lost a few so far."

"And we're the hunted. How long is it going to take for him to catch up with us?"

"Not long. Which is why you are going to have to take the Branch to Bijfhaaf."

"Me?"

"Best thing would be to get lost in the woods. But with this trail and Busby hot on it, we'll be shot before long. So we have to double back and find friends."

Just as he said that, I heard a rumbling above us. It was the engine of an airship.

Grundel shrank against a tree, motioned to me to do the same. "They're searching."

"They'll find Busby."

"Maybe. Keep moving.

We ran, or tried to, with our heads down, for another half-hour or so without stopping. The Branch was giving me strength again, and Grundel must have been on 200-year fumes. But it took all I had to keep moving.

One last push got us to a ridge, and there was a little view in the direction we were going. Lots of trees. But on the horizon, a little creamy wisp of low cloud.

"The coast," said Grundel. "Follow the fog."

"Once we get over that last ridge, that's where Bijfhaaf is?"

"No, but you'll see railroad tracks. Follow them. You'll come to a village, and someone will get you on a train."

"And how do we disguise the Branch?"

"Here," said Grundel. He took off his backpack, and got out an oilskin-- like a canvas drop cloth, but lighter.

"This will also keep the petals from falling out. But before you meet anyone, collect some petals and put them in your pocket. If anyone should ask you what is on your back, tell him you are a musician. No one will question you, even though you are Sherm Reinhardt from North America. The Loflins revere musicians. You will no doubt get a lot of invitations to dinner, however."

"So the Loflins don't know about the Branch? They don't read the papers?"

"Of course they will know about the Branch. But they will think that you must have a good reason for lying, and let you go."

"One other thing. What do you mean by 'finding friends?' Do you mean the Saints of Light?"

"No, indeed. Willem is not your friend, Sherm."

"But not the Shadows, either."

"No. Neither of them."

"Then--"

"You will find someone who has good sense. Put these petals that have fallen in your pocket now," said Grundel. "They'll be like money later. You have to go down into a valley before you get back up to the last ridge. This will be the hardest part of the journey. Down below, it's hard going. So don't stop."

"You're acting like you're not going with me."

"I'm not. I'm staying behind to slow Busby down. I have some crossbow bolts for our Loflin friends, and he won't get by me without a fight."

"You're fantastic with that shield," I said, motioning to the metal circle on his shoulder. I didn't want to leave him. Dude was a hero.

"Remember that drum?" said Grundel. "I was hiding behind it."

We laughed. Laughed pretty loud, I have to say.

"Go on," said Grundel. "Go on, the airships will be back, too."

"Okay, but can't I give you a couple of petals for the road? I don't want you to die just yet. Come on, Grundel. I can't be responsible for you kicking the bucket."

"I will take one, because I am tired and Busby has gotten strong. But that's the only one."

"The only one," I said, picking out a little snow-white piece of velvet from my coat pocket.

He took it on his finger, nodded at me, and caught the petal on his teeth. "Thank you, Sherm," he said after he lifted his head up and let the petal flutter down his throat. "*Life is sweet, for a time; for a time, it is bitter. This is life on the tongue of our hearts.*"

He gave me the rest of his jerky, as well as a metal cup, and a flint and stone in case I needed to make fire.

Then we said goodbye.

I scrambled down a rocky, bare slope, kicking stones in front of me. I looked back. He was facing the other way, the crossbow slung over his back.

CHAPTER 26 - RACHAEL

I woke up lying on a divan of some sort, across from a polished wood desk with a dual-shade lamp, both sides illuminated. On the walls were pictures of sailing ships.

The she-bear sailor standing at the door left as soon as she saw I was awake. Not long after, Man Greatbear appeared, stooping through the door. He really was a "great bear," much bigger than the normal.

"You are all right? Rested some?"

I nodded, rubbed my eyes. And noticed a bandage on my arm.

"The doctor said it was fatigue and dehydration. We took the opportunity to get fluids into you intravenously. I apologize for not taking care of this straightway."

A knock came on the door. More sailors came in, bearing a table, chairs, and dinnerware.

"You should eat," said Greatbear.

As they set up the table and place settings, Greatbear pointed to one of the pictures of the sailing ships. "That is the original *Integrity*," he said. "She was a British cutter out of Sydney, Australia, in the early nineteenth century. Her original destination was Chile, but soon after putting out, the crew revealed to the captain their intention of diverting to the

Continent for the purpose of economic adventure. The Continent was a destination for fugitives from the prison colonies of Botany Bay, once they heard the fabulous yarns from others about phase shifts and invisible lands. The sailors of the *Integrity* went to the gold fields above Brownbearking, and the captain became rather a famous missionary in Bearland, and the founder of the Bearish Anglican Church."

A steward arrived with covered dishes, and served us.

"It's salmon," Greatbear said. "Not very imaginative, I know, but they do a good job."

Even if I hadn't been pregnant and ravenous, I would've eaten well. I enjoy Bearish cuisine, and I am not the type of person whose stomach goes queasy under stress. And the "fluids" seem to have helped as well.

"Our infra-red cameras detect life forms in the dark quite well," explained Greatbear as we ate. "There is little doubt we will find Sherm. When we do, we will deploy a small team of experienced professionals, led by me, to collect him. Hopefully we will find him alone and ready to be rescued. If not, we will do what is necessary to... ah... disperse the captors."

"That sounds quite dangerous, Commander."

"Well, it won't be to Sherm," he said, and took a sip of the Bearish mead that I had declined. "Quite conveniently for him, he must remain alive in order to transport the Branch, and so he will be everyone's first priority for preservation."

My eyes fell to the honey-drenched square of Bearish baklava to the left of my dinner plate, and I knew I wouldn't touch it.

"Are you quite sure you won't take any mead? It has medicinal properties."

"Quite sure," I said. A little trickle of sweat passed down my temple.

"I will be flying out in about six hours," he said, and checked his watch. "That's about three in the morning. As soon as we locate him, we will radio back to the ship and you will board the rescue helicopter. In a matter of minutes you and the children will be overhead and encouraging him to join you."

"We cannot stay behind and talk to him over the wireless?"

"We discussed that," said Greatbear, and tapped a claw on his dessert plate. Bearish baklava was their very favorite. "We feel for the sake of... ah... persuasion, it is best for you to be there."

I nodded, and smoothed the napkin on my lap.

"Try the bureaucracy," he said. That was what they called the baklava. "It is a pistachio, as is only proper."

"There is no other kind of bureaucracy than a pistachio? I did think there was a walnut, at least."

"The walnut is not worth mentioning," he said. And as I had not picked up my fork, he took that as an invitation, and tackled his.

"This is one way," he said, "to cut through a pile of paper." And the crisp dough, impregnated with honey, cracked noisily.

A steward showed me to the cabin where the children were sleeping, or in any case where they were supposed to be sleeping. They were still awake and Melissa was telling them a story of Bearland when I came in.

"We must get some rest," I said. "You will need to get up very early to see your father."

"Where is Daduj, Mamuj?" said Connie.

"He is guarding his ice hockey stick," I said, and Connie said nothing, knowing as every Borschic boy knows that among the most important things in one's life is one's hockey stick.

I glanced at Melissa, and she gave a little apologetic grunt, but we said nothing, and after the meal, I was tired and fell asleep quickly.

The children and I slept together on the cabin's bed, quite soundly, for when Melissa woke us at something like half past three in the morning, it was as if I had just laid my head on the pillow.

"They have found Sherm," Melissa told me as we bundled the children in heavy blankets and carried them down corridors and up stairs. "We are to depart straightway."

On the flight deck, floodlit and with safety beacons twinkling like a dragon's horde, a helicopter was already beating its rotors noisily. In Borschland we called this unfamiliar machine a hummingbird, but when Connie asked what the thing we were climbing into was, I knew I couldn't call it that. It was just too big and windy.

"It's a helicopter," said Melissa.

"Helic-popter?" said Connie.

That was all that could be said. Two sailors closed the hatch door, the engines roared, and we were off with a stomach-turning lurch.

We sat on benches facing each other much like in a railway carriage. Melissa helped us strap into metal and canvas safety belts. There was a single window in the hatch door, but I could see nothing from it. The overhead light in the cabin was dim, so we all looked a bit green. Lily sat in my arms, gazing off at I know not what, and clutched her charms. Connie bounced up and down in his seat, and more than once dropped his puck, which would roll away to the other side of the cabin. Melissa would carefully unhitch herself to retrieve it, until I told Connie to put it in his pocket.

For a few minutes we sat there in enforced silence, the rotors beating away mercilessly, and we with no earmuffs, and for those few minutes I began to imagine the whole adventure as that type of journey where your original train breaks down and you must take a relief train miles out of your way. It is an inconvenience, and one is likely to arrive at one's destination much later than one anticipated, and there are telegrams to be sent to inform those at the other end. But eventually you get there, exhausted, discomfited, but hopefully with having made a great dent in one's reading load.

All of that went right out of my mind as soon as the cannonball exploded next to us.

We had begun to circle, and the co-pilot had made his way back to us in order to rig up a harness that could be lowered in order to pull Sherm up to safety. He was almost finished and warning us to hold on as he opened the hatchway when there was a bright light shined on us, then a report, a boom, in the distance, and then a much louder crack that sounded as if a lightning bolt had hit us directly.

The children screamed. There was the sound of breaking glass and the ping of metal. The helicopter lurched and descended. The co-pilot lost his balance and fell forward. He tried to hold onto the harness, which was tied with canvas to an apparatus in the ceiling, but failed. He knocked his head hard on the hatch door and slid to the floor.

The helicopter turned swiftly, and the engines roared. Melissa unbuckled herself and examined the co-pilot. She looked up at me and gave me thumbs up, which to me seemed wildly optimistic considering the circumstances. Then she crawled towards the cockpit, and was gone such a long time that I unbuckled myself and crawled forward, over the protests of my children.

The forward windows were smashed, and the wind was fierce. Melissa had taken over controls in the co-pilot's seat. The pilot was slumped in his chair, blood having trailed down his muzzle.

"What are you doing?" I screamed.

Melissa motioned to the pilot's headphones. I pulled them off his ears and put them on mine, and was able to hear her, along with squawking radio communication from the *Integrity*.

"Whoever found us got us a good one," Melissa said. "But we're all right. The pilot is still alive. The engines and rotors are intact. There's only one thing."

"What?"

"The fuel tank was holed, and we're leaking."

"The fuel tank was HOLED?"

"Go back to the children. We're going to land somewhere, and there needs to be someone back there to unharness them when we do."

"Will there be a relief humming-- helicopter?"

"Just go back, please, Rachael."

The children were screaming, but I couldn't hear them, and when I saw the co-pilot again, I felt dizzy and sick to my stomach. I managed to buckle in again and clutch the children to me, but I had the impression that any moment I would black out.

The engines roared again, and we pitched to one side, and I held Connie and Lily. Then we came back upright, Melissa let up on the throttle, and there was a crunch below us. The whole machine rattled like an old coffee wagon.

Then the engines eased, and shut off. The rotors went *whup whup whup* as they slowed.

Finally, there was quiet except for the panicked cries of the children, and the faint squawk of the radio talk coming from the pilot's headphones.

"We're all right, we're all right," I said, over and over.

Melissa entered the cabin. "Happy landings," she said.

"Where is my hockey puck?" asked Connie.

CHAPTER 27 - CATHY

It was Thursday, 16 Detzember, nine days before I was supposed to take my comprehensive exams, and two days before we were set to play a team from Vinasola in the tournament.

I didn't get to see Rachael, Melissa and the children when they got on the train, but I was assured via telegram from Roald the media maven that they were being well taken care of. The Borschic government had provided a first-class compartment where pressmen were not allowed. They rode in the next car: writers, photographers, a big entourage.

As for me, I spent the morning packing and worrying. It was cold, as usual, and cloudy, but it hadn't snowed in several days. Just low clouds and a cutting breeze.

The *Starfire* had arrived from its fight with the Loflin rebel ship the night before, and the team and I were on board by eleven in the morning.

It was a beautiful craft. It had a grey, ribbed balloon that was about a football field long, and was painted with thin black and gold stripes at its middle. The Borschic flag, black, gold, and white, flew on both sides from metal arms attached to balloon ribs. The gondola was of polished wood and brass, with spider-webby metal catwalks in front and in back. The engines powered eight propellers, and as it was a military ship, it had three cannons, fore, aft, and a 360-degree rotating one on its underside that the airmen called the navel.

I had only been on one airship, the Bearish passenger airship *Goshawk*, which made the regular service between Waterbrownbear in Bearland and Staff Borsch. I knew the Continental airships were buoyed by helium, not hydrogen, so they wouldn't explode if someone shot a hole into them. I also knew that we wouldn't be flying above 500 meters of altitude, just in case a phase shift happened. If you did, you'd be left behind in the previous world as the Continent shifted to the other.

The team boarded the ship with their suitcases and hockey equipment, shepherded by Fleemisch, who looked very worried to be going up anywhere near 500 meters.

"*Alles ergut?*" I asked him.

"*Alles ergut, Madaam,*" he said, though he was pale as a sheet.

In the *Starfire*, we'd arrive in Bijfhaaf in about 3 hours-- its top speed was 50 miles per hour, unlike the *Goshawk*, which was lighter and could go up to 90 miles per hour with a following wind. But as Willem had told me we would be doing an aerial search, we were guaranteed to get there later. How much later was anyone's guess.

"The cloud deck is above one thousand meters," said Henrick as we stood on the bridge. "So we'll be traveling just under the cloud at about 250 meters."

"Pretty close to the ground, isn't it?" said Willem. "Hopefully no obstacles."

"We'll go in north of Matexipar and across the Oondujn Peat Bog. There's a ridge of hills next to the Loflin border. They've telegraphed fog this morning. We'll be over the search area and will take a look as we go. I'd wager with our telescopes in the lookout bays, we'll be able to see a glow from the Branch."

"Mostly evergreens in that forest. One doesn't necessarily see to the ground."

It was strange to see both Henrick and Willem, working

together, like a couple of aging rock stars who have come together for a farewell tour.

I spent some time in the crow's nest with one of the airmen. The crew gave me a helmet and goggles, and I carefully pinned my hair so the wind wouldn't scalp me. I have no fear of heights, so getting out on that catwalk to the lookout was among the best things I have ever done. The wind whipped against my cheeks; I would've been completely happy except that I was worried about Rachael and the children, and worried more about Sherm. The airman who accompanied me out showed me the telescope. We focused on a young boy waving at us from a country lane, and the airman said, "He's on his way to hockey practice." We could see his skates slung over his neck by the laces. He carried a stick over his shoulder.

We reached the western outskirts of Matexipar and turned northeast to avoid downtown. We passed over the river and canal and in between smokestacks. The ground rose a bit, tree cover got heavier, and then we were over the hill beyond Matexipar and into wild country-- peat bogs and forest, the same type of terrain where Sherm had been lost. A hundred miles to Bijfhaaf, and in between almost nothing but this wilderness.

There are almost no towns in Oondujn Peat Bog, the biggest swamp between Matexipar and Loflinland. We passed over one of the only ones, St.-Rachael-Loflin, which is a peat-gathering center, and then it was nothing but iced-over streams and ponds and beech trees with snow topping their branches.

I tried to watch, first from the lookout, and then, when I got too cold, in the forward observation room. But after about twenty minutes of trees, I was fatigued and felt overwhelmed. I went back to the galley, where the kitchen crew were serving tea, and had a mug. Bep came by, took one look at me, and walked out.

What was there to say?

I went up to the bridge again, where Willem and Henrick stood with their hands on their chins. The captain didn't speak. The helmsman's hand didn't move from the wheel.

Then, almost on cue, I heard "Check starboard!" from a speaking tube. It was the lookout on the right side of the ship.

"Reverse engines," barked the captain. "Rudder port hard."

We made a very wide right turn, and descended. We were bearing straight for a clearing in the trees. It was somewhere around two-thirty in the afternoon. The light was good.

We drifted over it, and the captain ordered another pass. The ship was so large, we weren't going to be able to stop over it easily, but we kept descending till the navel reported we were brushing treetops.

"What is it?" I asked.

"Maybe nothing," said Willem. "But we're close enough to the area where Sherm disappeared that it may be something."

"Are you going to investigate?"

"Yes," said Henrick. "But you're not."

"Oh, come on," I said. "If it's the Branch, I have to carry it."

"We don't know the danger," said Henrick. "If it's the Branch, we'll send for you."

"Let her go," said Henrick. "She's right. We may need to move the Branch quickly. Arm her if she wants."

"You perfect idiot," said Willem.

"Nevertheless," said Henrick.

And he won.

The clearing was not large enough to accommodate the length of the airship, so we were lowered down by harness, a kind of zip line that ended with my turning my ankle on a tree root.

While I sat on the snow and winced, the rest of the team landed. There were a number of small buildings made out of sawed tree trunks and other pieces of scrap lumber. In the center was a building with stairs and a porch and a second floor.

"*Ergut?*" Willem said, pulling me up.

"*Ergut,*" I grunted, though for a second I buckled and almost sat back down again. But fear of embarrassment and adrenaline helped me stand.

"What's wrong?" said Willem.

"Nothing," I said, and limped after him.

It was the kind of situation where, if somebody had decided to ambush us and opened fire and we had to scatter and take cover, I probably would've been the first one shot. I have played paintball, tomboy that I once was, and I know how easy it is to be caught with your pants down. But Henrick, who was the military type and had let me go down, had probably already guessed the truth: whoever had been in the camp was already gone.

The airmen who came with us investigated the small houses and found no one. Then we climbed the stairs to the main house. Inside, a fire was going in the hearth, and two old women were sitting next to it. Cooking pots sat on grills above the fire, and a table filled the middle of the room, with chairs that looked like they had been found in a thrift store dumpster.

One of our party was a Loflin interpreter, who asked the women what was going on. They looked at each other, said nothing, and one of them got up to put another log on the fire.

Then the interpreter asked who they were, and where they were from. Still nothing.

Finally, one of the women croaked a short speech, pointing up.

The interpreter asked her to repeat herself, and she did. "It's a poem," he said. "A kind of cryptogram. If we're smart enough to solve it, then we'll get useful information. She isn't going to give anything out for free."

Willem then said something in Loflin. The woman who had spoken the poem shook her head and pointed at the interpreter.

"They clearly know something," said Willem.

"We could torture them," said Henrick. "It's worked before."

"Great starfire and heavenshine," said Willem, and did a real face palm.

I had to laugh, and when I did, the Loflin woman gave me the stink eye.

"It's too bad Grundel isn't here," said Henrick. "He'd be on to them faster than tea water boiling."

"Grundel?" I said. The name sounded like what you'd say when you got hit in the stomach.

Willem said, "Mittelmascht. The Swamp Saint. He's been living out here for a couple of hundred years. Henrick's grandson."

Willem and Henrick were facing each other, and I was facing the two women. When the name "Mittelmascht" came up, they both startled and their eyes bugged out.

"Look at them," I said, and Willem and Henrick looked.

The spokeswoman said something to the interpreter. "She wants to know if we're friends with Mittelmascht."

"Tell her no," said Henrick. "The Loflin are no friends of Mittelmascht. Maybe it will ingratiate her with us."

The interpreter translated, and the woman said "Liar" in Borschic.

"Oh, for pity's sake," said Henrick. "Write down the poem as you heard it, Vlissingen, and let's be off."

"Wait," said the interpreter. "She's changing her tune."

The woman spoke again, another poem.

The interpreter said, "This one should be much easier. They clearly have respect for Sankt Bogg."

"Thank them, and ask if they want to be transported back to their village," said Willem. "They are twenty miles from anything here."

The interpreter offered the ride, and they gravely shook their heads.

"They think their grandsons are coming back," said Henrick. "For all we know, they could be twenty meters out in the woods right now."

"Let's go," said Willem.

We were winched back up to the ship, and the interpreter and intelligence officer on board gave it a go. They brought the results within half an hour.

The Branch that blooms is what you seek
The blooms that are rank and of death reek
You are the only who quest for this trifle
No one from outlands has ear full or eye full
Of petals or wood or stems that break off
As soon as one takes to it finger or knife
None of the saints that ventures through swamp
Nor of outlands who can carry it aloft
Save two of the brandy men, one tall and one taller
And one of the outlands who helps the Lofler.

"No one is helping, save three people," said Willem, with a grim smile. "Loflin irony at its finest."

"What does this mean, the brandy men?" I asked.

"That's what Loflins sometimes call the people of Borschland."

"So the woman identifies two Borschic folk, and one foreigner," said Henrick. "*One of the outlands who helps the Lofler* sounds like Sherm, except that he wouldn't help Loflins, would he? And who are the Borschic folk?"

"I'd wager one is Grundel," said Willem. "This is his country, and he is likely to have a friend with him."

"He usually walks by himself," said Henrick. "He always was a solitary lad."

I said, "Is there any possibility that the woman was referring to Sherm and Grundel as Borschic folk, and someone else as the outlander?"

"Anything is possible."

"Continue the search," said Willem. "It is all we can do. We have evidence the Branch and Sherm were here."

So we searched. A long time. Dinner came, then coffee, then more coffee. We used searchlights, but it seemed useless. Still, I didn't say anything. It was the saints' decision, the saints' game.

Around three in the morning I woke up, and joined Willem and Henrick on the bridge.

"...Going to have to break off the search and refuel," the

captain was saying. "Our peat load gave us just under 5 hours' full-speed flight time, and we are approaching that limit. We can make it to Bijfhaaf, but under quarter engines."

"How long can we stay before the engines fail and the wind takes us?" Henrick said.

"Holding present course, till nine of the clock. But we will be fifty miles from Bijfhaaf in a forest or a bog or both."

The alarm sounded again.

"Airship ahead," came the call from the starboard lookout.

"Origin?"

"Correction," the lookout reported. "It is a hummingbird."

"A hummingbird?" I said, not realizing what they meant.

"It is a Bearish craft," said Henrick. "They are trespassing in Borschic airspace. Fire forward battery."

"Fire forward battery," the captain said into the speaking tube.

"No, for heaven's sake, what are you doing?" Willem cried.

Borschic gunners are well trained. Before Henrick had a chance to reply, the airship shuddered with the boom of a cannon, and then the distant crack of a cannonball exploding.

"Cease fire, cease fire, you idiots," Willem yelled.

"Cease fire," the captain ordered, eyeing Henrick.

"If it is Bearish, all they want is to take the Branch," said Henrick. "We need to scare them away."

"Damage report?" Willem asked the captain.

"Lookout reports hummingbird is no longer in view."

"Did you shoot it down?" Willem said.

"Can't tell until we overfly the area," said the captain.

"Do it," said Willem, and glared at Henrick. "And after that, we are going to Bijfhaaf. We've fooled about here long enough. Everyone will be worried sick."

"What is more important than the Branch?" said Henrick.

"What is more important than shooting guns, to you?" said Willem.

Under quarter engine power, it took us some time to arrive at the site where the lookout thought the hummingbird-- helicopter-- was spotted. The navel shined spotlights all around the area, and found nothing.

So we turned our nose towards the capital of Loflinland.

It was the weirdest all-nighter I'd ever pulled, and I didn't even study.

CHAPTER 28 - SHERM

It didn't take long to get very deep into that hollow. The sides of the slope were steep, and when I got down to the bottom, there was an iced-over swamp. But it wasn't like a pond with some trees on the side and some reeds in the middle. It was a serious bog, with dead and fallen trees, and masses of thick, dead grass where there weren't trees. It was the kind of a place no one would find you, not if you wanted them to, not if you didn't.

Since I had the power plant of the Branch slung over my back, I didn't feel too bad about my energy level. And I had the jerky Grundel had given me. I knew the general direction I needed to go, and the light was still good and would be for another several hours.

First I tried to move along the ice where it was thick, but that was impossible. I was always up against a dead tree trunk or a line of bushes. Then I tried to walk on trunks that had fallen, but they were slippery and didn't last long. In some places the ice would crack under my feet, and once, I put my shoe through to a shallow puddle.

And it was cold. That's the thing about Borschland in winter: it's just cold. I grew up in Minnesota so that type of thing doesn't bother me if I've got the right clothes on. But I'd been out in the wild for over 48 hours now and it was getting to me. If not for the Branch, I'd probably have died from exposure.

Many hours later I had no idea where I was; it was getting dark; I was starting to talk to myself.

"One more trunk, Shermy, one more trunk," I began to say, or "More trees now, less swamp." But for some reason the bog wasn't done. How wide was it? A mile, two miles? Or only a few hundred yards? I couldn't say.

I stopped to chew on jerky. It tasted like jam in a way-- really hard, chunky jam. With a big overlay of salt. I wished I could drink some water; that was a big thing as I kept going.

Before I knew it, it was dark, and I was very stupid for continuing on, but I found a patch of ice that allowed me to walk for more than a couple of feet. I must have been out in the center of some pond, because the ice broke.

I was in over my head and thrashing, and I kept thinking, *don't break the corners down, don't break the corners down once you get back to the surface.* I had to pull myself out and I hoped the ice would hold. It didn't, of course. Several times ice broke off in my hands before I was able to grab a hold, and even then I just barely crawled out and off the thinnest part before the path I'd taken split like a broken window.

It didn't take a genius to figure out that without a fire I was going to die. The Branch gave me only so much energy, and I was shaking violently and couldn't feel that energy at all when I finally got to a patch of dry ground. It was pitch black but at least there was no wind, and a lot of dry grass sticking above the water level. I made a big pile of it and then spent pretty much what was left of my strength on whacking the stone that Grundel had given me with his flint.

When the grass caught it smelled bad and was just smoke, and it smoked so much I began to cough, but that one little piece of hope kept me going. And when the grass wasn't getting any flame and I was wondering if I could find any dry sticks while the grass was trying to catch, I had an idea.

I undid the oilskin. There were about twenty little petals on it. I picked a couple up with a tip of a finger, pulled them off with another, and lay them next to the grass.

One of them singed a little, and curled up, but not much.

Then there was the explosion, and the fireball.

It was like I was in front of a grill and had put lighter fluid on an open flame. It went WHOMP, and I was engulfed in light for a second. I opened my eyes and the grass was nesting around this intense white flame. I had enough sense to notice that second petal was getting drawn into the flame coming from the first, and I scrambled away and put my body over the top of the Branch, shielding it as the second WHOMP came, and there were sparks all over and cracklings as whatever wasn't wet or frozen was burnt in the flare-up.

Then there were two columns of intense white flame, burning as if from a gas leak, and I hurried to get as much wood as I could while the petals stayed lit. Funny how easy it is to gather wood when you have light to see it by.

Pretty soon I had a big bonfire going, and the petals themselves flamed out, and I took off my clothes because it was that hot, and I had the bright idea of boiling some water in Grundel's little tin cup.

"Survival, a piece of cake," I said out loud as I went out to the broken ice, scooped a cup of muddy water, and came back to the fire. I knew if I could boil the water, it would be okay to drink, despite the dirt, and I laid it on top of some coals and waited. Before long it was pretty darn hot, and I was happy to remember that I needed to touch it with something other than my bare hand.

I clamped the cup with two sticks and put it on the oilskin to cool just a little bit, and that was when I realized Grundel had given me the tools of my own downfall.

Petals were lying there on the oilskin, right there, to be eaten or made into a *tisande*. And I had boiling water.

Grundel must have known-- petals, flint, cup.

And what would he have done?

Immortality, Reinhardt, I heard Henrick say in my head. To play hockey as long as you like, without fear of your skills diminishing. The security to your family, knowing any injury that might befall you is only a temporary setback.

Then I thought of Rachael, and the baby, and how they needed the *tisande* more than me. Could I make some of this, and somehow hold it, and give it to Rachael, so that our third child would be safe?

I was really thirsty, and I drank some hot water just to get something on my tongue. *More water*, I thought. *Get more, boil more*. The *tisande* needs to be made in boiling water. I drank some more. It tasted good. All the dirt had settled to the bottom.

I went out to the pond again and scooped, scavenged some wood that was not quite dry but would do, and set the cup in the embers.

While the water got hot I didn't think much, because I was dog-tired and just enjoying the fact that there was something warm in front of me. And so it wasn't that difficult to take a few petals from the oilskin and drop them into the water just to see what would happen.

Immediately the smell of roast meat came straight up into my nostrils. And it wasn't just any roast meat, it was the hamburgers and hot dogs my dad used to make in the back yard summers back in Minnesota, the type of smell you never forget but that I had not ever smelled in Borschland, because they don't make hamburgers and hot dogs here, and the only thing even remotely close is the grilled sausages which are, in my mind, a hundred percent better than hot dogs. But they don't smell like my dad's hot dogs.

A whole cup will make you a saint, said Grundel.

Maybe he wanted me to be a saint. Maybe he wanted the tradition of the saints to go on. That would be good, wouldn't it? Even if the others died, I would go on. Borschland would still have its saints.

But did I want to be a saint?

Then I realized I was hungry. Hungrier than I'd ever been. Hungrier than after those camping trips where you come back from the woods, and the first thing on your mind is a burger and fries.

Fat hungry is what I was, and that *tisande* was calling me.

And there was no way anyone was getting in the way of me drinking down that *tisande* meat broth-smelling drink.

But fortunately or unfortunately, whatever way you look at it, I forgot that the cup was hot. And man, that thing branded me on both hands as I picked it up.

I let the cup go and yelled a couple of choice words. Maybe more than a couple. And for about ten minutes all I could think about was getting out to the ice and sticking my hands in the water. Yow, that stung.

The pain wouldn't have stopped me. I would've gotten another one going.

But I didn't have time.

CHAPTER 29 - SHERM

While I wrung my hand from the pain, I heard whistling. Some kind of military march. And out of nowhere, twelve very large bear commandos surrounded me.

They had big helmets on with headlamps. Dressed in black jumpsuits and watch caps.

One of the whistlers was wheezy.

"Sharpclaw!" I said.

"The same," he said. "What is this? A half-naked human with an out-of-control fire?"

Another bear loomed up into the circle of light and spoke in a voice I recognized. "Where are your eyebrows, Mr. Reinhardt?"

I laughed, and touched my forehead. Eyebrows, singed off. "Man Greatbear. I thought you had a desk job."

"Not where the fate of the entire continent is at stake. That's a fine fire, by the way."

"I found out the petals are flammable. Like, very flammable."

"You have petals?"

We looked over at the Branch, propped against a tree trunk and lying on the oilskin.

"It's well on its way to losing them all, sir," said Sharpclaw.

219

"And what's that?" Man motioned to the cup in the fire. "It smells like death to me."

"That would be *tisande*," I said.

"Did you drink any?"

"It's too hot. I was waiting for it to cool down." And I looked down at my burned hands.

"All right. Well..." and Man went out to the fire and knocked over the cup. The smell of burnt fur came up, like a hot dryer. He wasn't wearing shoes; bears almost never do.

"That's too bad," I said. "I was looking forward to that."

No one laughed, or even grunted. The remark had gone over like a lead airship.

"Well, let's get out of here," said Man, checking his watch. "We're not safe. Call in the helicopter, Sharpclaw."

"Heli-- what?"

"The Bearland Navy does have aircraft carriers. The Royal Air Force supervise us. And they are in accord with us to violate Borschic airspace in order to find you and rescue you. It may not be what the Borschic government want, but what they want is not always what is best, I would venture to guess."

Just then the sound of rotors came from above, and we were bathed in light.

"Get ready," he said. "You're going up."

"Wait a minute," I yelled over the noise. "Where am I going?"

"Back to the carrier," Man yelled back. "We're rescuing you."

"What are you going to do with the Branch?"

"Don't worry about that. Everyone and the Branch are going to be perfectly safe."

"Wait."

Man faced me, loomed over me. He wasn't happy. He was showing his teeth. But he couldn't do anything about the Branch without me.

"Sherm," he said next to my ear. "Up in that helicopter, right now, someone is waiting for you. Your--"

The next was cut off by a bang, a big gunshot like a cannon, and then an ear-shattering explosion that sounded like it was right next to us.

A bearish voice squawked through static. Man unbelted his walkie-talkie and said something like "Roger" except it was in Bear language.

"They're peeling off," Sharpclaw said. "They're not staying."

"A rescue helicopter versus a fully armed air frigate. I'm not surprised. Everyone down. Put out that fire."

The airship approached, drifting with very low engines. Searchlights tracked along the ground, white-blue.

I didn't make a sound. What was I supposed to do? Hail the airship, and take the Branch back to the saints? Or give it up to the bears, who had no right to it? I thought of what Grundel had said: *you will find a person of good sense.* I figured I hadn't found him or her yet.

It took about ten minutes before the airship left for good. Man said, "We've got a hike ahead of us. We need to make it to Loflin territory, gentlebears and gentleman. Or it will be an international incident. How much darkness do we have, Sharpclaw?"

"About three hours."

"Not enough. We will have to be crafty. Headlamps off. Reinhardt. Get dressed. We don't have much time. God knows how far away that airship is."

I got dressed in my still-damp clothes, and we double-timed it back the way they had come. Only a few minutes' walk and we were going uphill again. I'd gotten pretty close.

With the Branch in the oilskin and slung over my shoulder, we walked uphill for a couple of hours, and often heard the sound of airship rotors and were almost caught in search lights several times. But Man always poked me with a claw at the end and said, "They are idiots."

At dawn we stood on top of the ridge and watched the airship fade into the distance.

"They need to refuel," said Sharpclaw.

"All right, here's where we split up," said Man. "Helicopter will pluck us bears into the air now that we're in Loflinland,

and you, Sherm Reinhardt, must find a way to keep the Branch hidden until it sheds all its petals and no one is able to use the *tisande* for any purpose whatever."

"Wait a minute. Don't you want me to hang with you bears? You were so big on it before."

"We've had our chance, and bollixed it," said Man. "It's daylight, and Borschland now know that we are involved. They will have notified the Navy, and they will be after us. We will need to get our paws out of the honeycomb, if we don't want to start a war with Borschland. No, you, Mr. Sherm, are going to have to make it seem as if you've been protecting the Branch from foxes and Loflin insurgents all this time. And, conveniently, well, it seems as if all the petals have fallen off in the process, dash the luck."

"You know that if there is no *tisande*, all the Borschic saints will die."

"I didn't know that," Man said, and grunted an *imagine-that* grunt. "But it makes sense."

"So what if I make some *tisande* for them? I mean, who wants someone to die?"

"It's not that we want them to die. It's that they are long past when they should have died, and we are setting it all straight."

"But the whole culture is based on the saints."

"What will change if they die? Nine hundred ninety nine out of one thousand Borschers have never come close to seeing a real, living breathing saint. And yet they believe."

I shook my head.

"Well, Sherm," said Man, "it is entirely up to you. I have confidence in you, however, to do the right thing."

"Wow. Thanks so much, Man."

"You're very welcome."

There was a logging road cut near where we parted. I took the road, and the bears got lost in the wilderness again, hoping to come out again in friendly Loflin territory and take a train back to their embassy, no doubt.

Pretty soon I came to a hut with an old man sitting outside

on a log cut short enough to be a stool. He was bundled up, with a scarf over his mouth and nose, and a heavy fur cap. He was whittling. There were wood chips all over the stone patio in front of the doorway.

I asked him for a drink in Borschic, and when he just stared at me with a dreamy look in his face, I put up my hand to my face and said, "glug, glug."

He nodded, and stood up, brushing the wood chips off of his lap. He motioned me inside.

It was warm inside the hut. There was a fire going. That fire felt so good, so much better than the petal fire I had made when I was wet.

He poured me out a cup of water from a clear glass jug. Then he pointed to my eyebrows.

"Yeah," I said. "Ugly, I know."

He pointed to the Branch wrapped in oilskin and slung over my shoulder. "Music," I said, and made a sound like a horn.

He nodded again, and asked if I wanted more water.

I said yes, and suddenly couldn't stand up. I sat down on his little bed, and lay down. "Just need a sec to..." I began, and closed my eyes.

And didn't wake up.

CHAPTER 30 - RACHAEL

When we woke up, bundled together in blankets on the helicopter's bench, the pilot and co-pilot were warming their hands in front of a fire they'd made. The pilot's arm was in a sling.

Melissa, who was sitting on the bench opposite, grunted at me. "*Alles ergut?*" she asked.

"*Alleskeet ergut*. It's cold."

The children were still asleep, thank heavens.

We were in a clearing, surrounded by trees on three sides. A path led out of the clearing. It might have been seven of the clock. A bar of white sunlight illuminated the treetops under low-hanging clouds.

"It's a clear cut," said Melissa. "They harvested the trees here. I was lucky not to touch down on a stump."

"Are we in Loflinland?"

"It's likely. We were right on the border."

"So what are we to do?"

"Find some breakfast, I should think," said Melissa, and gave a little regretful grunt. "There are emergency rations in the 'copter, but we need to leave those for the pilots. I don't know when they will be rescued, now that Borschland know we are involved in this."

I looked over at the fire, which was crackling nicely, and had a beautiful orange glow.

"How close were we, Melissa," I said, "to losing our lives last night?"

She didn't answer.

"And you've been with the Bearish Intelligence Service this whole time, haven't you? Lieutenant Shepherdbear?"

She gave a growl, and rolled her head. "I'm sorry, but it couldn't be helped. There are..." and she searched for the right word, "...causes greater than ourselves."

I thought of the children in the helicopter, sleeping next to each other, bundled in blankets.

"You are certainly a bear of your convictions," I allowed.

The fire crackled.

"You have lovely children," said Melissa. "And they have done so well so far."

They had done so well. They had hardly complained. Maybe adventure agreed with them.

"You are a good nannybear," I said.

"You are a good mother."

It was the best we could manage on that cold morning, before coffee or tea.

I said, "Well, then, we had best be on our way."

"Yes," said Melissa. "We shouldn't be seen near the helicopter, just in case the Borschic authorities take it upon themselves to overfly Loflin territory."

We woke the children, gave them water, and something to eat from the emergency stores. Neither of them was keen to walk on a cold morning, but Connie got warm in front of the fire and spoke with the pilots, telling them of his adventures the night before.

"I lost my hockey puck, and I'm not even sad," he said to them.

"We'll find it for you," said the pilot.

Lily put her arms around Melissa's neck, saying *Issa, Issa, Issa.*

We walked on a frozen cart track for about a hundred

meters, and the sun showed its face from the clouds, so that all the trees went a-sparkle. At the end of the cart track there was something like a road, well graveled under the snow and with ditches on either side.

One way went in the direction of the rising sun, and downhill; the other, uphill.

"Which way?" I asked.

"Do you want to find Sherm?" asked Melissa, and pointed to the uphill direction. "Or do you want to go back to Bijfhaaf? Breakfast--"

I immediately set off walking uphill.

Melissa laughed under her breath, almost barking.

We hadn't walked very far when the sound of horses' hoofs, and the tinkling of bells, came from behind us. It was a lumber cart, driven by a youngish Loflin.

"I wish it were a sledge, Mamuj!" cried Connie.

"The horses!" Lily said.

We spoke to him in Borschic, of which he understood little, but he could see our predicament. Lily insisted on patting the horses' faces first, but we climbed into the cart and rode, with the lumberjack doffing his cap repeatedly and pointing down the road.

As we rode in the hard wooden bed of the cart, and the sun tried out its winter strength to shine behind a procession of clouds, Melissa assessed our chances of finding Sherm. "He can't have gotten far," she said. "There can't be many roads in and out of here. Unless I miss my guess, we will meet him on the way."

I was glad of her company, truth to tell. And I was especially glad of her company when I began to feel poorly.

I don't have a weak stomach, as I have said before, but being with child makes me perpetually nauseated. Early in my first pregnancy, I threw up everything I ate. For Lily, it was a little better. With this one, I was hoping for nothing at all. But in the morning I appreciated a mug of tea to settle my insides.

At first, when the cart driver stopped at a house occupied by two old men and an old woman, who (he made clear) were his relations, I thought that the Loflin tea we were offered would make me feel better. It is an herb tea that is quite nasty in some ways, but many Borschlanders swear by it.

Then, I thought that the simple warm cakes that they griddled for us would do the trick. Connie ate everything given to him, but I felt weak and dizzy.

Then, when one of the old men offered to drive us further into the hills towards the border, telling us with no teeth and no Borschic that something very interesting was up there, which included, over and over again, Borschic, I fell on the front steps of the porch into the snow.

Melissa put a paw to my forehead, and it came off warm and wet.

"You are burning up," said Melissa.

I suppose it made sense. I probably should have been on bed rest the entire pregnancy based on my experience with the first two, but there is something about losing one's husband that makes one restless.

With the first two I had had no fevers, but they had both come early and unexpectedly. Not early enough that they were miscarriages, and both children miraculously survived.

This one felt like a miscarriage.

The old woman motioned to the bed in the house, but I would have none of it. The old man seemed to believe the solution to my problem lay in the hills. He got into the cart and motioned for us to climb up.

It was very late when we came to the place the old man had been seeking, and I was near delirious.

The old man knocked on the door, and another old man emerged. As it was nearly dark, I could not see any of the features of the one who had opened the door. There was a discussion in Loflin. The old driver shook his head at us, and motioned to me. Then money was exchanged, Borschic was spoken, and Melissa had me inside the hut, where, I must confess, I do not remember anything more than seeing someone asleep under a quilt in the one-room structure.

The rest is a blur; I did not come to my senses until I felt someone giving me a draught from a cup. It was warm, and the drink was so restorative, I was immediately aware of all my surroundings.

There was a fire, and a deep, tin pan filled with rose-colored, boiling water. The room smelled like Eden. In a corner, there was a long branch with flowers that had shed almost all their petals. Lily was sitting quietly, stroking the hair of the person asleep on the bed. Connie was holding my hand. Melissa was sitting on a stool near the door.

"What is it?" I whispered.

"The *tisande*," said Melissa, "has saved you and the baby."

And it was like the full moon times one thousand.

CHAPTER 31 - SHERM

The first thing I saw on waking was two really big eyes.

"Daddy, Daddy," somebody was saying.

And there was this little hand touching my face.

As the room came into focus, I figured I was still asleep and dreaming, though I hadn't had any dreams in the however many hours I had been asleep.

There was Lily, her hand on my face, breathing cracker and apple breath on me, saying Daddy.

And there was Connie, behind her, staring at me and picking his nose.

A fire was going in the hearth, making shadows flicker all over the room. The old man who had helped me was sitting on the floor with his back next to the wall. Over next to the fire, a big kettle. And next to the kettle, the Branch, its flowers all shed.

Sitting on the end of the bed was Rachael, looking tired, with dark circles under her eyes, but with her eyes shining like stars, and her cheeks as red and healthy as I'd ever seen them.

Melissa Shepherdbear sat on a stool near the door.

"Lilujbeest," I whispered, and took her hand off my face.

"Daduj!" she screamed, and jumped on top of me. Connie wasn't far behind.

It was pretty painful being wailed on by two little kids, but it was the best pain in the world.

"How did you get here?"

"That's a long story," said Rachael. "It may be that Miss Shepherdbear is the one to tell it, as for much of it I was in no condition to remember anything."

"We were in the helic-popter last night," said Connie.

Melissa explained the whole journey. The delay on the train, the boat ride to the aircraft carrier, the flight out to rescue me.

"So you were in that helicopter?"

"Yes. We never got a chance to bring you up."

Then she spoke of the next day, the help of strangers, and Rachael's illness.

"We got here last night at dark," said Melissa. "The children were all in, and Rachael was terribly sick."

"How in the name of all that's holy did you think you were going to take an all-day cart ride in the snow and pregnant?" I wanted to know.

"Well, it was touch and go. But thanks to this man here, everything is all right."

The old man stood up, went to a table under the window, and picked up a leather wineskin.

"He made the *Bloomentisande* for me, darling," said Rachael. "And now I am right as rain. Now we never have to worry about the baby."

The old man handed me the wineskin, then went over to the corner of the room, where he threw on his winter coat and began slinging things over his shoulder.

"Jesus Christ," I said.

Melissa said, "An appropriate name to invoke at this time."

The old man faced us, bowed, and made a sign like wood chopping. "Brrrr.... crash," he said, as his imaginary tree fell.

Rachael tried to pay him with schillings, but he refused. In a few seconds, he was gone.

Connie ran around the room, cutting down trees with his hands the way the old man had done.

"So why haven't Henrick and Willem found us?" I asked.

"We don't know. They have been unaccountably delayed," said Melissa.

"And what about the bears?"

"They would have been back if they could," said Melissa. "But the Borschland Navy may have persuaded them to leave."

So here we are with a half-gallon of *tisande*..." I said, hefting the bag.

"It's very concentrated," said Melissa. "He boiled it down quite a bit."

"...And the Branch with no flowers."

"And two children," said Rachael. "We have made rather a big batch of coleslaw."

"And this dude just hands it over to me?"

"He refused even a sip," said Melissa. "The Loflins are wise. They want nothing to do with the *tisande*. Better to have Borschland rip its fur out over this."

"So what are we going to do with the *tisande*?"

"If you ask me," said Melissa, "we need to take it out back and pour it on the snow. But to honor this man's generosity, perhaps we should wait until he is out of sight."

"This is where we disagree," said Rachael. "The *tisande* belongs in the hands of the Borschic church. It is a holy elixir. And I mean to give it to my father, who with his colleagues will determine the best use for it."

Melissa frowned; Rachael raised her head and set her mouth the way she does when she thinks she's going to get her way.

And I was the one with the wineskin. It now felt heavier than a half-gallon.

"Well, let's wrap the Branch in the oilskin again," I said. "We have to get that back to the Rijksmuseen and start the countdown at three hundred years again."

I had just finished the wrapping, and tied it securely with twine, when there was a rapping on the door, and a hallooing in Borschic.

But the accent wasn't quite right.

Melissa opened the door. Busby stood in the threshold, and

his holster was full again. He'd replaced his lost gun.

"How do you do it, Buzz?" I said in English. "How do you manage it?"

"Call me a cat. Where is the Branch?"

"It's in the oilskin."

"Has it lost all its petals?"

Melissa said, "I wouldn't risk opening the oilskin."

"Why not?"

"It's in such a fragile state now."

"What do you know?" he said, and pointed the gun at her.

"Don't be an idiot," snapped Rachael. She had never liked Busby.

"It's good to see you again, Madaam," said Busby, switching to Borschic. And he looked down at the children, who were holding on to Rachael's skirts and glaring up at him.

"So," I said. "Did you defeat Mittelmascht on the ridge where I left him?"

"I don't know what you're talking about. It took a while to figure out where you'd gone in that muck of a swamp, but I found your fire finally and your tracks. Super-strength did the rest."

"What did you do, Busby? Did you shoot him?"

"Come off it, Sherm. I'm telling you I didn't see him, eh?"

He holstered the gun. "Bring the Branch to me. I'm headed for the hills. Original plan intact."

"You're not going to get away with this, Busby. Why don't you turn the Branch in? We'll say that you were the hero: you found it, you rescued it. That ought to cut you some slack with the courts."

"Yeah, right," said Busby. "Nice try."

"We're not giving it to you," said Rachael. "It is a holy relic."

"Suit yourself." And he pulled out his gun, cocked it, and pointed it at Rachael.

Rachael screamed. Connie said, "Bad gun! Bad English!"

Melissa menaced him, and he said, "What, do you want it?" She withdrew.

He nodded. I took the Branch and handed it to him.

"So long, suckers. By the time you see me next, I'll be a full-fledged saint. Saint Kevin von Busby, the patron of Canadian bad guys. No hard feelings, Sherm. We've all got to do what we've got to do, eh."

"You bet, Buzz," I said.

And he backed out of the hut and closed the door behind him.

We waited for what seemed like a really long time without saying anything.

Then Connie said, "Why are we being so quiet?"

"I can't believe he didn't notice the *tisande*," said Melissa. "Once he opens the oilskin and sees no petals, he's going to come straight back here for them. That's why we need to pour out the wineskin right now."

"I don't know about that," I said. "The Branch itself is worth a lot of money. He's got to make tracks quickly to avoid airships and helicopters."

"In any case..." said Melissa.

"We're not dumping out the *tisande*," I said.

Melissa made a low growling sound, but thankfully didn't go for the *tisande*. I wasn't up to wrestling bears at the moment, especially after having a gun put to my head.

"Hear me out. We need to give the *tisande* to the saints. They'll die otherwise. Grundel told me as much. Once that's done, they can track down Busby. Otherwise he is going to disappear and the Branch will disappear and Borschland will be down one holy relic."

Rachael shuddered. "We must get it back," she whispered.

"So it's flat out for Bijfhaaf, then," said Melissa, who sighed and gave a little woof that sounded like she was giving in. "These children have had quite an adventure and it would do them good to get back to a warm hotel room and a proper meal and nap."

"Not tired," Connie said.

"Yes, you are," Rachael said.

Lily said, "Want a drink of water." And she pointed to the

wineskin.

"That's not water, darling," Rachael said. "That is not for you. It is only for sick people."

"It is water," said Connie. "It is water. I want a drink, too."

"Water," said Lily.

"It's not water, kids," I said. "We can't drink this."

"Yes, it is," said Connie. "It is water. It is water."

"Well, it is water," said Rachael, "but it is a special kind of water we shouldn't drink. It's the water the old man gave us."

"No, it isn't," said Connie. "It isn't. It's water."

"It's special water," I growled. "It's the water mommy drank. It's for medicine."

"No, it isn't," Connie kept insisting. "The man took the medicine."

"Stop it or you will get a spanking," Rachael said. "You must listen to your parents. This is unacceptable."

Lily began to cry; Connie stamped his foot and yelled. I said we would take the kids out to the well and show them how to work it, but they were beyond talking to.

Finally, over the yelling, Melissa knelt in front of Connie and said, "Connie, what did you say? The man took the medicine?"

Connie wiped his nose, which had begun to run. "Yes, he took it. He gave us the water."

"Sherm, give me the wineskin," she said.

"What are you going to do?"

"Please. Just give it me."

I took it off my shoulder, handed it to her, and she unstoppered it. Then she squeezed. The liquid made a pencil line on the wooden floor.

"Whee!" said Connie. "Do it again."

The liquid was clear. If it had been *tisande*, it would have been pink.

Melissa squirted some into her mouth. "Water," she said.

Rachael and I exchanged bewildered glances. Melissa gave a drink to the kids. They immediately calmed down.

"What happened?"

"The old man clearly switched wineskins when we weren't looking, and kept the *tisande* for himself."

"A Loflin wouldn't do that."

"Maybe he wasn't a Loflin."

"A saint?"

"Grundel?"

Just then there was the sound of whirling rotors. We looked up.

"Helic-popter! Helic-popter!" cried Connie, and jumped up and down.

The copter passed over us, then circled back.

"It's ours," Melissa said, as if there was another kind of helicopter.

The area was clear enough for the copter to land. Once its pontoons were safely on the ground, out came bears and saints.

There was Man Greatbear, in a Bearland Navy uniform and hat, and next to him, looking very old and tired, were Willem and Henrick. Bearish sailors supported them as they came.

"Where is the Branch?" asked Greatbear.

"Busby took it," I said.

"Busby?" said Greatbear.

"An old friend," I said, and pointed. "Hills."

Man nodded, and Henrick fell to one knee. A Bearish sailor helped him back up.

"But there's *tisande*," I said. "Grundel has it."

"Mittelmascht?" said Henrick.

"Where?" Willem wheezed.

I shook my head. "Hills."

Man said, "Borschland and Bearland have negotiated an agreement. Our technological support to find the Branch, their pledge to hand over the *tisande* to us to be disposed of. You say the Swamp Saint has the *tisande*, and Busby the Branch. We'll find both. Meanwhile, we'll take you back to Bijfhaaf. The newspapers need to have good news about you, disappearing Reinhardts. And apparently, there is a hockey tournament."

"What has happened?" Rachael said. "Have we missed it?"

"Your sister's team is playing their first game as we speak."

"How long-- how long--" I began, and motioned to the saints.

"Hours rather than days, I'm afraid," said Man. "But don't worry. We'll find Grundel and the *tisande*. We have infrared cameras."

Well, I thought. *Infrared cameras. That ought to do the trick.*

Man had the radio operator relay the news to the aircraft carrier. "They'll scramble aircraft," he said. "The search is already underway. Meanwhile, we need you to make your away overland to Bijfhaaf. Our communications officers have prepared a statement for the press."

"Saying what?" asked Rachael.

"That you got it into your head to go off in search of Sherm on your own, and that by the kindness of Loflin strangers you found him."

"Nothing about Bearish aircraft carriers, I expect?" said Rachael.

"Not a word," said Man, and put a claw to his mouth.

I thought of something. "One more thing. Since Grundel has the *tisande*--"

"Yes?"

"If Kasmahlov is well enough to travel. Bring him to Bijfhaaf. Once we find Grundel, we need to help him out. It wasn't his fault he picked up the Branch."

"We will do that, Sherm."

CHAPTER 32 - GRUNDEL

Perhaps it was selfish of me to try to make Sherm a saint.

I knew that it was time, our time, to pass from this world and not be seen again. I'd known it for many years. We had outlived ourselves. We had outlived our purpose. And the Shadows and the Lights had come into a situation where it was one side versus the other, with no clear goal in mind. No good goal.

But may the Creator pardon me for sending Sherm into that swamp by himself, with the tools to make *tisande*, and the occasion-- even the necessity-- to do it, when, I felt sure, he would get lost and need to warm and nourish himself.

For it is a grand tradition, the saints of Borschland, and a shame that there should be none left.

But there was no fair way to choose which people would drink, and which would not.

And so Sherm was to be an accidental saint, a saint of opportunity.

As soon as he left and I knew he was facing forward, towards his task, I began to follow him. If Busby came down after us, then I knew we two could beat him, especially if Sherm took the *tisande*.

Sherm blundered for a long time, and I felt sorry for him,

but I kept my distance. I was patient, as is required of someone like me.

When he fell through the ice, I considered saving him, but held back at the last minute, and it was nearly providential, for he was wet and needed to make a fire with the flint I gave him. And as the hours went by it must have become inevitable for him to think of the *tisande* as a way of surviving. And once you drink the *tisande*, you cannot stop at a sip. You will drink the amount needed to be bound to this strange world my ancestors discovered so long ago.

But of course I had not reckoned on the bears, who are well meaning at the same time they are paramountly self-interested. I cocked my crossbow as they tramped in like hibernators searching for berries in the spring. But when I saw their numbers-- a dozen at least, a standard Bearish commando team-- and saw that most of them were very big and there was at least one grizzly, I knew that I wouldn't be able to shoot enough bolts to put all of them to sleep before their wicked little submachine guns found me.

When the helicopter came I began to resign myself to the failure of my plan, but I didn't reckon on the Borschic Navy showing up. So I changed tactic, went on ahead of Sherm and the bears, and looked for a likely place to intercept Sherm. There was the woodcutter's hut, and the woodcutter, who gladly accepted the antique gold coin I offered him for the use of the place until I should call around for him lower down in whatever music hall he'd ventured into to break his hard money into negotiable Loflin currency.

We saints are, always have been, masters of disguise, but when Sherm arrived at the hut, he was so exhausted that it could have been the president of North America sitting on that log whittling, and Sherm would never have recognized him.

And, of course, when Madaam Reinhardt and her family arrived, quite miraculously and in the nick of time, they could not have recognized me. Borschic children are taught of Sankt Bogg quite thoroughly, but the pictures in the books hardly do me justice.

Madaam Reinhardt, in fact, omitted some things from her account to her husband that would have caused him undue concern. She implied that I had made the *tisande* simply because I had white petals floating free.

That was not the case. I would let Sherm make *tisande*, but I would not choose to do it myself, unless someone were ill, and gravely so.

For you see, when she arrived at the hut, on foot with her nannybear and the children in a pallet behind her, she had been experiencing labor pains for some hours.

She was deathly pale, and collapsed on the bed next to her sleeping husband, and Demouzeel Shepherdbear expressed grave doubts about her ability to hold the baby she was carrying, or even survive the night.

I put my hand on her forehead. It was hot, and slick with sweat, though she had been in the cold for many hours.

There was nothing to be done, no diagnosis to be made, no treatment to be ordered. I was not a doctor, nor was my borrowed hut a hospital. This is why the Shadows believe we should progress-- for medicine's sake.

So I put a pot up on the fire, and went to the well for water-- good, clear, mountain water-- and poured it into the pot. When the water boiled, I undid the oilskin from the Branch. Several petals fluttered down. The she-bear did not protest-- much-- she is of the Bearish Intelligence Service, and her mission is to see the *tisande* done away with. But she is also a compassionate creature and she would never want two tiny children to be deprived of a mother and another sibling, especially when only a sip would make her right again.

"Ah! Ah!" Madaam Reinhardt cried out in her delirium as we fed her three spoonfuls of the cooled heavenly-scented juice. It was all I could do not to gulp the stuff down myself. But as I told Sherm, I am a man who has mastered his body's desire to survive.

It was a small thing to locate one more wineskin-- the woodcutter had three-- and fill it with plain well water, and switch it with the *tisande*. I had great expectation of having fooled everyone, though the little boy was very observant, and spent nearly all the time that he was not sleeping staring intently at me. So the girl, too, although she slept like an angel once she found her father. All four of them-- or five, should I say-- together on that one rough couch with its deep, heavy quilt for the winter, sleeping like a litter of puppies.

Miss Shepherdbear knew very little Loflin, and conversed with me politely as she could, until she, too, succumbed to some sleep, as is the habit of civilized bears.

Finally I dozed for a few hours before dawn, though I never need much sleep. That is, not until now, and the petals falling from the tree, and my strength beginning to ebb.

I intended to take the *tisande* into the woods and pour it out, and then return to my fellows somehow to make a clean breast of all we'd lived, to say our apologies and goodbyes.

I was hardly out of the hut, however, when I heard a crackling of boots on snow. I hid myself, and saw Meester Busby forcing his way out of the woods and onto the logging path.

Busby came to the hut, looked back and forth, understood this was the first place anyone coming from that swampy valley would see, and investigated, crouching to look through the ice-encrusted window.

When he had satisfied himself, he called out in Borschic, and opened the door. There was no doubt he was happy to see the Branch wrapped in my oilskin, for it was not long before he was out again, carrying the wrapped treasure and hoofing it quickly down the hill.

I followed him, and he took a fork off of the main road. Within a mile or so he reached a railhead with a lumberyard attached. He picked up his pace, and it was difficult to follow, for my strength was going now, and he had motivation and the pollen still coursing in his bloodstream.

Another mile on, he hallooed, and there was a handcart manned by two Loflins. He waved to them, and they waved back, and I knew he would get on that handcart, bound no doubt for Bijfhaaf once the spur lumber road united with a main track.

There was only one thing to do. I cocked my crossbow, put a bolt to it, shot.

And missed.

So, then, winded, bent over, my head spinning, I unstoppered the *tisande*, squirted some in my mouth, and followed.

CHAPTER 33 - CATHY

We limped in to Bijfhaaf somewhere around 5 AM, and stayed at the Borschic naval base across the harbor from the team hotel. I found out later that all the journalists assigned to us slept in the lobby waiting for us to arrive.

Sorry, guys.

My first thought was a mattress and a pillow, but it was not to be. We got a briefing as soon as we arrived: Rachael's train had been delayed in Bevinlunz; the track near Hijluj Moruu had been sabotaged; Rachael, their nannybear, and the children had gotten off the train there and disappeared.

"Didn't you have someone watching Rachael?" I asked Willem and Henrick. We were in a situation room, and it was still before dawn. Harsh electric lights shone down.

Both of them looked like they'd been punched in the stomach. Their eyes were bloodshot, and they stooped over. Henrick said in a grouchy voice, "We don't consider them high priority."

"He was investigating the sabotage," said Willem.

Then Bep came into the room. I gasped. Her hair had gone gray.

"What's going on?"

"Dearest," she said, "The Branch is losing its petals."

"And we are dying," said Willem.

Bep broke the nauseating silence that followed. "We must contact the Upright Bears."

Henrick turned to me. "Katharujna, you must play your part now. You have a tournament to coach, and it is important that you do so. If the bears and their helicopter were involved here, it is doubtless the Branch is being moved and that Sherm is still alive. We will take over from here. If we need you we will call on you."

"Fleemisch can coach the team," I said.

"Karolujna Kretschmer cannot disappear," said Willem. "There is no reason to panic the press and the people even more."

"But what about you? How can you do anything, if you're dying?"

"That's where the Bears come in. They will help. We have to get the Branch back, and we have to find out what is going on with the petals-- whether *tisande* has been made from them."

"Coach well," said Bep. "You must make the country proud, my dear. That is your patriotic duty, even though you are Anvorian."

She laughed, and it was almost a cough.

I lay down for a few hours, but we were scheduled for a practice skate that day, so no real sleep.

When Fleemisch joined the team for the boat ride across the harbor, I thought I might take back what I said about him coaching the team. The airship ride must have taken a lot out of him. I hadn't seen him at all on the bridge or the observation rooms. He looked sunken and beaten, yet somehow just as stubborn as ever.

About a thousand boats were bobbing in the harbor, each one painted black with eyes on either side, no pair the same as another. Some were just dots of green or blue; others were very elaborate, with lashes, lids, and brows.

I said to Fleemisch, "Do they think their boats are alive? Like, with spirits, or something?"

"No," he said. "They know the boats are just pieces of

wood. They do it for a joke. If a tourist asks why they make the eyes, they tell them the most outrageous stories. The Loflins are great liars."

We maneuvered between the boats and into a wide canal that was bordered on both sides by stone walls. Soon after, the canal narrowed, became filled with floating ice, and finally terminated in an ice sheet. We got out of the boat and put on our skates.

Bijfhaaf, the Venice of the Continent.

I asked Fleemisch if the Loflins really skated to their greengrocer.

"Most assuredly," he said. "And in summer the whole thing stinks to the starfire. You've never smelled such a stench."

Then I realized that was the most I'd ever gotten out of him on anything other than hockey.

"Fleemisch," I said. "Are you married?"

"My wife has predeceased me many years, Demouzeel."

It turned out we were in for more than a skate that morning. All the teams were assembled in a big, open square. There was a crowd, dignitaries on a platform, and a band to welcome us, all set in front of a large stone building that must have been City Hall.

It was the strangest band I've ever seen. There wasn't a single conventional instrument in it. Most of them were about as big as the people who played them, and many were connected to a steam engine huffing off in a corner with a pile of peat next to it. One of the instruments had a seat built in with pedals for your feet and levers to pull with both hands. Another was a horn with several mouths that was connected by what looked like a fire hose to the steam engine. And there was every kind of percussion instrument imaginable, sheet metal hanging from frames that people banged on, conventional drums but with metal drumsticks operated by bike pedal and chain.

The noise that band made was incredible. It sounded like a drone of fifty foghorns and the whomp of a hundred drums, with twenty thousand kinds of animal hoots above it, all going at the same time. Basically Dr. Seuss on steroids.

Then it all stopped, after about two minutes, and out of the crowd came these tiny eight-year olds with the tiniest piccolos I've ever seen. They piped a heartbreaking song, almost inaudible because the instruments were so small, but so beautiful. Then the band started up again, gong-whomp-boom-hoot, and went on for another couple of minutes until they all kind of petered out like fifty pot lids dropped on the pavement and rolling around crashing into each other and rolling in a tight circle until they vibrated to a silence.

The crowd applauded, and the mayor-- or whatever he was called-- came up to us and shook our hands and made a short speech in Loflin that no one translated. The Borschic press took our pictures with the mayor, and then we migrated over to the hotel, which was across an arched bridge from the city hall town square. It had tables set up in the foyer and on the tables there were shots of weshnak.

"Nothing like starting the day with a pick-me-up," one of the coaches from the University of Borschland said. "Don't eat too much, girls. After our skate, we are set for a tour of their musical instruments factory." And she put her finger in her ear.

The press were seated at the far end of the foyer from us. I could see Roald at a table, and wondered how I could get to talk to him.

We were brought a succession of courses that would've done anyone in for three days if they'd tried to eat everything. Not that it was appetizing. Much of it was some kind of puree of something colored and shaped to look like something else. The best thing I had was a fried potato croquette with a filling of seasoned fish inside.

After lunch-- about three hours later, in fact-- we got to check in to our rooms, and then hustle over to the rink with our equipment to get in a skate.

The rink had been laid out between two dry-dock shipyards. In fact, it looked like it had once been a dry-dock shipyard itself, because the ice was almost perfectly rectangular, with only the corner boards diagonal, and it was sunken about

12 feet below street level. That meant that if you lifted the puck above the boards, it stood a good chance of whacking against a concrete wall and coming back to you at high velocity. There were plenty of depressions in the walls where hot pucks had gouged out a little concrete.

In the middle of the far side of the rink, the concrete had been cut out for the team benches and for a seating area. Here, nets were set up to catch flying pucks. Besides there, the only place to watch the game was from dock level, leaning over a railing. Behind the railings, someone had set up strings of lights held up by poles, a bit like Christmas lights. That was all connected to another steam generator with its pile of peat and attendants at the ready. The effect was somewhat magical, throwing light and shadows everywhere, though that wasn't going to help our defenders locate the puck along a corner board.

The rink itself was narrower than normal Borschic rinks, which meant that theoretically there would be opportunities for more contact between the players.

Not that the referees would allow that for a second.

Behind the landward goal there was a gate to a canal, frozen, that led to other street canals and eventually the Paas River.

"This is a skating rink when there are no games being played," Fleemisch said, and pointed to the canal. "In winter there is nothing but skaters on the Paas. It is shallow and freezes easily."

Oststaff and Bijfhaaf would be skating tomorrow evening in the third round of the Flowering Branch Cup. We would play tomorrow twice, and Sunday in the finals if we won.

When we got to the rink, Oststaff was already in the middle of their workout. We sat in the seating area, pulled laces on our skates and retaped sticks until they were done. When we got out there, the Bijfhaaf women's team was congregating at the railing above us.

"They are in the other group," said Fleemisch. "They play today, then rest overnight. We will play two games tomorrow."

We went back to the hotel after the workout, on strict orders from Bep to rest up. I slept like a saint between phase shifts.

CHAPTER 34 - CATHY

The next morning it was even colder than the day before; the first game was scheduled for 10 AM that morning, the University of Borschland versus the Anvorian team. Fleemisch came down to breakfast looking green. He slumped over his coffee and hardly ate anything. I knew he wouldn't tell me what was wrong, but I asked anyway.

"Please do not trouble yourself over me," was what he said. "We must put all our attention on this game to come. I have gotten word that the Anvorian teams were delayed by weather in Celtlands. They won't be here. It just came through in a telegram."

"And what happened with the games yesterday?"

"Loflinland won in a shootout versus a Gimrothian team, and Queen Maeve College won by forfeit." He coughed into a handkerchief.

"You're sick," I said.

"No, I'm not," he said. "I'm not sick. I'm just a little... old."

We played the Vinasolan team first, at noon. Philbuja came back from a shift with news that the whole Vinasolan team was hung over. We won, 2-0.

Roald watched in the press house. After the game, he came down to the benches, and I said, "Aren't you going to get my thoughts on the game so you can file your story?"

"I'm not assigned. Look, here is your reporter."

A young woman with a turned-up nose and freckles was taking the stairs down from the press house.

"Anna-Danielujna van ter Roost," she said. "Te *Taglik Staff*, Women's Pages."

I sighed. At least we were getting coverage.

At noon, it was the Loflinland National Women's Side versus Queen Maeve College of the Celtlands, the ones who had routed us 7-0. I wanted to scout this game, but I ordered Fleemisch to get into bed and not get out until he felt better.

The Loflin women came out in forest-green jerseys and bloomers, with black stockings. *Very chic*, I thought, as I looked at all of our players in their gray skirts and shirtwaists with military insignia. The crowd, leaning over the side of the railing, shouted encouragement.

The Loflins also held sticks taped like Sherm's, on the handle, the blade, and all the way up and down the shaft. It had become the rage, among many amateur teams, though Te Staff's BHL foes refused to follow suit. And they had written things on the tape with some kind of black paint. Maybe it was Loflin script, but it was impossible to see clearly.

Queen Maeve were pretty good. They were small and skated fast, and passed well, too. Sometimes a little too well. They would go through several combinations and look like magicians, then forget to shoot on goal. When we lost to them, we played so badly we probably should have lost twenty to nothing instead of just seven.

But that was weeks ago. We were much better now.

The Loflin women were good skaters, too, but awful stickhandlers. During the first few shifts they tried to pass to each other, but half the time the puck would go under their stick and get stolen. The other half, it'd smack off the stick and get stolen. After two periods it was 3-0, and the big crowd had thinned noticeably.

But on the face-off after the third Queen Maeve goal, the center won, collected the puck back from her defender, and went on a kamikaze rush to the goal. The defenders converged on her, sticks at the ready, but she weaved through them like they were stationary. She then bore down on the goalie, who crouched and braced herself.

Zing! Quicker than I could see, the center had directed a wrister past the net minder's blocker-hand side. The puck rattled around in the back of the goal.

The referee tweeted up a goal, pointing to center ice.

And just like that, it was 3-1.

"Who is that?" I asked Philuumeena. "Has she been playing the whole game?"

The Loflin fans celebrated by ignoring the center and hanging their heads as if some disaster had occurred.

"I think she's new," said Haanelore.

"Want me to find out?" asked someone else.

But before I could say something, the new center had won the face-off, collected the puck from her defender, and made another charge on goal. The Queen Maeve team surrounded her, and the puck came out to a Loflin wing. Left completely alone, she shot, and the puck came off the goalie right in front of the net, where the center swept it home.

3-2.

Queen Maeve stood around the goal with their sticks in hand, huffing and puffing. From all the steam rising, it looked like a factory with a bunch of smokestacks.

The center took the next shift off, but within a couple of minutes was back again and causing havoc in the Queen Maeve side of the rink. Their defenders were overmatched, and their forwards had little idea how to help back and forecheck.

The action got chaotic, with women in big knots at the boards, or in front of the nets. When the puck came free, it was always a Loflin who picked it up, because the Celtlands women had lost any idea of what spacing meant.

One of the free Loflins took a shot from point-blank range and almost completely missed the puck. But the goalie was anticipating a heavy shot, and stood up to brace for it. This allowed the biscuit to glide between her skates and into the goal.

3-3.

About three minutes were left in the game. Both teams settled down a bit with the ringer center out for a shift or two, but with a minute and a half left, the new center bounded over the boards and immediately stole a pass. She skated in, loaded up, and narrowly missed, the goalie doing the splits and making a save on the tippy end of her left skate blade. The puck skittered out to the boards, and there was a melee to get it. Someone knocked someone over, the referee kept his whistle in his pocket, and the puck came out between the circles, where a Loflin skater whacked one that the goalie melted down.

The Loflin crowd was deadly silent.

The center won the draw, and it slid back to a Loflin defender. She pushed it to her wing, who skated in and tried to shoot. A Queen Maeve player hacked down on the Loflin's stick, however, and the puck continued to run towards the goal crease.

Another melee, more stick whacking, and the center took it, whirled around, whirled around again, was lost in the crowd, somehow got it out of the pack, and a Loflin wing tipped it in weak side.

Final score, 4-3.

More bedlam from the Loflin crowd.

More suspicion of the center on our parts.

Next up was us versus the University of Borschland at 4 PM. We owned them. Final score, 2-1, and we were in the finals.

"Our opponent," said Philuumeena, pointing at the ladies in the bloomers watching us from the stands.

Fleemisch reported that we were expected to stay for the Oststaff-Bijfhaaf game and that we had seats behind the Oststaff bench. That meant back to the hotel for heavy coats and to stow our equipment.

A big crowd had gathered, zanier than the one for the women's game that afternoon. They brought their own temporary stands-- stepladders. They positioned the ladders behind the railings and sat on the steps. There were children sitting on fathers' shoulders at the apex of the ladders.

Many of them brought noisemakers, and others were playing miniature versions of the instruments we'd seen in the band that morning. The whole place was one clanging, oinging madhouse, and the game had not even started.

Then as soon as the game started, all the music and the banging stopped. It was preternaturally quiet except for the smacking of the puck and the sound of the skates cutting into the ice.

When there was a pause in play, the music and the noisemaking began anew, along with cheers for the Loflins that sounded like ah-nee, ah-nee, ah-loaf-loaf-loaf.

The first period was scoreless, and my butt was going from ice-cold to totally numb when Oststaff scored and the crowd went wild.

It was amazing, the screaming, banging, tooting for the opponents' goal.

Then Bijfhaaf tied the score, and no one said anything, except that a little child, dressed in an ankle-length robe with silver stars on it, skated out to retrieve the puck out of the goal and presented it to the mayor, who bowed very deeply and put it into a glass case with about a hundred other pucks.

During the third period, however, all bets were off. The score was tied, and no one, not even the it's-opposite-day Loflinders, were going to keep quiet. In fact, the whole Borschland contingent-- we were seated with the University team, too-- spent the whole period standing and cheering as the cadets furiously tried to break down the Loflin wall of defense.

"If Bijfhaaf manage to hold on to the tie," said Fleemisch over the din, "There will be a shootout to determine the winner. They have already tied the game played at Oststaff."

And I thought of what Roald had said, in the face of all these great events. *Oststaff have a clear road to the fourth round. Bijfhaaf are twelfth in the table out of fourteen.* I looked behind me, at the press house. Roald was there, on the front row, giving a piece of paper to a boy, no doubt telegraphing his editor back in Staff Borsch. He was a hard-working man, and I wanted all of this to stop, and to be back in that barracks with him at that table, with the champagne and lobster.

Then I saw someone else: sitting next to Roald, in a wheelchair, and bundled up, Urdan Kasmahlov.

I looked again. Someone was giving Kasmahlov a drink of something from a wineskin.

Fleemisch was right. Oststaff wanted to win, and they were taking the play to the Loflins, who had retreated all five skaters into their end, a failure of courtesy according to Borschic hockey etiquette. Oststaff put shot after shot on goal, and shot after shot came back at them. There seemed to be no way that the cadets were going to get through.

But then a defenseman, who had been pinching in to the Loflin zone, let fly a slapshot from behind the right circle that went through about three people, and one of his teammates redirected it past the goalie.

You never heard such screaming, but it was cheering that was really anger and despair. *Wow*, I thought. *This is very emotional. This is very rough.* And I looked back at the press house again.

There was about five minutes left in the game, and the Loflins, at a sign from the mayor, completely quieted down again.

This time, the Loflins put their engines in gear and began to bear down on the Oststaff goal. The referee called a penalty on Oststaff, and Bijfhaaf went up a man.

Fleemisch whispered, "I was afraid of this. We had better have scored three or four goals when they were turtling. No referee can resist calling a penalty when the home team is down one goal."

"Is it a Loflin referee?"

"Of course it is. The Loflins would trust no one else in so crucial a game."

As the players lined up for the first draw in Oststaff's zone, the entire crowd unfurled red bed sheets and covered themselves in them. It was unnerving. A couple thousand people-- I have no idea how many there actually were there-- pulled out blood-red sheets and stuck them over their heads so they couldn't see.

Then they all howled like ghosts.

"It is the Spirit Cheer," said Fleemisch. "The hidden ancestors of the sunset come back to help the Loflinder warriors."

Meanwhile, Kasmahlov had left his wheelchair and walked down to the Oststaff bench. The team cheered.

Flash bulbs went.

Kasmahlov was standing there with a greatcoat and scarf on, behind the bench with the coach.

The men on the ice were all rubbernecking Kasmahlov's way. Which is why, when the Bijfhaaf center won the next draw and it skittered to the left point, the defenseman let it pass under his stick and the right wing shot it hard at the goalie, who just managed to get a skate on it, just enough so that it landed on the center's blade and he put it home.

Deadly silence under the red bed sheets as the child skated out to get the puck to give to the mayor.

"What is Kasmahlov doing up?" Fleemisch said. "What is going on?"

On the scoreboard clock, which was analog, the little hand was on zero and the big just less than two. So we had less than two minutes to win in regulation.

Oststaff was scheduled to put in their third line for the next shift, their least potent offensively. So the coach skipped their shift and put in the first line.

After the goal, Oststaff was back at full strength, and even when Bijfhaaf won the face-off, they pushed the Loflinders back into their own end, stole the puck, and smacked one hard on goal.

The puck flew off the goalie's blocker and into the netting over the gate to the canal. The referee tweeted another face-off. Oststaff won the draw and the puck came back to the right defenseman. The center went after him, and he sent the puck around the backboards. One of the cadets picked it up and cycled it back. The defender won it from the Bijfhaaf left wing, danced back towards the blue line, then, quicker than I'd ever seen, snapped off a wrister that took the goalie-- and everyone watching-- completely by surprise.

It went into the goal, bounced off a pipe, and came out fast, straight to the Bijfhaaf center, who collected it, raced down the ice and beat the Oststaff goalie in a one-on-one.

The bed sheets came off. The noise was ear-splitting. People were jumping up and down and dancing.

The referee pointed to center ice, signaling a goal. But whose goal?

"This can't be," said Fleemisch, pointing at the scoreboard. The attendant was putting up a "3" placard under Bijfhaaf's name.

Both coaches were leaning in, trying to listen to the referee. The Oststaff coach was shaking his head and pointing.

Kasmahlov was shaking his head and pointing.

Finally, the referee pointed to the Bijfhaaf bench, then to center ice.

The scoreboard attendant wasn't moving. 3-2, Bijfhaaf.

The Oststaff coach went crazy. The Oststaff players were shaking their fists. The crowd was still going wild. Garlands of dried herbs were being thrown on the ice. The smell of spice filled the air. I wondered if we were going to get out of there alive.

Finally, the referee indicated by hand signals that there were 27 seconds on the clock. The big hand on the scoreboard was about on zero. And that was not enough time for Oststaff to come back.

Bijfhaaf won, and the whole city erupted in music played by strange instruments.

"*Unglaaberlickt*," I shouted in Fleemisch's ear.

He wouldn't say anything, just shook his head and scowled.

I made my way up to the press house, where bespectacled Roald was furiously scribbling again. He saw me, and put down his pencil.

Some kind of firework went off. Light. Boom. It lit up his face, made his spectacle lenses shine.

"Did you see?" I asked

"What?" he said.

"Did you see who gave Kasmahlov that drink?"

"I'm on deadline," he said.

Another *boom*, and several *pop pop pops*.

"I know you're busy," I said, "but I can't--" I wanted to say "wait anymore," but I couldn't even wait to finish my sentence. I took his head in my hands, pulled him to me, and gave him an honest kiss that was so honest I could feel it all the way down to my cold-numb fingers and toes.

Wow. Fireworks.

"I'll see you after," he said. "Dinner?"

"Love to," I said.

We went back to the hotel, where they had scheduled another huge meal. But this time it was not inside. The entire square of Bijfhaaf's city hall had been converted into a camp with about five hundred bonfires. Waiters went around with trolleys full of fish on spits. Some of it was whole fish, some in chunks. There were other waiters with trolleys full of round loaves of bread out of which they were cutting the middle. You were supposed to grill the fish over the fires, then set the fish in the middle of the loaf. No knife and fork needed.

Then other waiters would go around with wineskins and spray cider or weshnak into your mouth when you wanted a drink.

It wasn't just the hockey teams. About the entire country was in that square, and they all had spits, even the little kids.

Roald found me about a half-hour into the ordeal, and asked if I wanted to go on a skate.

We went back to the hotel for our skates, and truth be told, we never exactly got our skates on. We never made it out of my hotel room until much later that night. By then, I had a ring on my finger, and the party was going full blast. There was music and dancing and skating and bonfires and strings of lights everywhere.

We found Kasmahlov was in the middle of it, dancing with a young lady I later found out was named Danielujna van ter Roost.

Later on, we definitely skated. We gave the impression we had been skating all along.

"I know these canals like the back of my hand," Roald joked to Philbuja.

Fleemisch was nowhere to be found.

Well, I thought, in my Roald-induced euphoria, *it's only a game.*

CHAPTER 35 - CATHY

The next day we were to play at 11 AM, the final, Sunday. It sleeted a bit early on, but we hardly noticed, ending the first two periods with us leading 2-1.

Then their new center came into the game.

She won the first face-off of the third period, took it into their zone, and within a minute the Loflins tied the score.

Next draw, the new center again. She skated fast, handled the puck like a champ, and shot a laser beam by Greetje.

3-2.

And she took a shift off.

"What's going on with this lady?" I asked Fleemisch. "Is there anything we can do?"

Fleemisch said, "Her name is Waatat Uuduu, so it says on the roster."

"That's a fake name if I ever heard one," I said.

"There's no other information about her. She hasn't been a part of the Loflin hockey program."

"Are there any rules against that? Obviously she's a..." I wanted to say, "ringer," but I didn't know the word for it in Borschic. So I said, "a foreigner," though I didn't mean that exactly.

"If Waatat Uuduu is a foreigner, yet this is lawful. The only thing the rules state about a team's composition is that the roster of eligible players be submitted one hour before the game. Fifteen players can dress, and two players can be healthy scratches."

"So she could be Vinasolan? She could be from Anvoria?"

"Yes," said Fleemisch. "She could be from anywhere, except the wide world. The rules prohibit these women from playing in the game."

"Well, we need to find this out," I said. "She could be from the wide world. She could be playing under an assumed name. She could..." I was going to say, *she could be a man*, but I thought that was just silly.

Out on the ice, we'd failed to score on the next two shifts, and this What's-her-face was getting ready to step back on to the ice. We were going to go down 4-2 and the championship was going to slip through our fingers.

So I called the next two defenders in line over to me and said, "Next time that center gets the puck, we need to stop her. Some kind of hard check. I don't care if you take a penalty. A trip, crosscheck, it doesn't matter. I want you to make it tough on her to keep the puck. Let's see if she still flies as fast once she's gotten her feathers ruffled."

The women nodded. "Understood, Coach," said Philuumeena.

Fleemisch had been listening. He said, "I have a suggestion, Demouzeel."

"Quickly."

"Knock the stick out of the woman's hands."

Philuumeena stared.

"You know what I mean," he said.

"What? Why?"

"Bear with me, Demouzeel. I have an inkling."

Philuumeena and Roxanne went out onto the ice as the other two defenders came skating in. They skated out to where the center was poised and waiting for the puck to come out of the Loflin offensive zone.

Philuumeena looked back at Fleemisch. He nodded.

She whacked at the center's stick. She wasn't at all ready for it, and it went flying, spiraling along the ice towards our goal. The tape split, exposing a strip of dull wood underneath.

Fleemisch came out from the bench to intercept the stick. He bent to pick it up. Then the center was there, hip-checked Fleemisch so that he spun around, and kicked at the stick with her skate. More tape unraveled.

The referee was blowing his whistle and waving his hands over his head, but no one was paying attention.

The center picked up the stick, but at the same time, her wig went askew. That silly little thought about she could be anybody, she could be a man?

She could.

The center picked up the stick, tore away some tape, looked left and right, and then skated for the gate to the canal.

Greetje lumbered out towards him. She had her goalie gear on, so when she tried to dive at him and stop him, he just skated around her. He could skate very fast.

My team sprang into action. They tore away their uniforms. Yes, tore them away. Underneath they were wearing something that looked like rubber diving suits. Sheaths with little daggers inside were strapped to their shins.

They skated towards the impostor, knives drawn. But he wheeled around, leaving his wig behind, and opened a gate to the canal. He got out into the canal a second before the women met him, and was off like lightning.

I bent over Fleemisch. He was bleeding at the mouth.

"Are you all right?"

"*Alleskeet ergut*, Demouzeel," he managed to say, though he was clearly having trouble breathing. "It is the Branch. Go after it. You are the only one who can handle it besides that imposter. For Borschland."

"What is it? What? Why? You tried to pick it up?"

"I knew it was here. I could sense it."

"How? What?"

"I am a saint, Demouzeel," he said. "Now go, and let me die."

I skated towards the gate, knowing that the others had a big head start. I raced down the canal that took me to the River Paas. When I got there, there was no one.

Then I looked to my right, and there was the impostor, out in front, with fifteen ladies in rubber diving suits hot in pursuit. He'd taken a roundabout route, but he'd finally made it to the river.

There was no time to think. I skated out just as the impostor was turning his head to see how much of a lead he still had. He didn't see me until I gave him the hit of his life.

When a skater is going that fast and gets a big jolt like that, he flies a long way. The Branch flew even farther. When he stopped rolling end over end, I figured they'd have to take him away on a stretcher.

But he got up quickly, and he went for the Branch, which I was just picking up. Good thing it was heavily taped on the handle end. I slipped my fingers under, flipped it up, and had it in my hands with just enough time to trip him at the ankles. He fell badly, and didn't get up that time. He cursed a blue streak, and then said in English, "Well, thank you very much."

"For what?" I asked.

"I blew out my knee," he said. "Again."

"Wait a minute," I said. "Are you Busby? The Busby?"

"Yeah," he said, and cursed. "The Busby. Anyway, thanks."

"What the hell for?" I said.

"For ordering your goon to stick-hack me. I was on my way to my second hat trick in two days. You know how long it's been since I did that?"

The girls surrounded him.

Then the Loflin police surrounded him.

"Keep hold of the Branch," said one of the officers. "We cannot touch it, or we die."

Philbuja said, "*Alles ergut*, Coach?"

"*Sankthelejnakorps*! Saint Helejna Corps! I can't believe you all played like you were such sissies," I said. "You could've kicked all those teams' behinds up and down the ice."

"Fleemisch told us not to," said Philbuja. "He said he'd

have our commissions if we did."

"We always had your back, Coach," said Philuumeena. "You never had anything to worry about."

I looked over at the big dog pile on top of Busby. Then I looked down at the Branch, with its tape split and feathered out.

"What happened to the flowers?" I said.

"I've got them," someone dressed in a police uniform said. "St. Grundel Mittelmascht, at your service, Demouzeel. Well done, by the way. One more thing. Could you please help us by transporting the Branch back to base?"

"It would be my pleasure," I said.

CHAPTER 36 - CATHY

Not long after the game, all the saints assembled in the chapel of the Borschic navy base. It was not the most beautiful place I've ever seen, but having Grundel Mittelmascht there with a wineskin full of *tisande* more than made up for it.

"Every saint will drink," said Grundel. "I'm not going to live another three hundred years and let you return forever to the starfire."

Twenty-seven saints had gathered, including Bep, Henrick, Willem, Wolfenstejn the detective, and Fleemisch, who it turns out, was named St. Karolus of Matexipar, officially a Saint of Light.

"But I want you to promise me something," Grundel went on. "From now on, the rivalry of Light and Shadow is no more. We are all to work together for the good of Borschland. And we will all meet..."

Dramatic pause.

"...with the permission of Meester and Madaam Reinhardt, in their home in Staff Borsch."

"You mean they're safe?" I said.

"Most assuredly," said Grundel. "And they would be with us, except that Connuj and Liluj have come down with colds, and we are keeping the whole family in quarantine."

"Well," I said. "If Willem promises to make his *terrijn*, I'm sure they'll say yes."

They all laughed, and Willem nodded.

"And now, Cathy," said Grundel, "We would be honored if, as the youngest subdeacon in our midst, you would all give us our dose of *tisande*."

"How many squirts?" I asked.

"Three is enough," said Grundel. He held the skin between saints, and gave it to me to administer, a real acolyte.

I held it together until I got to St. Elisabeete.

"Bep," I said, tears streaming down my face, "I don't know how to thank you."

She looked very old, very care-worn. "For what, darling?"

"Everything. My team. Protection. What I needed."

"Give me the *tisande*, child," said Bep. "We can talk afterwards."

Squirt. Squirt. Squirt.

Henrick next.

"I hope," he whispered, "you don't think I'm an evil man."

"There is no light without shadow," I said, "and no shadow without light."

Squirt. Squirt. Squirt.

Then it was Willem.

"What a strange man you are," I said.

He nodded. "You have done everything I knew you could, and more," he said.

"I don't know. I just stepped in at the end."

"And defended the goal," said Willem.

I wiped my nose with my hand, and Grundel gave me a handkerchief. After I blew, and composed myself, I said, "I wonder how many women have been broken-hearted over you through the centuries?" I said.

He ignored the question. "I think this means that they will make you a deacon without sitting for your exams."

"Horse chestnuts!" I said. "Anyway, after this, what's an exam? Child's play!" And I laughed and cried at the same time.

When I came to Fleemisch, he shook his head.

"What?"

"I picked up the Branch," he said. "I touched it."

I couldn't see for the new tears.

"Karl," said Grundel. "Take the *tisande*."

"No," he said. "I will not take it. I have touched the Branch."

"You would've died on the spot if you touched the Branch."

"No," he said.

Grundel took the wineskin from me.

"Karl, what is the first letter of your name?"

He shook his head, kept his mouth closed.

"First letter?"

He held his mouth away, like a baby that doesn't want its strained peas.

"Come on!"

"*Nej!*" Fleemisch yelled.

Squirt went the *tisande* into Fleemisch's mouth. He coughed, and swallowed.

"Why did you do that?" Fleemisch said, wiping his face.

"Because you are an idiot. And I am going to dedicate the next three hundred years to making sure you smile once per phase shift. Now open your mouth again and let's get the rest of this over with."

Later, Sherm and Rachael came down and we ate supper in the company of the surviving saints of Borschland.

After I told him the whole story, Sherm said to me, "Fleemisch must not have touched the Branch."

"I'm sure he touched it," said Grundel. "If he said he did, then he did."

"But why didn't he die on the spot?"

"I do not know," said Grundel, and laughed. "Remember, only one saint ever did die on the spot from touching the Branch."

Sherm said, "I'm going to kick your tail if I find out anyone could touch the Branch."

"I'm strong again. I don't think you could do that."

I laughed.

"So what is the story with Fleemisch?" Sherm asked.

Grundel said, "You do not know of the tale of St. Karolus of Matexipar?"

"I know," said Rachael. "He was Willem van Noos' great-grandson. He grew up when the city of Matexipar was still a mixed town of Loflins and Borschlanders. He loved greatly. He loved a Loflin. But neither of their families would allow it; no saint can marry a non-saint. So he did not marry, and when she died, he never got over it."

"He told me his wife had died," I said.

Willem said, "He was among the few of us who never wished to be a saint. Never embraced it. But he knows his duty. And he did it."

"He sure did," I said.

EPILOGUE - SHERM

Well, first off, I have to say that that was the most exciting tournament I've ever been to where I spent most of the time in a hotel room looking after sick kids and a pregnant wife.

Connie and Lily both got temperatures and perpetual runny noses and life without Melissa, who had to go back to duty on the aircraft carrier, was a big snot-filled mess.

But we got through it, and both Rachael and I learned once and for all that having a little help when you've been stupid and had three kids in five years is the biggest gift anyone can receive.

I'm sure you're wondering about Busby. The Borschic government didn't end up hanging him, though they were in their rights to do so.

No, they figured Busby was more valuable alive. After he rehabbed his knee, again, they made him the practice goalie of the last-chance division zed hockey team that plays in the provincial territories league where they mine rubies. Not a fun job, no indoor toilets, but at least he was on the ice. In the summer, he got to break rocks in the mines. And once he'd done his time, maybe he could coach. I wrote him, and he wrote back. Mostly cursing.

And Cathy? The tradition in Borschland is that once you

have decided to get married, you do it. Long engagements don't happen, especially if the two people have been courting. That's what happened with me and Rachael, and I recommend it.

So Cathy and Roald got married in the Chapel of St. Noos a couple of weeks after the tournament. It was a simple ceremony, attended by a couple of dozen saints and about a thousand reporters.

The following Christmas, Cathy passed her deacon exams with a triple first class, which is the highest grade you can get. She told me it felt like cheating because she got an extra year to study up. But I think hanging out with saints had a little something to do with it.

And the predictions did come true. The phase shift ended almost six months after it had begun, and lasted the whole hockey season.

I played right wing on Lavishbear's line, and we mopped up the competition. We ended up 21-5-6 and Kasmahlov scored seven goals, more than I did. Lavishbear was the top goal scorer with 30. Bijfhaaf won the Flowering Branch Cup, by the way. First second division team to do it in 27 years. No, they didn't beat us. Itasca smoked us the weekend of my disappearance. The guys blamed it on the stolen sticks.

At the end of the season, they made me an official player-coach, which makes sense, since you can't play forever. Of course, they didn't raise my salary.

And what about the saints? They scattered to their various hidey-holes for the shift back to our world, and right about the time I began to miss them, we had another shift.

One late summer evening, just after Schmeecks had delivered a big wheel of Schijnenfvaas, the doorbell rang.

I went to the door, and there was Willem.

"I thought I might make the terr--" he began, but didn't get a chance to finish. He got a puck in his eye instead.

"Goal!" screamed Connie, and his sister danced around like he'd won the championship.

There is always a big racket in the Reinhardt house, even

with our new nannybear, Honoria (Melissa writes often; she can't tell us any details about her job, although Connie loves to collect the international stamps from the envelopes). Honoria has learned from Lily how to make a fine chocolate cake, and she does a great job with our new arrival. We called him Willem, of course.

Willem Henrick.

ACKNOWLEDGMENTS

"A wise person says that poems are one's children," Rachael Martujns Reinhardt opines in her 25-year old wisdom. She's right. Creating a world from nothing is like conceiving children: easy and fun. Much harder is the birth, the nurturing, and the final *tah-loo* as you send your little creation off into the ranks of the millions all vying for reader's hearts. It takes a village to raise a novel, and I have a village to thank: for continuing support, encouragement and sweat equity-- Lyn Fairchild Hawks; Bob Mustin; Phil Naessens; Pete and Andréa Taylor; Richard Abbott; my family, and especially my wife Celeste: publicist, marketing strategist, and chief optimist. I would also like to give special thanks and hats off to the Naykki-Emery family, who have been tireless supporters and co-creators of Borschland from the beginning, and whose enjoyment of Borschland and my storytelling help me to believe in Borschland's worth. This time around, I would like to give especial thanks to eldest son Ross, whose careful proofreading saved me from numerous headaches. Finally, I write these words in loving memory of Jo, one of my first enthusiastic readers.

AUTHOR'S NOTE

Alleskeet ergut is a Borschic phrase that can mean a lot of things, depending on the context. It literally means "All's well," but it can mean "I'm doing fine," "It's going to be fine," even "Don't worry, it'll turn out fine, you'll see." Which, taken together, is the motto of the Borschland Hockey Chronicles. I started this series a long time ago when I created Borschland and the other nations that make up the mythical Continent on which it sits. Maps, short stories, blogs, and one novel later, this second book stands as humble witness to the truth of the Borschic phrase. With luck, and the grace of the saints, a third book will appear under the BHC rubric, and it will concern Willem Henrick Reinhardt. While you wait, I hope you will tell all your friends about the first two books, and that you will visit **breakfastwithpandora.com** and the **True North Writers & Publishers Co-operative Facebook page** for news, updates, short stories and articles, and other fun stuff. And please let me know what you think of all this.

Until we meet again, *Tah-loo, tah-loo, alleskeet ergut.*

www.ingramcontent.com/pod-product-compliance
Lightning Source LLC
Chambersburg PA
CBHW071233250626
47163CB00001B/159